STORM RIDER
RIVER OF FIRE

ROBERT BARON

JOVE BOOKS, NEW YORK

For Ernie
Thanks for lending me the borrow of ya.

*   *   *

And for Arthur, wherever you are.
Ride with the wind, bro.

STORMRIDER 2: RIVER OF FIRE

A Jove Book/published by arrangement with
the author

PRINTING HISTORY
Jove edition/March 1993

ISBN: 0-515-10976-2

Jove Books are published by The Berkley Publishing Group,
200 Madison Avenue, New York, New York 10016.
The name "JOVE" and the "J" logo
are trademarks belonging to Jove Publications, Inc.

PRINTED IN THE UNITED STATES OF AMERICA

10   9   8   7   6   5   4   3   2   1

1

The Taos Rendezvous lay in a broad, flat, spring-green valley east of the ancient Pueblo proper: a garden of bright color, loud voices, and engine snarl, fenced with tall straight ponderosa pines on the slopes to either side and overwatched by Taos Peak and mighty Wheeler Peak, both still capped with snow. Into the midst of it all rode the Jokers Motorcycle Clan, dirty, wounded, and triumphant. As the Law demanded their holsters were empty; you didn't carry weapons into Rendezvous. With them they brought a rich booty of bikes, towed on ropes, loaded onto open flat trailers, crammed into a trio of trucks and vans.

For a wonder the skies were clear, so bright they ached the eyes, except for the ugly black column of smoke rising from Capulín Mountain away to the east, which had been throwing its guts up for a week. The gathered clans greeted the newcomers with whoops and joyous disorder. Ugly John Stovic of the Nighthawks was so mightily cranked by the arrival of his long-lost bros that he rode his big-ass Iron Mountain sled into the middle of the creek that ran past camp. It promptly stalled and had to be hauled out at the end of a rope by a gang of laughing bare-breasted biker babes, under the disapproving gaze of Dog Soldiers in their orange armbands, who were charged with maintaining the sanctity of Laughing Girl—as Plains myth personified running water—as well as cracking heads in the service of Peace. But that was Rendezvous.

Skinny, blond Zonker of the Jokers was so inspired he laid

his own bike down and rushed into the stream himself, shedding clothes, to catch Ugly John in a flying, naked embrace and plant a kiss on his black-bearded lips. It was an ancient greeting, rooted in the deathless desire to freak out the Citizens that had existed among the brethren since before the Star fell and ended the old order of Earth. Neither bro was a noted backroad rider, at least where boys where concerned; it was just Rendezvous.

At the head of the Jokers rode their Prez, Jovanne, a tall woman with brief amber hair roached up in front. She was grim today, and ignored the ritual importunings to show her tits, which was cause for hoots and groans of disappointment. She was accounted quite a looker.

Beside her rode a stranger. He was tall, taller than Jovanne, which not that many men were. His hair was black, with short-cut top and sides and long in the back. A wicked bandido mustache hung over his mouth. His eyes were gray-blue and keen as a red-tailed hawk's. The stranger resisted the equally ritual cries of the sisters for him to unbutton and hang Iron John in the wind. The grin he showed them made many of them regret that, as sincerely as the bros regretted Jovanne's uncharacteristic modesty.

Despite his pride of place he wasn't wearing the Joker colors: the head of a man with an elephant's trunk, tipped with a human hand, in place of a nose. He showed no insignia at all, just a loose canvas shirt, somewhat the worse for wear, twill trousers with a red stripe down each leg, and high black boots. The fact that Jovanne would permit an unaffiliated rider at the head of Joker line had the gawkers winking and digging one another in the ribs, not without jealousy.

The Jokers stopped in the center of the vast encampment, where mounds of brush and wood had been piled to await the night's Circle Fires. Electric music crashed over them like prairie thunder. They put their boots in the dirt and waited.

Between the polychrome hemispheres of the tents of the High Free Folk strode Fat Ed, President of the Diggers MC and Grand Wazoo of the Ron D. Voo. A crown of thick gold paper with great gaudy paste rubies and emeralds set into it was crammed down on the tangle of his curly graying bark-brown hair. A buffalo robe was thrown over his mountain shoulders, and he wore a quiltwork tunic, faded grease-blackened jeans, and knee-high Apache moccasins beneath. His smile was wreathed in beard, and his wonderful belly was wreathed in gold and silver tinsel. He held a six-foot oaken staff likewise wreathed in tinsel and crowned with a gilded soup ladle, the symbol of his double office.

"Jovanne!" he exclaimed, holding wide his arms. "Good to see you, girl! How you've been keeping your lovely self?"

She accepted his hug. He did not look especially tall, but when he folded his arms about her she almost disappeared into him.

"Fine," she said, pecking his bearded cheek.

" 'Fine.' You don't *sound* fine." He had no difficulty making himself heard above the screaming din. His voice boomed like the wind of a blue norther. "C'mon, tell your bad old uncle what's happened to his favorite niece." All sisters were Fat Ed's nieces, as all bros were his nephews. He wasn't the Grand Wazoo for nothing.

But for once he found resistance to his jollying. Jovanne pulled away. "Nothing, Ed," she said. "I'm okay. Nothing wrong with me that food, sleep, and a long hot bath won't set right."

He shook his huge head, then spied the man who rode behind her. *"Jammer!"* he yelled, and raised a wailing coyote howl. The black man in the silver mirrored shades unforked his bike, grinning enormously, and let Fat Ed catch him up in a spine-creaking hug.

"How are you, my man?" the Digger straw boss roared.

"It's been times, my man," Jammer said, struggling free. "It's been times. And I'm making some songs for them that'll put you in the dirt."

"I'll damned well bet they will!" Fat Ed gave him a happy blow on the shoulders that would have been enough to settle a good many face-up fights. Jammer rode it with barely a flicker of his tooth-baring grin. You didn't get to be the Main Bard of the Plains without having the sand of a samurai. "And we'll be listnin' to 'em with our tongues hanging around the Git-Down Fire tonight, or I'm a Pawnee."

He turned his head and spat. The craftiest horse-traders between the Big River and the FlameLands of the Cascade Range, and not by repute the most scrupulous, the Pawnee were not universally loved. Since they skirted the same rap, the Diggers made a particular point to disdain them.

"Or the Council Fires," Jammer said, and inclined his head significantly in Tristan's direction.

Fat Ed's eyebrows rose like humping caterpillars. "Oh?" He turned to scrutinize Tristan with his tiny happy-grizzly eyes and his hands on his hips.

Tristan gave him a quiet smile and nodded his head in acknowledgment. "What have we here?" Fat Ed said, not unkindly.

"His name's Tristan," Jovanne said from back in the saddle of her lean Quad Cities softtail. "He claims to be the last of the Hardriders."

"He *is* the last of the Hardriders," Jammer put in emphatically as Tristan shook hands with Fat Ed. Tristan was ready for the knuckle-crushing game, a favored Plains greeting ritual for which he knew a remedy or two, but the Digger boss's grip was child-gentle. "And you know I should know, for I saw 'em fall. Done sung it oft enough."

Fat Ed nodded, frowning appraisingly at Tristan the while. The Hardriders' Last Stand, when that small but proud clan burned its lacings and died outnumbered by hated City soldiers and their war-machines, had taken its place among the foremost of the Plains' thousand sad epics, thanks to the Electric Skald.

"So one survived," Fat Ed rumbled.

"Two," Tristan said. "There's Jammer."

"Ahh. Yes."

"He says he's not a Hardrider anymore," Jovanne said. "He's got a new name now."

"He got his *Sign*," Jammer said. "Mind that new Guest Star, in the head of the Bull?"

Fat Ed nodded. The High Free Folk dwelt with the stars for a roof, and knew them all as friends.

"It struck my man Tristan *here*." He slapped himself softly on the breastbone. "It's his SoulStar, if you follow StarLodge ways. When it lit up, three days ago, it brought right clear to him a dream he'd been having since first the townies captured him. It was his Sign and Symbol, the burning skull of a longhorn steer."

The other Jokers, those that weren't cavorting in the creek with Ugly John and his helpers, had hung back, letting the important folk palaver. Now they crowded forward in their eagerness to tell what they'd been part of.

"He got him a lodgepole and a skull old Zonker found," said Tooth, so named for what he was prominently missing, though by that logic he might also have been called *Size* or *Cleanliness*. "Poured Mother's Milk all on it, and torched it right off."

"He swore he'd set the Plains on fire with his Sign," said white-blond Pony, blue eyes shining so hot you expected the drum-tight skin of her face to commence to blacken and crisp away. "He lit the Catheads off right enough, the very next day!"

"I saw some faces missing as you rode in, and some bikes I knew with no riders to go with 'em," Fat Ed said. "So you got in a shooting-scrape, did you?"

"We only kicked the ass off old Drago himself," said Emilio, whose arm rode in a sling. A Cathead bullet had smashed his elbow. The Jokers' supply of City Medicine had run dry, and herb cures hadn't helped; the arm was festering up, and the color was unhealthy high in his cheeks.

"Teal did him," Pony said, with a nod back toward the Jokers' diminutive female wrench, who stood back with arms crossed beneath her small breasts and a wedge of bangs hanging almost in her eyes. "From five hundred yards out, one shot, *bang!* through his fat neck. Drago's boys did Big Jupe."

"Sister, your grief is mine," Fat Ed said. Little Teal said nothing. She did a lot of that these days.

"There must have been four, five hundred of 'em!" enthused Tooth, not to be drawn off the scent.

"Two hundred," said Pud, one of the two newest Jokers. He was a small, pale, prematurely balding man with bulging eyes.

Emilio cuffed him upside the head with his good wing. "Shut the fuck up! Wasn't that Burningskull has a merciful streak, your hair woulda been all of you to make the Rendezvous, just flapping from the Prez's buckhorn bars, you sag-nuts Cathead shit."

"Slack it," Jovanne said as Pud cowered. "He's taken the colors. He's a Joker now."

Wiry Red Dog stroked his red Vandyke. His thin face was grim. His platonic saddlemate Sooz, the Jokers' Singer, had left her ashes by the wash where the Burning Skull fight went down. "Once a Cat, always a Cat," he said. Jovanne glared at him.

Then she glared at Tristan. *I'm losing them*, her fierce brown eyes said. *It's all your fault.* He shook his head.

"Any Catheads in camp?" Jammer asked.

Fat Ed instantly went into guarded mode. "Now, Jammer, this is Ron D. Voo. You of all people should know everybody checks their disputes at the Party Line."

"I mind that, my friend. But there's more here than a dustup between clans, even if it'll make a hell of a song. I'm bound to speak in the Circle tonight. Now, have the Cats come in?"

"Oh," Fat Ed said, subdued. "No. None yet." He was starting to sweat. For Jammer to talk, rather than sing, meant very heavy things in motion. The Digger chief had a powerful allergy to anything that might bring discord to Rendezvous.

Looking for a flying subject change, he noticed the bike with the flame-painted gas tank which Tristan still stood astride. "Is that how you come by the ride?" Fat Ed asked him, waving a hairy paw. "That there's John Badheart's hand-built Big Twin, I'm bound."

"It is," Tristan said levelly, "but I didn't pick it up after the Cathead fight. I beat Badheart in a duel. Face-up."

"He bashed his chest right in with his knees," Thin Lizzy said admiringly. "He's one hard motherfucker." He had clearly won as much of her affection as she would give to any man.

Fat Ed pulled a mouth. "Oh, so. So he must be; Badheart was a stark warrior." He raised a hand, made a fist, and unfolded it with a push of fingers toward the horizon, consigning the dead man's smoke to Brother Wind. "May he have a wing to himself in Heroes' Holm; Mother Sky preserve me from bunking with him, when my Road runs out. He was a handful."

He looked at Tristan with his body language speaking of new respect. "So you've come into a Power," he said. "Right on. May you ride hard and long as your grandfather Anse the One-Eyed."

"Call him Burningskull now," Jovanne said. "He has a lot of names; up to not so long ago he went by the handle of Outlaw One."

Fat Ed's jaw dropped till it looked like his bottom teeth would get tangled in his chins. "You're jacking me! You're trying to wire me right up, girl."

Tristan grinned. "No such luck. I'm Outlaw One. The one and only."

Fat Ed's eyes grew wide, and he stared around in comic alarm. "Are you—wait—but you're a *Striker*."

"I *was*." Tristan's eyes grew dark. "Then the City bastards turned on us, tried to wash us all away. I escaped, and spent the better part of a year making them pay."

"C'mon, Ed," Tooth said excitedly. "You've heard about the vengeance road of Outlaw One."

Fat Ed nodded, never taking his eyes off Tristan. "That's true. It's sung, how you laid the brothers waste in the City's name, and how the City betrayed you."

Tooth spat. "Can't trust City scum."

"But—what does that make *you*, my friend?" Fat Ed asked.

"A true man to ride with," Tristan said, "and a deadly one to cross."

Fat Ed chewed the gristle of his underlip. "You vouch for him, girl?"

"We were bringing him here as a captive, to be sold to his enemies, whom I'm sure the Circles are full of," Jovanne said, with a smile that hung down at one end. "Now it's him who brought us here. I *am* riding with him, Ed, and you don't see any guns pointing at me."

Fat Ed nodded. To ride with a man was to acknowledge him your brother. He embraced Tristan. "Then you're a bro, no matter what's rolled down the Road before. Welcome to Rendezvous, my friend."

"Thanks," said Tristan, considerably muffled.

Fat Ed turned away with a grand sweep of his quilt-clad arm. "Welcome, my children. Welcome to Rendezvous. I see you have brought much rich booty. So join us. The tents await, the Fires are laid and ready for the Circles. The clans are gathered to greet the spring. It's Ron D. Voo, and all the High Free Folk're here that ain't back-broke or staked to a fire-ant hill!"

2

"Who-*ee*," Tooth said, stretching. "It surely is a kick to be flush for a change."

The tent was roomy, long as three men laid pate to sole, wider than Tooth could span had there been two of him—which thankfully there weren't—and high enough for Tristan to stand full up in and not keep wanting to stoop. It came courtesy of the Diggers, that Motorcycle Clan whose duty it was to provide the hospitality of the Plains.

Of course, it didn't come *cheap*. Like many of the Clans, the Diggers could trace their roots back before StarFall, to a time when they didn't even ride, though since then they'd wheeled across miles sufficient to wash away that stain. Since their very borning days their mission had been to feed the hungry and shelter those in need.

But along that Road they'd passed enough markers to learn that someone always has to pay. For all the tales of the Big Rock Candy Mountain and the Free Lunch Café, in the burning heart of the FlameLand—or maybe it was away East across the Mississip, among strange folk and unknown perils—the Stormriders all knew that chocolate didn't spring from fountains, or new drive-belts grow wild on bushes like buffalo berry.

If you were in *need*, the Diggers would provide and never keep a tally. But if you could pay, you did. As sutlers and hostlers they knew no master, not the wily Pawnee, and not Rendezvous' tight-fisted hosts, the Taoseños.

The Jokers, while they had tents of their own which they would also use, could afford to pay. Their victory over the Cat-heads had been lucrative in terms of bikes and guns. Better, they had captured a hefty stock of ammunition, scarcer and much more valuable outside the Cities than firearms themselves. They could afford to splurge. And they had been riding a hard road, and had lost brothers and sisters in their victory, and what the hell? It was *Rendezvous*.

"Yeah, Tooth," Jovanne said pointedly, "it's great. Now, would you mind *excusing* us for a little while?"

"No, uh, sure no, y'all just go on and get to whatever you're minded to do."

She glared at him. He stopped, blinked, and broke into a gap-tooth grin. "Oh. I see. I got it now. You two wanna be alone for a little, uh, you know . . ."

He raised grubby hands. Before he could start poking the stiffened forefinger of one hand into a thumb-and-forefinger O of the other, Jovanne shouted, *"Roll!"*

Tooth rolled.

Jovanne dropped her bedroll and possibles bag on the fabric floor—these Digger tents were first-class, and no mistake—and sat heavily upon them. She crossed one long leg over the other, rested elbow on knee and chin in palm, and looked at Tristan.

Tristan had pulled out Cubby, the little stuffed grizzly bear his City stepmom Mrs. Tomlinson had given him, and was holding him, smiling and stroking his round brown head. He bent and gently set the stuffed toy on his possibles. He and the little griz had been through a lot together. Then he turned to raise an eyebrow at Jovanne.

"Moving in? I guess there's plenty of room for two rolls spread out in here. Though we're a pretty leggy pair of humans."

She leapt to her feet. "Fine," she said, and started hauling her traps up onto her shoulder.

"Whoa," Tristan said, raising a hand, "settle down. You're welcome to stay. Or, what the hell. I can move, if it's that big a thing."

She dropped her bag with a thump and turned away, standing with arms tightly crossed. "I know I don't smell too good," she said in a strained voice, "but you know I'm clean. I'll scrub my-self pink at the first opportunity. Or am I just ugly?"

He laughed. She jerked as if slapped.

"We've been through this before. I like women, and I've been a long damn time without one." A very long time indeed, he realized with an uncomfortable south-of-the-belt-buckle twinge; his fiancée, Elinor, whom he'd been forced to leave behind in Homeland when conspirators caused the death of his commanding officer—who also happened to be her father—had insisted on waiting for marriage to go to bed with him. To his own surprise he had agreed, and stayed faithful to her. "And you're beautiful, hon, it's not like I fail to notice.

"But I think you're still afraid I'm going to take the Jokers away from you. And I don't want you believing you've got to fuck to stay Prez. The Jokers are yours; you've led 'em well down a long, bad road, kept them together and most of them alive."

He shook his head. "It's not that I don't want your tender body, babe. I just don't want your *pride*."

Her face went white beneath suntan and road-grit. "So you're a mind reader now, are you, you cocky son of a bitch?"

"Tell me I'm wrong."

"Lava take you, you bastard! Who the *fuck* do you think you are, to tell me what I can do and what I can't?"

"Nobody," Tristan said. "I can only tell you what you can do to *me*. And what you can't."

She deflated onto the possibles bag again. "What is it you want?"

You, he knew. He liked a woman with her fire, her hard-won Plains skills—her ferocious Plains pride. But he needed her, with both her skills and pride intact.

And also, every time he looked into her doe-brown eyes, so big and deep and deceptive-soft, he saw Elinor's ice-blue eyes behind.

"To make a new nation of the Plains, under my Burning Skull sign," he told her. "To mash the Catheads so flat they'll never trouble the bros again, and squeeze those yellow-robe Fusion devils out of them like pus from a pimple and send them back across the Missus Hip where they belong. And then I want to plow through the wire strung round Homeland, and smash City Hall flat, and tear the heads off those backshooting Purity minges and then shit down their necks. Okay?

"I don't want to take the Jokers from you. I don't have *time*."

• • •

Puffing, Tristan slowed to a trot as the bustle of Rendezvous came into view up the creek. A band of Ghost Riders with blue and silver beads woven into beards and hair blatted past on their cruisers. They turned their heads to stare at Tristan, laboring in his shorts and T-shirt. To be a *walking man* was a considerable stigma, and running wasn't much better; songs were sung about warriors who stood to fight against fatal odds when their bikes went down, even though cover lay a short sprint away, because they would not deign to run from foes.

Tristan was unarmed—which was to say, he wore his foot-long Arkansas toothpick strapped to his hip, but no firearms. He just nodded and waved to the Riders. As Outlaw One he hadn't had any dealings with them, though you could never tell whose friend or ally it was you'd scragged—Plains alliances shifted like Plains wind.

After slowing slightly to gawk, the Ghost Riders accelerated and blasted away out of sight. Tristan let himself breathe easier. Here beyond the Party Line was where disputes were settled—but that meant face-ups or, occasionally, prearranged battles between groups. By long-standing custom bushwhacking was forbidden within a five-mile radius of Rendezvous. On the other hand, the nomads regarded laws as meant to be broken, even their own.

Which he thought about as soon as the pack's engine noise died away and he heard cries coming from some rocks on the other side of the creek.

He ran into the creek, splashed across, and ran up the bank to the clump of boulders at the top of a short slope.

On the far side of the rocks the land dipped down in a small depression. Four bros with long blond hair swinging around muscle-swollen shoulders and Sons of Thor colors on the backs of their leather vests were holding a Pueblo girl in the air by all four limbs. The pair nearer Tristan, their backs to him, tugged the girl's jeans down her plump legs. They were cursing, while their brothers who held the captive's arms jeered at them. They showed no sign of noticing they had company either.

Tristan plunged ahead. He announced his presence with a savage straight-fist rabbit punch to the base of the skull of the nearest bro, who had just got a leg free of the pants and was holding an ankle and crowing. He fell onto the captive, pulling the other leg from his partner's grasp.

The second man turned to gape at Tristan with total incomprehension. Tristan kicked him in the balls hard enough to lift his feet off the grass. The Son of Thor dropped to his knees. Tristan drove an elbow straight down into the nape of his neck, flattening him.

Still posed above his victim, Tristan showed his teeth to the two still on their feet in a killer's grin. They let go of the shoulders of the girl, who had been pretty well brought down to the ground by the first rider falling on her.

The one on Tristan's left was young, just a kid. "Hey!" he exclaimed, still more surprised than anything else. "If you wanted a piece, why'n't you just ask?"

The other whipped out a huge Bowie and dropped into fighting stance. "C'mon, you fucker," he snarled. "You just bought yourself a bad damn death."

"Oh, did I?" Tristan asked. He drew his own knife and advanced as the girl, gathering her wits, rolled to the side and out of the way. As she kicked free of the remaining leg of her jeans and scampered off toward the woods, her bare bottom twinkling, the kid's eyes flipped aside to follow her. Instantly Tristan did a sidestep hop and drove a side-kick into the pit of the boy's stomach. The kid went flying backward, cracked the back of his head on a rock, and lay still.

Tristan glanced back at the first two he'd nailed. The man he'd rabbit-punched was moving. The one he'd nut-kicked wasn't.

He switched his attention back to the knife-handler before the man could take advantage of his distraction. Tristan could not count on having a clear backfield for any length of time. That was just too damned bad.

He grinned at his opponent. *I'm not doing too bad for going one-on-four, am I?*

The Son of Thor took the smile for taunting, which wasn't altogether wide of the mark. "You *fuck*," he hissed. "I'll cut that smile right out of your face!"

Tristan turned his hand palm-up and made a come-here gesture. "Go for it," he said, still smiling.

The Son was in a fencer's stance, very popular on the Plains, with right foot and knife-hand extended, left hand low and near the hip. Tristan held himself low, feet wide, left hand advanced in front of his knife-hand. The way Ferret and the others had taught him in Dorm C. It wasn't a pretty style; he could see the Son's blond-bearded lip curling with contempt. But it was a stance developed from tens of thousands of kid-hours of practice with sharpened spoons.

The Son took a forehand cut at Tristan. Tristan easily leaned back out of the way. *He's trying to see if I'm as open as I look.*

Tristan swayed in. Predictably the Son came back with a savage gut-cutting backhand. Apparently taken by surprise, Tristan leapt back, way farther than he had to. He overbalanced, threw his hands up and wide, leaving himself wide open.

It was the Son's turn to grin. He lunged, slashing for Tristan's exposed belly.

Tristan pivoted his hips and whipped his knife-hand across his body. His straight-edged blade bit the inside of his opponent's forearm to the bone.

The instant Tristan saw the Son's fingers slacken and the knife start to fall he whirled toward him, smashing a spinning back-fist to the temple. The Son staggered. Tristan snapped a right front-kick to the solar plexus, folding his enemy. A left knee straightened him back up with blood starting from his mashed-in nose. A spinning hook kick to the temple put him down.

Tristan spun, knife at the ready. The Son he'd hit first was just getting onto his feet again. Tristan knew it was sheer stupid luck he'd stayed down as long as he had.

He heard engines gunning, heard shouts, and his peripheral vision caught people running toward the fight from inside the Party Line. It occurred to him that he was reenacting one of his own father's legendary deeds, one he himself had witnessed. Wyatt Hardrider had stopped three Scum of the Earth from raping a local girl, back in the days when SOTE were allowed into Ron D. Voo.

Of course, that had happened inside the Party Line, where such behavior was distinctly uncool. Outside the Line, the rules were different. Tristan had to grin at himself. Not only had he acted without thinking, he had acted on his old Striker reflexes.

He hoped a lot of Jokers were among the first spectators on hand. He might just have hung his own ass on a wire for true.

Then his opponent brought his hands out from his hips with a

double wrist-flick. There was a sliding rattle, and twin glints of
sunlight on steel, and Tristan realized that unfriendly spectators
were the least of his worries.

The Son was big, with a scarred face. He looked to be in his
mid-to-late twenties, and he held himself like a fighter. A tough
bastard, and if Tristan hadn't blindsided him he would likely not
have downed him. But that wasn't what raised the hair on the
back of Tristan's neck.

In either hand the Son held a short-handled hammer with a
head shaped like an inverted V. Thor's hammers, symbol of the
clan. A ten-foot length of chain fastened at the end of each haft
joined them. The Son slowly began to swing the right-hand
weapon around his fist in an eighteen-inch circle.

He smiled.

Tristan felt himself break a fresh sweat. A samurai, an expert
who devoted his life to weaponscraft, found the Double Trouble
a lethal challenge to sword or axe. All Tristan had was his dirk.
Stacked against the glittering steel circle, it suddenly seemed
about as threatening as a butter knife.

There were people close by, ringing them in. Tristan had to
let himself be aware of them in case someone tried to stab him
in the back, but his vision narrowed to a tunnel with his opponent at the other end.

He circled right, hoping the man would trip himself up in the
loose chain pooled on the black earth at his feet. No luck; the
man gathered the slack with his left hand without losing the grip
on his hammer. The Son smiled again.

He wasn't wasting a lot of air on threats, Tristan noticed. He
was smarter than the knife-man.

Tristan darted forward, slashed for the left hand. The circling
hammer angled around with an angry swish and struck sparks
off the blade of the Arkansas toothpick. Tristan danced back
hastily, just avoiding a second rotation tilted toward his head.

Fuckard's good, Tristan thought. He moved back. The man
smiled. Unless Tristan was planning to make a break for timber,
increased separation was all to the Son of Thor's benefit.

Tristan let his right hand stray forward. Instantly the spinning
hammer shot toward him, wrapping its chain around knife and
wrist and practically torquing the weapon from his hand—
practically but not quite. The Son showed teeth in a victory grin

and yanked hard on the chain to jerk his victim into range of the hammer in his upraised left hand.

Tristan launched himself forward with all his strength. He got his left forearm above his head, taking the swivel in the muscle and stunning his hand but jamming the hammer.

His right hand plunged his knife into the hammer-man's belly to the hilt, just to the right of his navel.

They went down in a seethe of limbs slick with sweat and sudden blood. A piercing scream came whistling out of the Son as he thrashed. He didn't give up, though; he kept trying to free the tangled hammer with one hand, or get enough of a stroke with the other to open Tristan's skull for him. Tristan kept a deathgrip on the left wrist. He plunged his Arkansas toothpick repeatedly into the Son's body, until he felt the fight go out of him.

He let go of the man and stood up, leaving the Son doubled around his ruined torso making mewling noises. Tristan took a couple of steps to the side to clear the man, in case he had a last leg-sweep in him, or a back-up dagger to hamstring his enemy with.

The first face he saw was Tooth's. That meant at least one Joker was on hand, though probably not the one Tristan would have chosen for backup. There were also Sons of Thor on their bikes, big and blond and angry.

There were Dog Soldiers too, looking grim, toting quarter-staffs and side-handle nightsticks. They were using them mostly to keep the onlookers back; they didn't look too sure of what to do.

The knife-man, clutching his spurting wrist, was more than willing to tell them. "The fuckard jumped us! We were just having us some fun, and he just backstabbed us. You gotta let us have him. We'll *cut* him."

"They were trying to rape a girl," Tristan explained, in the direction of a Dog Soldier who looked like he might be senior. He noted more Joker faces in the growing crowd, including that of Jovanne, who wore a little half-smile.

"Hey, we're outside the Party Line," the injured man said. "Anything goes, right? We're Stormriders, right? Anything goes. Who the fuck does he think he is, a Citizen?"

"That's Outlaw One," a voice said in a none-too-friendly tone. "Bastard was a City trooper. A fucking Striker."

The knife-man stared at Tristan. "You puke. You fucking *fuck*."

He fought his way to his feet. "You think you're gonna come here and play City Cop with us. You got another fucking think coming, Asshole One."

He held his left hand out, letting his right arm spurt. A fellow Son flipped him a knife with a staghorn handle. He caught it deftly.

"Grab his arms," the bleeding man said. "It's time he learns who the law really is on the Plains." He took a step toward Tristan.

A burst of full-auto gunfire opened his chest, bare beneath the leather vest. He sat down on his butt in the dirt, staring at himself in total astonishment. He put a hand to his chest, raised it to his face, and carefully studied the blood-dripping fingerprints. He raised his face, looked past Tristan with huge blank blue eyes, and toppled over.

Slowly Tristan turned. His ears still rang from the burst, and he had felt the wind of the bullets' passage slapping his cheek.

A stocky horseman with long black braids was gentling his nervous pinto mount. In one hand he held the reins. In the other he held the pistol grip of a Water Horse M52 storm carbine.

Other riders emerged from the woods. Like the one who had shot the Son of Thor they wore yellow headbands and matching brassards. They all carried storm carbines.

Behind one rode the girl Tristan had rescued, still naked from the waist down.

3

"Burningskull!" exclaimed the burly Loco, greasy hair hanging to vast shoulders. "My *man*. Gimme five!"

Picking his way through the various bodies and body odors around the Council Circle, Tristan grinned and slapped hands. He tried not to breathe too vigorously. After his years in the City he found himself strongly aware that hygiene wasn't real important to all of the High Free Folk.

"Showed those Son of Thor dickwads," another Loco exclaimed.

"Thor Losers!"

"Righteous."

Stone righteous, in fact. That was Fat Ed's judgment of Tristan Burningskull's intervention in the Sons of Thor's impromptu gang bang.

Fat Ed was a gentle soul—even some outlaws drew the line at gang rape, and he was one of them. A lot of High Free Folk did not. However, squeamishness wasn't the main reason for giving Tristan the nod.

The Jicarilla Apaches were that. Tough brown bastards, traditional allies of the Taoseños, the Hickories provided the Pueblo's security force. The intended rape victim had run right into a mounted patrol.

The girl was a Taoseña. That the locals were *not* fair game was the most unbreakable of the conditions under which the

17

wealthy and powerful trade center gave permission to the High
Free Folk to hold Ron D. Voo in its traditional locale. Because
two of the assailants were dead—the samurai Tristan had
stabbed bubbled his last while things were in the sorting-out
stage—and because a Stormrider had saved the girl, the Hickories felt magnanimous: If the remaining Sons of Thor pulled up
stakes and left at once, the Hickories would not insist on taking
possession of the surviving attackers for some edifying torture
sessions, and would even forgo levying the fines the treaty permitted them to demand from the High Free Folk for misbehav-
ior of this sort.

Subdued but surly, the Sons of Thor had gathered their
wounded brethren and launched their hogs northeast in showers
of dirt and grass, followed by shouts of "Thor Losers!" From almost being the guest of honor at a lynching bee, Tristan became
Rendezvous' hero of the day.

The stars glittered like silver studs set in Mother Sky's favorite
black-leather party skirt. She and Brother Wind were smiling
yet upon Ron D. Voo, blessing it with fair weather and clear
skies. They dug a good Git-Down as much as flesh-and-blood
bros.

Between the Council Circle and its Fire of piñon, piled higher
than a man's head, crackling and pouring out that tangy smoke
that got in your blood and damned near made you high, a wispy
youth was singing the legend of how Electric Bill met Mavis
Mankiller many years before, how they fought and fucked an
entire fortnight. His watery voice did not match the subject matter.

The grit from Old Cappy crunching beneath their boots, Tristan, Jovanne, and several of the Jokers followed the gestures of
silent, watchful Dog Soldiers to their appointed places in the
Circle. Stiff, the hugest of the Jokers, looked at the young
Singer with disapproval as he settled his bulk on the bare
tamped soil.

"Blood must be getting thin," he said, and spat into the fire.
The spittle, heavy with the grease of venison and buffalo hump,
burned with a crackle and brief yellow flare. "If *he's* the best we
can do, I fear for the Stormriders—not that you'd ever see the
likes of *him* Dancin' with Mr. D; he'd soil his breeches at the

first sight of a Stalking Wind sticking its tail down from among the Witch's Tits."

Sitting crosslegged, Jovanne eyed the young man thoughtfully. "I don't know. I think he's very sensitive."

Stiff emitted a buffalo-bull snort of scorn and rolled his eyes at Tristan, as if to say, *She's our Prez, and we follow her forever, but see how she is?* Tristan began to understand why a sis as easy on the eye as Jovanne could stay so long without a blanket-mate.

Emilio stared at Tristan. The Diggers had poured City medicine on his wound and dressed his wound up proper, but his eyes still looked like holes in a sheet. He probably should have been lying down, but this was the first night of Ron D. Voo.

"You ever Ride the Storm, Hardrider?" he asked.

Tristan met his blacklight gaze. "I said I did." His voice was perfectly calm, the language of his rangy body relaxed to the point of being languid, but something in him said that to ask that question again—implying he was a liar—would be poor policy. "When I was just a stripling, on the back of my Dad's Osage scrambler. There were five of us—my Dad and me, Quicksilver Messenger, Stony Bill, and—and a girl. Daughter of an independent who was riding with us then."

He thought then of Jamie, little and stringy and tough as any boy. There had been no other children near his age among the Hardriders. She had been his only true friend as a child, and even if there had been a passel of other kids, she would have been his best one. He hadn't seen her since a couple of days before the Hardrider massacre.

The memory caught him by the throat and gave him pause. He had known few friends in his life. First Jamie. Then Ferret, quick and clever and savage as his namesake, who introduced him to the closed knife-play circle of Dorm C at the Homeland reform school, where he lived before the Tomlinsons adopted him. Mal and Leo and Billy, his fellow Strikers, who rented a house with him on Homeland's outskirts, in the happy times, when John Amos Schenk and the Reconciliationists were making the City someplace a free man might choose to live, when Outlaw One had made his name feared among the renegades and rapers of the free-ranging clans and was sparking the daughter of his CO, and the future stretched as high and bright and filled with potential as the Plains that rolled away from the Front Range foot into the eye of dawn . . .

He wondered where they all were now. Ferret, a year or two older than Tristan, had been adopted out of McGrory a few months before Tristan. Unlike Tristan, he didn't luck into a kind and loving family; he went off to become a virtual slave, a far more common fate for McGrory kids. When he himself got out, Tristan had tried everything he could to track him. But he had never known Ferret by any other name, and if Homeland's Administration kept track of Citizens by nickname, they didn't share the knowledge with lowly Clients, especially when they were caught and half-tamed scooter trash. What had become of Ferret Tristan didn't know. He doubted he ever would.

Of his three housemates, Tristan had last seen Leo—call sign "Big Bear"—lying on the living room floor clutching his thigh, into which a mortar blast had driven a six-inch splinter of wood. Mal Veeder had already been blown down by a .50-caliber, fired by HDF troops treacherously attacking the old house as part of a City-wide coup by the reactionary Purity faction. Billy had been out on a mission, Brother Wind be thanked, so he might yet live, if the Cats hadn't trolled him in yet. Leo—Tristan hoped he'd found a quick, clean death. Leo was a good man, and didn't deserve what the small-man's malice of Purity would do to him.

Jamie—*I wouldn't even know her now. If she's even alive.* The High Free life was not without its costs. If you hadn't seen a ride-mate in as many years as had rolled past since he'd seen her, odds were you wouldn't again.

"You knew the Messenger?" Zonker asked respectfully. Quicksilver Messenger was one of the greatest pure *riders* to ever fork a bike.

"We Danced with Mr. D then. Me clinging to my daddy's back like a possum baby." Tristan raised his head and stared through the fire, not seeing it or the bearded laughing faces beyond.

"We made it—the only rider better than my dad was the Messenger himself, of all the whole wide Plains. Mr. D got his payment for the dance, though. He took Stony Bill."

A shudder ran through the clump of listeners, which had invisibly expanded to take in the bros sitting to either side. There was something uniquely terrible about death by Stalking Wind. Terrible and holy.

"So you really are the Hardrider of the Hardriders," Emilio breathed.

"I was. I'm Burningskull now."

The dozen or so Tommyknockers seated to the Jokers' right parted with unaccustomed respect. Black Jammer came walking through. Despite the mountain blackness, out of which the high-jumping flames took the merest bite, he had his silver wraparound shades on. A Bard had his image to think of; he had to show as much class as anybody, maybe more. Jammer yielded to none in that line.

He sat down next to Tristan, on the other side from Jovanne. "Hidy," the Skald said, nodding and grinning across Tristan's shirtfront at Jovanne. "Sorry I'm late, Prez. I was making palaver with the Big Boy."

Warily, Jovanne nodded back, looking sidewise at Tristan. The Electric Skald didn't have to account for his motions to the Prez of a sad-nuts little club like the Jokers. She suspected a trick.

The weedy Singer finished his number and vanished. Jovanne was the only one who clapped; her riders looked at one another and rolled their eyes. A skinny adolescent girl in buckskins blew a startlingly loud fanfare on a bugle. Fat Ed rolled into the Circle between bodies and flame, looking grand and not at all ridiculous in his cardboard crown and buffalo robe and quilted tunic.

"Brothers and Sisters," he began, his bass voice loud as thunder, "I bid you welcome to Rendezvous."

That won him a round of whistles and clapping and lusty wolf-calls. This year's Ron D. Voo was three days old, and every night Fat Ed had opened Council Circle with those selfsame words. But they were words that always got a big response. Like a Git-Down Circle standup's challenge, "Are you ready to *par*-tay?"

Fat Ed stood there and took it with a smile. He was a man who appreciated appreciation, no matter how *pro forma*.

After a moment, though, he frowned and spread his arms wide. The crowd quieted.

"Tonight I have serious business to lay upon you. Business of the heaviest import for every last Son and Daughter of the Two Mothers Earth and Sky, for all of the High Free Folk."

That drew a scatter of derisive whistles. The Council Circle was drawn up each night to tend to Plains business, but taking that too seriously offended the pure party-hearty spirit of some. This was Ron D. Voo, after all, the partiest of parties.

He held up his soup-ladle scepter. Silence came down again. The Dog Soldiers were on hand to enforce unaccustomed order in Council, and a bro didn't join the Society because he disliked busting heads.

"Stormriders, I give you—*Jammer*!"

The applause was loud and sincere. There was hardly a rider there who hadn't grown up with the Electric Skald's songs in her ears or on his hairy lips. But there was a puzzled note too. Jammer wasn't often seen inside the Council Circle.

Jammer grinned and raised a hand. "Thanks. I'm used to singing, not jawing, so I'll try to keep this brief.

"Children, I come before you as a captive freed. The Cathead Nation made me their prisoner."

It was as if each man and woman listening had taken a hard blow to the brisket. There were heartbeats of breathless, impending silence, broken by the distant sounds of songs and laughter and engines racing in an impromptu drag, the trill of leopard frogs from down along the creek. Then the Council Circle gave out with a single moaning growl of outrage.

Zonker caught Tristan's eye, held up a thumb, and grinned. It was not a good kind of sound to hear if you wore Cat colors.

The riders of the Plains were outlaws, by birth, by preference, by style. But every society has laws, even an outlaw society. Maybe *especially* an outlaw society; Bro Wind knew a lot of the clans weighed down their members with as many rules as ever a City hung around its Citizens' necks. But the difference was, they were *voluntary* laws; if you couldn't abide the bylaws of any club, you could hit the road and seek out another, more congenial one, or try to show enough class to found your own, or even become a wave-man, an independent, a one-percenter's one-percenter.

Likewise the High Free Folk had laws. They were damned few. One of the foremost was that *he who hinders a Bard must die*.

"I was going solo on the Apishapa," Jammer declared. "They came upon my campfire after dark. I welcomed them, for aren't all bros my bros? I offered to share with them my meager grunt.

"They laid the hard arm on me, my friends. Busted up my axe

and tossed my skinny black butt into a van. The old ways are
gone, they told me; what the Plains need now are spreaders of
the Truth, not Bards."

The crowd was on its feet now, fists clenched, spittle flying,
screaming its collective fury. The Bards were the thread that
held the loose tapestry of the High Free Folk together. They
were more than just a source of entertainment for diversion-
hungry nomads. They witnessed agreements, oversaw duels, ar-
bitrated disputes. They carried messages too important or
personal to entrust to uncertain, open airwaves. They served as
go-betweens in negotiations.

They remembered a bro when he fell, with a sword or bullet
through his lights. They were the memory of the Plains; they
were its soul.

"Death to the Catheads!" the crowd screamed. "Lay 'em
waste!"

Jammer held up his hands. The turmoil quieted.

"I don't ask vengeance for myself; it's not fitting for a Bard
to call bro down upon bro—on his own account. Besides—" he
chuckled "—my lady Jovanne and her Jokers and a certain
friend of theirs settled my personal debt to the Cats and more,
when they matched their forty against two hundred of the Cathead finest, sent 'em packing, and set me free."

The spectators broke out in wild cheering, this time directed
toward the little clump of Jokers. Jovanne smiled tightly and
nodded.

"But, my brothers and my sisters, I have to tell you: The Cathead Nation is massing, away in the East, under the eyes of their
yellow-robe advisors. They aim to sweep the Plains clean in the
name of the Fusion."

"Is it true the Fusion demands human sacrifice?" a voice
asked from the back.

"I don't know. There were two Fusion priests with the band
that took me, and they didn't exactly argue mercy for me.
They're keen on having their friends the Catheads take over the
whole Plains. One thing I do know: Unless someone stops them
they'll do that thing. And if they do, from that day on the High
Free Folk will be neither high nor free."

He stood a moment, head bowed. Then he slipped back to
Tristan's side as the crowd again began to cry blood and devas-

tation upon the Cats. Into the firelight once more stepped Fat Ed.

"My friends," he said, "it isn't my place to take sides. But I have to admit I'm glad there's someone among us who's ready, willing, and able to take up the challenge Brother Jammer just issued. We have a man among us who recognizes the threat the Cathead Nation and the Fusion pose to all of us. A man who is ready to act—to *lead*—and whom we all know is equal to the challenge."

Tristan sat there feeling unaccustomed warmth spread from heels to head. He was surprised. He hadn't expected Fat Ed to introduce him so soon, let alone give him so much of a buildup. . . . He started to rise.

And Jammer grabbed him by the arm, holding him unbreakably in place.

4

"Brothers and sisters, Stormriders, it's my pure pleasure to present to you—*John Hammerhand!*"

Into the circle of orange light and crazy applause limped a man, supporting himself on a crutch carved and painted and feather-decked like a Blackfoot coup-stick. He was tall, tall as Tristan at least, and though he obviously carried the weight of a good twenty winters more than the young Hardrider, his shoulders were every bit as broad, his waist as narrow, his belly as flat. His hair was blond and shaggy, thinning ever so slightly up top. Unlike most Plains men, his face was shorn clean.

It was a commanding face. It was rescued from City rich-boy prettiness by having taken some damned hard knocks in its day. His fine nose had a hump to it that hadn't been there when he was whelped. A long transverse slash crossed his right cheek. It had been left by the claw of an angry grizzly sow, not a foeman's blade. It still bore the perforations of the self-stitch job with a porcupine needle and gut its owner had performed by feel, after he had laid that grizzly in the dirt with his own Green River blade. And then he had knelt down to sing a death song for that opponent, for she had been protecting her tiny cubs, and afterward he'd adopted the cubs, which were raised up by his clan, and lived and fought beside them for years.

The most arresting feature of the man—once you got past the eyes, which were blue and clear as the sky over the Sangre de Cristo Mountains and caught up in webs of grin-wrinkles—

were his hands. They were big hands, big for his arms, which, while corded well with muscle, were not the tree-trunk black- smith's arms many of the beefier Free Folk boasted. Rather the hands were like maul-heads on good hickory helves, great with scar-tissue and cartilage. Hands a man might hammer nails with, or bend a nail in two between the fingers.

Hammerhand. Such was the man's name; such was his leg- end. John Hammerhand, council chief and warlord of the Wan- derers MC, walked with the mightiest Plains heroes in the campfire songs of the Bards.

He held up those terrible hands, open, like a bear presenting his claws. "The Cathead Nation has betrayed their colors," he said in a voice deep as Rio Grande Gorge and rough as a dirt road. "They've disgraced every one of us with their treachery. And now they say they'll put all true bros in the dirt, with their boots on our necks. I say . . ."

Rolling his hands over, he clenched them into fists, with such sudden force it seemed he could crack the world like a walnut between those scarred fingers.

". . . *this:* We fight. Who's with me?"

The crowd came to its feet in a screaming mass. Feeling as if maybe the Son of Thor had caught him a lick on the conk with his Double Trouble that afternoon and he was only just getting around to feeling it, Tristan looked to Jammer.

The Electric Skald just shrugged. But he was smiling a small, secret smile all the same.

"Ouch. *Crap.*"

Tristan jerked his hand away from the bike, growling on its kickstand, and waved skinned knuckles in the air. The short- shanked screwdriver kept slipping from the slot. *I'm not cut out for this,* he told himself glumly.

It wasn't news. His father, Wyatt Hardrider, had been charis- matic, a hell of a rider, and the bravest warrior on the Plains. One thing he had not been was a wrench. Okay, he hadn't been bright either, but that was not thought a major disability. A Prez was supposed to shine at everything—especially such funda- mental skills as keeping your ride rolling. A man who didn't have much hair with a wrench in his paw had to show some real class if he wanted to lead.

Of course, it didn't *help* that Tristan had been daydreaming about Elinor, the love he had lost when the City turned on him. But that wasn't the problem's root. He was just a terrible wrench.

I hope nobody's watching, he thought, *not that it matters, since Hammerhand's in as Main Man of the war against the Cats. . . .*

"Yo, Tristan," a voice said from behind him. "Havin' some trouble there?"

He glanced up to see half a dozen Jokers gathered around him. He gave them what he hoped was a confident smile. "Just a spot," he said, "but I'll handle it."

"When are you gonna call out Hammerhand?" Zonker asked.

Tristan froze in the act of bending down to pick up his screwdriver. He reeled it into his hand and straightened, very deliberately, wiping the shank down with an oily rag. Overhead clouds were piling up like mountains in the sky. They were still white and fluffy, but it was clear the weather reprieve the gods had favored Rendezvous with was coming to an end.

"Why would I want to do a thing like that?"

Zonker tipped his head to the side and looked blank. "You're the man with the *Sign.* That Guest Star in Taurus belongs to *you.*"

"Wind and Sky picked you," said Little Teal in a voice scarcely audible above the never-ending wind. "You're the man to lead us against the Cats."

He looked at her. The tiny wrench, blue-eyed and attractive in a tough round-jawed way, seldom spoke these days, since her mate Big Jupe had died in the Burningskull fight. That made it difficult to blow her off.

Then behind them he saw Jovanne, standing with her arms crossed and a sour half-smile on her face. *Great,* he thought, *fucking great.*

"I got my Sign, right enough. But it was for me. Finding your SoulStar is personal business for a man."

That quieted them for a moment, not to mention taking a little of the edge off their Prez, who was listening intently while managing to seem not to. Belief in a rider having a Star which was his soul—or hers—spread wide across the Plains, well beyond the women-only StarLodge cult within which it originated. It was the most private kind of medicine.

"Why does your Star shine so bright," Red Dog asked, "if it wasn't meant for everybody to see?"

Tristan wanted to kick him. The red-bearded man was more thoughtful than most of his bros. He had also been steadily skeptical of Tristan; it was even odds at least that he was intentionally trying to show him up.

Unlike his father, Tristan had no problem with cunning and misdirection. He prided himself, though, on knowing when you had to face something squarely. He reckoned this was one of those times.

"I'll set the Plains alight with the Burning Skull," he said, looking Red Dog in the eye, "*someday*. This is Hammerhand's party; I'm not going to crash it for him. My time will come when the stars are right."

"Yeah," put in Pud, the former Cathead. "Burningskull's just biding his time."

The other Jokers glared at Pud. Tristan ignored him. He wasn't sure how to read the little man. Though Tristan had executed with his own hand the Catheads who had been responsible for burning a captured Joker scout alive, he had kept the clan from massacring the remaining prisoners. Along with the aptly named Handsome, Pud had opted to join the Jokers—not an uncommon thing for prisoners to do, though their new brothers generally made sure they didn't have an easy ride until they had fully proved themselves, and this was no exception. Pud had attached himself to Tristan like a little dog, and insisted on pushing forward to help him whether Tristan wanted it or not.

"But why not now?" Zonker wanted to know. He was a persistent son of a bitch, you had to give him that. "Hammerhand's old. Shit, he's all crippled up. You could take him easy."

Tristan bent over his bike again. "Whether I can or whether I can't, I don't intend to try."

"Afraid?" Red Dog asked.

Tristan looked up. His gray-blue eyes darkened to a slate color like the clouds of a gathering storm. The others backed a step off from Red Dog. The redhead looked as if he wished he could grab the word and stuff it back in his mouth.

"What the hell would it prove?" Tristan asked, bending back to his work. Everybody there had seen him take on John Badheart with his hands in shackles, and whatever else Badheart was, he wasn't a weakling. He didn't deign to defend his courage. "Have a thought here. So I beat up Hammerhand. So the hell what? Buffalo Bull over there's a hell of a lot stronger than I am."

He jerked his chin towards a big A-shaped tent before which a gigantic Kiowa who rode with the Comanche Kwahadi MC, stripped to the waist and looking like his namesake shaved and oiled, sat taking on all comers at arm-wrestling. War had been decided upon, but much remained to be jawed over in Council. Meantime, Ron D. Voo ruled. "You want *him* leading you against the whole Cathead Nation?"

The Jokers laughed. Buffalo Bull was as dumb as he was strong, and there might not be a stronger man on the whole wide Plains.

"I'm riding behind Hammerhand," Tristan said, pressing his advantage. "And so's your Prez. And I'll follow my Star when the Cats are in the dirt, you can damned well bet to that."

He glanced up at Jovanne. She looked as if she had lightened up a shade or two. He noticed something unusual beyond her.

"But what about the prophecy?" Tooth asked.

Spotting the chance at a flying subject change, Tristan jumped on it and rode like the wind. "So who're the dudes in the red coats?" he asked, pointing with his screwdriver.

About thirty yards behind the Jokers two men stood slightly apart from the throng watching Buffalo Bull at play. One was tall, slim but broad-shouldered, his aquiline features emphasized by the receding line of his dark hair. The other was small, fair, and pinch-faced, as if he smelled a bad smell. Tristan sympathized. Both men wore long taper-tailed coats of brilliant red.

"They're Brits," Jovanne said, "down from Eddie City in the Federation. They're with the Honourable Company. Looking to do business of some kind. What, I don't know."

"Seriously? They're English?"

She nodded. "Right straight from the Queen Across the Water, Vicky Three her own high and mighty self."

Tristan thrust his lower lip out. "I'll be wired. The big dude with them?"

A man stood across the upended barrel from Buffalo Bull, shucking off a third scarlet coat. He was even taller than the dark-haired man, with orange hair cropped close to a bullet-shaped head and enormous orange whiskers flaring ferociously from beneath a much-broken nose.

Pud bobbed his head eagerly. "He sure is. 'Sergeant General' they call him."

"Sergeant *Major*," Tristan corrected. He straightened up. "This should be interesting."

The huge Brit settled down across the barrel from Buffalo Bull. He had removed his white blouse, revealing a great-muscled chest covered with bright orange fur. He wasn't as squatly massive as the Kiowa rider, sitting there smugly on his camp stool with his greasy black braids hanging across either thick shoulder. But his arms were like thighs, the same thickness from elbows to hands; he was a red bear to the Kiowa's brown bull.

The Kiowa smiled.

Music skirled from a boombox, the reedy jangly sounds favored by belly-dancers, a popular species of entertainer at Ron D. Voo. Some called it Mideastern music, which suggested to most of the High Free Folk that it came from somewhere just across the Missus Hip. Somebody cranked it high.

Buffalo Bull put his elbow on the barrelhead. The Brit did likewise. They clasped hands.

At a signal from a young woman flying Digger colors on her open denim vest—she was topless beneath—the two began to strain. Slowly the smile slipped off the giant Kiowa's face from behind the gloss of sweat. He seldom took more than ten seconds to put an opponent down; more often or not he pushed his foe's hand straight onto the table with little wasted time.

But the Limey's arm was unmoved. And then, impossibly, the Bull's hand began to be forced back and down. His eyes bugged out, his mouth worked furiously, and the sweat poured off him in rivers.

His bellow drowned the thump as his hand was pinned.

The orange-whiskered man stood up massaging scarred knuckles. The tall dark-haired man permitted himself a slight smile. His partner still looked as if he'd stepped in dogshit.

Tristan rubbed his jaw. "Interesting." Then, because there was no excuse for putting it off any further, he started to get back to work.

He felt presence by his side, and then Little Teal was hunkered down, studying his bike. "What're you doing?" she asked.

"Um," he said. He tapped the throttle stop-screw. "I'm trying to adjust the carburetor. I'm getting some ping."

"I think your problem is you need to advance your timing," the slight woman said. "You're firing too long before top dead center."

He looked at her. She smiled. "Badheart was a pretty lousy wrench. He was too big a jerk to listen to anybody, though. Let me give you a hand."

She turned and signaled for somebody to bring her tool kit. Tristan nodded. A smile unfolded slowly across his face.

Despite having fought beside the Jokers—led them to victory over one-sided odds, in fact—Tristan was still in much the same boat as Pud: a well-hated enemy who had recently switched sides. His acceptance by the Jokers—not to mention the High Free Folk at large—was a fragile thing, like a dandelion head gone to seed, awaiting the slightest puff of wind to blow it away. That was a major factor in his refusal to challenge Hammerhand for command of the Cathead war—though he wasn't stupid enough to say so out loud.

Maybe they don't think I'm a total sag-nuts for not knowing how to fix the sled after all, he thought. It seemed a hopeful sign.

"Tristan, look out!" Jovanne shouted.

As he spun his eye's corner caught a blur of onrush movement. Someone was trying to jump on his back, knife in hand.

5

Tristan pivoted on his left heel and brought his right elbow straight up from his side. It smashed the leaping knife-man's face. Tristan sensed his opponent go limp, start to collapse on him. He slammed his knee up into the man's body as he collided with him.

Tristan just kept from being knocked backward into his bike, which, supported on its kickstand, would've gone right over with him in a hell of a tangle. His assailant fell into a sprawl on the grass at Tristan's booted feet, groveling and gagging and clutching his spurting nose. His knife lay beside him. He gathered enough wits to become aware of it and his hand darted for it.

Tristan's right boot came down hard, pinning the hand to the turf like a Comanche lance spiking a rattler.

"Another sag-nuts who didn't get the word about what Tristan did to those Sons," observed Zonker, leaning forward with interest.

"New arrival," suggested Little Teal.

Dog Soldiers materialized to Tristan's either side. They were always alert for trouble—eager was more like it—and they clutched their six-foot staffs as if they anticipated being able to bounce them off somebody's head real soon.

"You know the rules," said one, whose face was dark and beak-nosed enough for a Lakota. "No fighting."

His burly blond partner was practically licking his bearded lips. Tristan thought fleetingly that he might be a Son of Thor or an ally seeing a chance for a touch of payback. He dismissed the thought instantly. No matter what blood his clan might owe Tristan, the Dog Soldier would never dare abuse his power in that way. Soldiers who betrayed the Society were taken into Dog Society kivas and never seen again. What actually became of them, no one knew, and no one was ready to find out first-hand.

"I was attacked," Tristan said calmly. He stepped back off his opponent's wrist. "I defended myself. That's permitted by the Law of Ron D. Voo."

"He—he killed my brother," moaned the man on the ground.

The dark Soldier's eyes glittered. "Here?"

The injured man shook his head. "Out on the Plains. He was a Striker. Mingy City scum-sucker!" He batted at Tristan. The dark Dog Soldier rapped him smartly on the elbow. He yelped and clutched it.

"Who was your brother?" Tristan asked.

"Easy," the man said between sobs. "Headhunters clan."

"He had it coming."

The man shrieked and tried to hit him again. More Dog Soldiers arrived at the run. The Headhunter was hauled to his feet while the darker of the two original Soldiers held his staff horizontally between him and Tristan.

"A Striker?" the blond Soldier said. "You're actually a Striker?"

"I was."

"We'd better take you along for a little talk," the dark one said. "We don't take kindly to spies in camp."

Pud thrust himself forward. "He's not a mingy spy. He's Burningskull!"

The dark Dog Soldier pushed him back. "And I'm Aching Piles. Go away."

Blondie took hold of Tristan's arm and pulled. Tristan set himself and refused to be budged.

"I'm a guest at Rendezvous," he said. "I claim full protection under its laws."

"Those laws only apply to bros, pal," the blond Dog Soldier said, still trying to pull Tristan off balance and trying equally hard not to show the effort.

"And a bro he most certainly is," a deep voice said.

Heads turned, which was a normal effect of that voice. John Hammerhand stood there leaning on his cane, grinning all over his battered boy's face.

Reluctantly the blond Dog Soldier let his hand fall away from Tristan's arm. "But he was a Striker," his partner said.

"He was more than that," Hammerhand said, his grin getting wider. "He was Outlaw One."

"Wind and Sky," the dark Soldier breathed. The Dog Soldiers actually edged away from Tristan. Members of the Dog Society were supposed to be fearless even by the balls-to-the-wall standards of the Plains. But over the last four years *Outlaw One* had become a name nomad mothers used to frighten noisy children to silence.

"You want us to arrest him?" the blond Dog Soldier asked, his voice cracking like an adolescent's.

Hammerhand shook his head. "Hell, no. He was born a Hardrider—he's old Wyatt's son."

"I thought the Hardriders all died," another Dog Soldier protested. "That's what Jammer's song said, and he was there to see it go down."

"So he did. But even Jammer makes mistakes sometimes. Who do you think it was told me about the boy?"

He limped forward to lay his hard hand on Tristan's shoulder. "You all heard about the fight the Jokers won over the Catheads up north? Here's the boy who led them. That new Guest Star in the Bull's his SoulStar; gave him a vision and a Sign. He's Burningskull now, and that name will shine bright on the Plains before he hits the end of his Road. I tell you this is true."

Nodding, the Dog Soldiers fell back and began to go elsewhere. Tristan frowned. On the one hand, Hammerhand's intervention had worked to the benefit of his personal ass, a very dear possession. And the Law was on his side: By custom, even as Outlaw One, the Striker and relentless City slayer of outlaws, he should have been as inviolate at Ron D. Voo as Fat Ed himself.

On the other hand, the Dog Society was supposed to be above personalities as well as clan rivalries. No man was supposed to have the kind of influence over Dog Soldiers that John Hammerhand displayed, not even an out-and-out hero of his stature.

"Come, boy," Hammerhand said, applying gentle but irresistible pressure to his shoulder. "Walk with me a ways. I understand you'll be leading the Jokers to the fight."

Tristan allowed himself to be pulled along. He rolled his eyes at Jovanne, whose fierce and lovely face was clouding up again.

They walked among the brilliant tents and brightly painted bikes and rowdy raucous mobs and hard-rocking sounds of Rendezvous, the gaming and the swearing and the lying and the haggling. Walking past the Kwahadi tent into which Buffalo Bull had retired to sulk, Tristan saw the three Brits standing together, the big sergeant major dressed again and standing like a redwood behind his superiors. The dark-haired one caught Tristan's eye, and gave him a nod and a hint of smile.

"I appreciate your speaking up for me, Brother Hammerhand," he said, using the form of address the nomads rolled out on the rare occasions when they felt called on to act formal.

"Call me John, boy. We're going to be brothers-in-arms soon; we're going to ride together."

Riding together was the sacrament, the cement that held the cranky and individualistic Plains brethren together. The ritual of blood-brotherhood was widely practiced on the Plains, along with a lot of other Indian rites—real and fictitious, as Tristan knew from his studies in Homeland's great but neglected Library. But that was window dressing in a way. All those who Rode were brothers; the Strikers, now defunct, who rode and talked and generally acted like the nomads whose archenemies they were, were actually more widely respected on the Plains than the Diggers, who seldom forked a hog. That had helped save Tristan's life to date.

To consent to ride with another was a bond as deep and wide as marriage—much more so, to many Stormriders. Tristan's parents, Wyatt Hardrider and Jen Morningstar, had been devoted to each other, happily if stormily married, but they were exceptional.

"Okay," Tristan said, "John. But I'm not actually leading the Jokers. In the Burningskull fight I was just their warlord *pro tem*—uh, for the time being. Jovanne is their Prez. Is, was, and will be."

Still smiling, Hammerhand shook his shaggy blond head. "Son, we've fallen on hard times out here on the Plains. The Catheads falling under the spell of these yellow-robe devils from the East is a symptom, but it ain't the sickness, not by a

Plains mile. We Stormriders have veered off the true Road, the old Road. We're in sore danger of losing the Way."

"How do you mean?"

"In the old days a man was a man and a woman was a mouse, if you catch my drift. She knew her place, which was serving her lord and master and keeping her mouth shut."

"Oh," Tristan said. That was the Trad line, fairly common on the Plains. "You mean like the slave girls there?"

He gestured toward the long low-slung pavilion of the Slave Drivers MC. As usual, a dozen or so women stood or lounged on carpets out front. Today they were dressed in loincloths and bangles that accentuated more than they covered, with weird mock-Egyptian patterns painted on their faces. Noticing Tristan's attention, they began to make yearning come-hither pantomimes with bracelet-hung arms. Tristan grinned in honest appreciation.

A burly Driver lounged against a tentpole keeping a bloodshot eye on the harem. He wore his colors vest without a shirt beneath, and a bare black-furred belly lopped over the belt of his grease-crusted jeans.

"Look all you want, buddy," the Driver said, "but beware of burning your eyes. You don't touch without our say-so."

"Oh, really?"

"Really."

"You're talking to the son of Wyatt Hardrider," Tristan said. "Care to place any bets on that proposition?"

The Driver sagged. Jammer's song of how Wyatt Hardrider—then known as Wyatt Octane—had stolen the beautiful Jen Morningstar from her clan, the dreaded cannibal Smoking Mirrors, was even more widely known and loved than the ballad of the Hardriders' Last Stand. A man as masterful as the Drivers liked to pretend they were doubtless would have undertaken to make young Tristan eat those words. But John Hammerhand stood right there at the offender's side, and the Dog Soldiers were never far, and unlike the occasional hapless vengeance-bent newcomer, the Driver *had* heard of the asskicking Tristan had laid on the Sons of Thor. Rather than tear himself off a piece of that, he scowled and spat and slunk inside the tent to sort things through.

Tristan laughed. Hammerhand laughed too, and slapped him

on the back. Tristan choked. It was like being given an affectionate pat with a maul.

"You've got the touch, son," the hero said. "You're a leader born, or this child's a Pawnee. And yes, our brothers the Slave Drivers have the right idea. Better than what most of us have allowed ourselves to sink to anyway."

That wasn't much of a ringing endorsement, but then again, the Slave Drivers were widely regarded as purely low-down, mingy, and mean. How they always managed to talk a handful of gorgeous babes into being their slaves was a mystery as profound as any StarLodge secret, and even more keenly sought after.

Tristan and Hammerhand entered the Huckster Zone, where there were for sale beads and baubles and timing lights, smokes and tokes and tapestries depicting brothers and sisters in the wind, after paintings of the ancient master Dave Mann. Here a selection of swords and spears and maces—hardware to be reckoned with on the Plains, where ammo was scarce—lay out in the sun, glinting hot on black velvet. Up-and-coming young Bards hawked their latest tapes, their own selections slotted in hopefully among classic songs of ancient times by Cinderella or Steppenwolf, or Plains greats by Dreamboat Annie and Twelve-String Jake, and Jake's son Jammer, of course.

"With respect, cousin," Tristan said, using a form of address that affirmed kinship without presuming on it, "I don't much hanker to ride the Slave Drivers' road myself."

With the trademark authoritative deep-throat roar of the true outlaw bike, a couple of clans began peeling out in high traditional style, one after another, raising dust on their way to a bonfire shivaree up at Lost Lake, along the ridge between Wheeler and Bull of the Woods Peak. It wasn't as choice a location as Blue Lake or Star or Waterbird Lakes, but they were on ground sacred to the Pueblo. Permission to enter that ground was not easy to come by, and if you entered *without* permission, the Hickories came and got you, and helped you get your mind right awhile before they let you die. The Taoseños' enforcers, the Jicarilla, were very concerned that not even the most dedicated party animals should get the idea it was worthwhile to crash the forbidden zone.

"It's not for everybody, the Driver way," Hammerhand agreed when they could hear each other again. For a man with fists that by rumor could bust chunks from living rock, he sure was an agreeable cuss. "But we've given up too much of our power to our women. It's sapped our strength. It's how come the Cats are able to threaten to put all the Stormriders in the dirt."

"Maybe," Tristan said.

6

"A man should never think," John Hammerhand said, "just *act*."

Tristan coughed. The sunken cylinder of the sweat-kiva was heated by a smoky fire of scrub cedar and piñon. It smelled great, but it like to choked you to death.

Stripped stone bare, Tristan sat cross-legged, facing Hammerhand across the fire. To left and right sat a pair of ManLodge initiates, glassy-eyed and sweating dutifully, pounding on little skin Pawnee drums with their fingertips.

"What?" Tristan managed to say.

"Thought. It's a trap for a man. The way of the Warrior means no thought and no intention. The action speaks for itself."

"Mother Sky," Tristan swore.

The drummers gaped at him. One of them missed a beat. He realized he'd commited a faux pas, invoking a female deity.

"Uh, *Brother Wind*, I meant to say," he said sheepishly.

The initiates nodded and went back to beating. Tristan sat there sucking the insides of his cheeks. *Great. He thinks we're going to whip the Cats without* thinking?

Not that Tristan always exactly thought things out before he leapt right in himself. There was that battle with the Sons of Thor . . . he'd won that one on sheer balls and meanness, no question.

Then he thought back to the Burningskull fight. Even with

the crazy courage of Jovanne and her dug-in decoy force, the Jokers had fought a ferocious battle. Once the enveloping sweep Tristan had led had crashed into the Cathead rear, the battle was all over except for running down as many Cats as had been caught. But if Jovanne's little group had been overrun, if the sweep had got hung up or lost its way . . . The song Jammer was composing in his head would make the victory seem predetermined, easy almost. Tristan didn't remember it that way, but he guessed that's how the Bards—and the straight world's historians—always called the shots.

It had taken guts and sharp shooting and strong arms to beat the Cathead war-band, sure. But without thought—and a big dash of luck—things would have gone the other way.

John Hammerhand rocked gently on the tamped-earth floor, smiling pleasantly. "I reckon you're wondering what my plan is when we come up with the Cats," he said.

"You reckon right."

Hammerhand beamed. "No plan at all. Attack, attack, attack! Grab 'em by the nose, kick 'em in the ass. Plans and schemes and strategies are women's ways. The Way of the Man is to charge—to bust right on through!"

"He's fucking nuts," Tristan said.

"Did he let you beat a drum?" asked Jovanne, all full of honey malice.

Tristan groaned. He lay on his belly, naked among wolfskins on the floor of the big rented tent he shared with Jovanne, with his cheek on the backs of his hands, staring into the unwavering glow of a kerosene lamp. The Jokers' Prez sat beside him, wrapped in a wolfskin robe, long legs bare and crossed at the ankles. Outside the night rang with songs and guitars and curses and laughter, but it seemed another world away, having nothing to do with this snug microcosm.

If he weren't so wound and worried he could get to like this.

"He said, 'Plans and schemes and strategies are women's ways.' Exact words. I'll hear 'em till I die—which won't be long at this rate." He shook his head. "Wind and Water, if we'd played according to his damned ManLodge code it'd be Drago's Cathead war-party playing drums tonight—made from our hides."

Jovanne laughed. When she wasn't uptight she had an excellent laugh, full-throated and rich. "So you're not a heavy Trad then?"

He craned back to give her a blue eye. "What do *you* think?"

"I guess not. Rub your neck?"

He looked at her a moment more, then nodded and turned his face forward. She began to knead the muscles of his neck. Her hands were strong, capable hands. Hands that could do far more than John Hammerhand would ever acknowledge.

"So how come you're not Trad," she asked, swinging a leg over to straddle him, "coming from a big, tough clan like the Hardriders?"

"We weren't big."

"Jammer's songs make it seem like the prairie shook when you rode."

"His songs make it seem like the prairie shakes when *any-body* rides. No, there was no way we'd be Trad, not with Mom riding right alongside Dad. And if my dad ever thought to play Driver to her Slave . . ."

He shook his head and laughed. "She'd have busted his ass in a hurry. She was a handful, even without all those witchy StarLodge Powers she was supposed to have."

"You don't believe in the Lodge? Or should I ask, you don't believe in Powers? Hold still, you'll get your neck all knotted again."

"You're pinching. I don't know. I always took for granted that my mom was magic—everybody said she was. I wonder now how much that was just being a kid."

He sighed. Jovanne had worked her hands down to his shoulders. She was good at what she was doing. "Hell. I can't *dislike* Hammerhand. I mean, he's dumb as an adobe fence post. But he's a good man, and strong, and his reputation makes him out to be pretty brave. And he does know how to make it feel good to be around him, if you catch my drift.

"Y'know what?" He grinned over his shoulder at her. "I think I just described my father."

Jovanne stopped and leaned forward with her hands on either side of Tristan's neck. "So what are you going to do?"

"I don't know. Sign or no Sign, I don't think enough riders would follow me to make much of a dent in the Catheads. A lot of people have trouble forgetting I was Outlaw One. I put a mess of the Folk not just in the dirt but under it."

"You got the Jokers turned around quick enough."

"Don't start. I washed away the unpopular but well-named Badheart, and I helped pull a quick victory out of what looked like a very deep hole. You have any ideas how I can manage that for most of the Motor Clans on the whole Plains?"

She leaned forward onto her elbows. Her bare breasts flattened on Tristan's back.

"If you take Hammerhand down," she murmured, "they'll respect you."

"But they'll probably hate me."

"Does that matter?"

"It does if they get the idea I'm still in City harness. They'll decide it's all a setup, and get a mind to use me for bike-polo."

"That would be a shame."

He turned to look into her face, so close to his. "You really think so?"

"I really do," she said, and kissed him.

She started on the side of his mouth, then covered his mouth with hers. Something snapped inside him. He'd been without a woman for a long time. Suddenly, whatever was keeping him from taking Jovanne up on her frequently repeated offer didn't seem so awfully important anymore. *Elinor*, he thought, and then he put her from his mind.

He rolled over. She raised up off him so he wouldn't bear her over. He grinned at her as she turned her lithe upper body to tug the wolfskins away from his groin. He was standing to full attention. She looked back at him, pursing her lips appreciatively.

Her fingers took light hold of his cock, and began to stroke up and down below the head. He moaned. He reached up to make play with her breasts. They were big breasts and round, without much hang to them, so that when she was clothed they looked smaller than they were. Her nipples were pale pink. They firmed and grew as he rolled them between his fingers.

She felt his cock start to quiver, and pulled her fingers back. "Not so fast, big boy," she said, low in her throat. She waited until the pre-orgasmic spasms safely passed. Then she took hold of his prick again. She thrust her rump back, dragging the head agonizingly down the cleft before socketing it in the moist snug vestibule of her pussy.

Both of them moaned aloud as she dropped her hips, impaling herself full-length on his cock. She crushed her breasts against his chest, which was lightly furred in black between powerful pecs. Their mouths locked, their tongues wrestled. She rolled her hips. He dug heels into the unyielding earth and thrust rhythmically up into her, hands locked in the small of her back.

After several minutes she broke the clench, sat upright, arched her back. He caught her wrists to keep her from flying over backwards. She threw her head back and screamed.

Tooth's head popped through the front of the tent. *"Prez! Are you all—Oh."*

Her right hand broke Tristan's grip and snaked into the robe she had let fall beside them. It came up with a slim straight-edge dagger, which she hurled at Tooth. He leapt back with a squawk as it bounced butt-first off the aluminum lodgepole with a clang.

Using the muscles of her thighs Jovanne pumped herself up and down on Tristan with quickening tempo, grinning down through her orange bangs at him until her head went back and she began to scream again. He felt her clench around him. He thrust upward with all the considerable strength of thighs, back, and belly.

"Ohhh." She collapsed onto him with a protracted sigh. For a moment she lay full-length on him, quivering slightly, breathing convulsively. Then she licked his ear.

"You're a tough customer," she whispered. "I like that in a man."

He showed teeth and started to drive upward again. She rolled off him, tugging him with her with such startling strength that it took nearly no effort to wind up on top of her.

"All right," she said breathlessly, "I've seen what you got. Now show me how well you can use it."

He began simply enough, arching his butt up into the air, driving into her with a long forceful stroke. She locked her ankles behind his back. Her face to the side, her teeth clenched, she pulled herself up into him at every thrust.

He worked his knees forward, under her thighs. He bent his back forward, so that his chin was between her tits and his hips were driving his cock almost horizontally into her. He began to slam into her, faster and faster, exploding the breath from her in short panting cries.

"Oh, now!" she cried. She dug her fingers into his buttocks

and pulled him into her with all the force of her wiry arms. He straightened his legs behind him, gripped the earth with his toes, and simply *pushed*, while she screamed and shook with earthquake intensity.

When she moaned for him to stop he relaxed and let himself lie, supporting himself on his elbows while he caught his breath. In half a minute he started to rock his hips again.

"Wait," she said, pressing fingertips against his sweaty chest. He raised himself. She disengaged, rolled out from under him, came up on all fours. The yellow light cast golden highlights on the curve of her taut-muscled ass.

He got up on his knees, took himself in hand, guided himself to her. He swirled the head of his cock between the lips of her pussy until she made a peevish, pleading sound in her throat and thrust her butt back into his belly.

Hands on those perfectly rounded cheeks, he began to work his hips back and forth, letting them both feel the full length of him working inside her. Slowly he built momentum, feeling her excitement build around him, and then he was slamming into her with piston force, and this time when she cried out and tightened he let himself go too, in a roaring, bucking, rattling surge of release.

When the shocks and aftershocks finally let him go he collapsed onto her. They fell facing each other among the skins, and into sleep.

Sometime later Tristan woke. He was lying on his back. Jovanne was propped on an elbow, drawing a finger down his chest. Out in the night a Bard was singing in a clear tenor of Heroes' Holm, the red planet that neighbored Earth, where true bros went after death to party down eternally with topless red-skinned princesses—and sisters with well-hung red-skinned studs—and hassle now and again with eight-foot green foes with four arms each.

"So the way you've got it figured," Tristan said, rolling to face her, "is if I push Hammerhand aside and take over the war, I won't be a threat to you keeping the Jokers anymore."

She kissed him on the nose. "You're not as dumb as you look, darlin'."

"Shit, I hope not." He reached for her.

7

Tristan raised himself high off the saddle as the yellow scrambler broke the rim of the arroyo. A moment of flight, that floating-the-edge feeling when your gut seems independent of the rest of you, and then the knobbed tires came down and bit the soft streambed sand as shocks and flexing strong legs took the impact. A wobble, a spray of sand, and Tristan blasted across the finish line to the accompaniment of cheers that went soaring up like a cloud of the migrating seagulls busy picking through the garbage dump downstream from the Rendezvous camp.

He threw the bike sideways and put a booted foot down in a victory slide that raised sand like a bow wave. The next rider behind crossed the line, hunched over his handlebars as if it mattered.

Though they did it a fair amount, the bros were not big on hard cross-country riding; there was no sacrament of the Dirt as there was of the Road. They were more at home rolling the Hard Roads on their big deep-voiced cruisers.

Tristan had a double advantage. The Strikers never rode full-out sleds; they forked nothing but scramblers, and were never happier than when they were busting brush or chewing sand with the cleats of their tires. Plains culture was built, almost defiantly, around the big bikes, the outlaw hogs, which were really little use off a solid road. The Strikers had no such hang-ups.

More than that, he was the get of old Anse the One-Eyed, the

45

original Hardrider, who had won the clan's name by pushing
WildFyre—the greatest bike ever wrenched together in all of
time—across a thousand miles of Plains, storms, Stalking
Winds, and earthquakes in three days to pull a one-man rescue
of his then-clan, the Prairie Hawks, from the Blackfeet—and, of
course, their uneasy temporary allies, the Cathead Nation.
Though WildFyre was a cruiser—the *ultimate* cruiser, the songs
had it—he rode her as if she were a scrambler. When there was
no road, or the road was blocked, he by-God made his own.

And Tristan had been taught to ride less by his father than by
Wyatt Hardrider's best friend and counselor, Quicksilver Messenger. The Messenger was reputed the best rider of his day, and
rare among the nomads, he owned no cruiser at all. Instead he
lavished all his care and attention on Silver Streak, his scrambler. Because no man or woman born could keep up with him,
on the Hard Road or off, his refusal to ride a big bike was held
to be showing near-ultimate class, not a quirk or disability. Out
on the Plains, damned near nothing was odd, if you did it well
enough and with sufficient style.

Tristan held up gauntleted hands in a victory salute. The Jokers clustered around him, hoorawing and slapping him on the
back. John Badheart had naturally owned a scrambler, which in
due course had passed into Tristan's possession. But the late
Joker warlord had disdained it in favor of his more macho
flame-painted sled. The scrambler had been thoroughly neglected. Accordingly, Tristan had appropriated the finest of the
bikes won from the Cathead scouts, with advice and assistance
from Little Teal and the ever—not to say *over*—helpful Pud.

A young Digger woman in a thong bikini came forward to
hang a wreath of mountain wildflowers around Tristan's neck
and give him a kiss on the cheek—lingering too long for
Jovanne's taste—and then Fat Ed stepped forward to raise his
gilded-ladle staff high and proclaim Tristan the cross-country
Grand Champion in his mighty voice.

And then from east up the valley, like harbingers of the black
and mighty thunderheads piling up above the Staked Plains beyond the ash-plume from Capulín, appeared a ragged straggle
of bikers, slumped in their saddles, their front wheels wobbling.

"It was the Cats," the leader of the newcomers said, after he had
drained half a skin of wine at one pull and sent the rest in a pink

jet all over his balding head and matted brown beard. "We wintered in Lakota territory, did some odd jobs for the Nation. Soon's we left the Black Hills the Cats were all over us like stink on shit. Big war-band, maybe a hundred bikes."

He looked grim. "Not that much bigger'n us."

The noisy mob surrounding the new arrivals quieted right down. Not more than thirty Sidewinders had ridden into Rendezvous, and no auxiliary vehicles—trucks and vans, what the nomads called "cages." Tears glinted in the leader's eyes.

"They 'bushed us, plain. We got away from them, though it cost us ten. But that was just the start. They're swarming all over the Plains, man. They just kept hitting us. We lost everything. All our supplies, all that shit we loaded up with on what the Sioux paid us."

He drew a sobbing breath. "We lost five of our *kids*, man. And we left sixty good riders lying out behind us as we ran."

He broke down and planted his face in fingerless-gloved hands. The onlookers stared at each other in shock. Tristan's gut felt as if he'd gone over the bank all over again. *Sixty-five Folk gone.* It was an epic catastrophe. Even the Hardriders' Last Stand had cost fewer lives.

The Sidewinder got control of himself. He wasn't the clan's President; the Prez had left his bones back along the line of the long flight. This man was no more than temporary trail boss. He might or might not be confirmed as Prez once the Sidewinders had a chance to catch breath and regroup—if they *could* regroup after their shattering experience. It was just as likely they'd disband.

"Last of our people went down not five miles from here." The Sidewinder spokesman waved a fingerless-gloved hand back the way they had come. "Cat band's no more'n fifteen minutes behind us."

The shock that ran through the crowd was so solid it was almost visible. People started peeling off and running for their bikes or clan tents, some to fight, others to pull up stakes and split while they still had wheels to split with.

Fat Ed thumped his staff on the ground and roared: "*Settle down!* God damn it now, *calm*, y'hear? Not even the Catheads are mingy and low-down enough to attack Rendezvous."

"What the fuck do they care?" somebody demanded. "They must know we're fixin' to fight 'em."

John Hammerhand had been beside the Sidewinder as he gasped out his story. Now he put his hand around the man's shoulders.

"Strength, my friends. The Catheads have to know that if they violate the sanctity of Ron D. Voo, they'll face the wrath of the Dog Society."

"As if they gave a rat's ass," another snarled. It was half-hearted; even the Cats had to take the threat of proscription by the Dog Society seriously. To violate Rendezvous would automatically mobilize all the clans of the Plains against them under Dog Soldier command—in theory, anyway, though whether any more would take up arms against them than had already was open to question. But all Dog Soldiers were also required to participate, *regardless* of clan—and there were Society members among the Cats, as among most of the clans.

"Will the Cathead Dog Soldiers honor their bond?" asked Jesse Keen, the young warlord of the Long Riders MC.

"Dog Soldiers've fought their own clansmen before, sure enough," said a one-eyed Desperado.

"I don't know," Pud said. Heads turned to him; he wilted, but drove on. "This Fusion medicine is pretty powerful. A lot of the bros are pretty caught up in it. The Enlightened One—that was the Fusion high priest, like—he said the time of the old laws was finished, that it was time for new laws."

"Fusion law might be more powerful even than the Dog Society blood oath," Fat Ed said, "but the Cats might not be eager to find out."

"Everybody honors the Diggers for what they give us," Hammerhand said, facing the mountainous headman squarely, "but they're providers, not fighters. We can't take a chance."

He raised his famous fist over his head. "Brothers, take up your arms!"

The crowd broke to obey. Jovanne stood there with arms crossed. "What about sisters?" she asked loudly.

Tristan touched her on the arm. "Come on."

Half an hour later the cry went up, *"Here they come!"*

The clouds were gathering to the east and the camp was still a-seethe as riders tried to jockey their sleds from the tribal encampments where they'd been parked to the perimeter. Tristan, lying on his belly with the Jokers to the right of the trail down

which the Sidewinders had ridden, with his Scout carbine ready
in his hands, was of two minds about that. On the one hand,
since not even John Hammerhand was dense enough to try to
make a defensive stand mounted, the bikes were not going to be
of any use, and fooling around with them was only slowing
things up and disorganizing the defense.

But a cruiser was the soul of a blood, brother or sister, far
more tangible and immediate than any Star. A nomad would
fight as fiercely for his ride as for mate or child. A Stormrider
separated from his bike, on the other hand, would worry about it
to the point of distraction. Tristan, who had studied history in
Homeland's cavernous Library, under the blind eye of Old Man
Bayliss, knew the tale of the Sacred Band of Thebes, away back
thousands of years before StarFall even, knew why they fought
as hard as they did.

He wondered what John Hammerhand would make of them.

Away up the valley he caught sight of three black-clad riders.
Not much of an attack. He switched his rifle to the tree that lined
the valley to the south, his right. It there was going to be an assault, likely these three were mere diversion for a short-range
dash from cover.

From the half-deserted appearance of the huge encampment,
and the lines of men and women lying on their bellies in the
grass, it was obvious something was going on. The three Catheads rode on, indifferent to the thousand rifles pointed at them.

Where the trail met the Party Line the Dog Society had
massed. The orange-armband boys were eying each other nervously. Swaggering around camp playing all-on-one and one-
for-all with pairs and small groups of troublemakers was one
thing. Preparing for a possible attack by the biggest, meanest
clan on the Plains was another.

From the very center of the Dog Society line rose John
Hammerhand—he was not a current Dog Soldier, though he'd
served as one, and so had no right to be there, but no one ob-
jected. Unarmed but for his knife, he stepped forward to block
the Catheads' path.

The lead Cat rolled until the front wheel of his sled was practically touching Hammerhand's shin. Hammerhand didn't
flinch.

The leading Cat put his booted feet in the dirt and his hands on his hips and glared at Hammerhand. He was a big man with a bristling black beard and a mighty gut.

"You deny us entry to Ron D. Voo, Brother Hammerhand?" he demanded. "That's bold even for you, all in the middle of the Dog Soldiers and all."

He glared at the Dog Soldiers. With his jutting bushy brows he was well equipped for the job. "So what's it to be, boys? Will you enforce the Law, or are you just a bunch of mingy puppies?"

A growl went up from the still-prone Soldiers. Fat Ed stepped forward to stand beside Hammerhand. "Our brothers the Side-winders told us you harried them down from the Black Hills," he said. "You last counted coup against them just minutes before they arrived."

"We obeyed the five-mile limit," the Cathead said. "If the Sidewinders told you otherwise, they're liars as well as weaklings."

"I have the right to ask your intentions, Charger Charlie."

"Why, we're here for the same thing as the rest of you," the Cathead said. "Hit Ron D. Voo, kick back, lift a few, bullshit with all our bros. Ain't that so?" He glanced back at his comrades. One was a slim red-haired man, the other a black woman with a shaved head. They both nodded, unfurling nasty grins.

Fat Ed set his bearded jaw. "They have the right of it, John Hammerhand. Stand aside and let them pass."

"But—"

"Are you ready to abandon the Law, brother? If it don't protect the worst of us, it protects none of us."

"Listen to him, cousin," said Charger Charlie with a sneer.

The Dog Soldiers rose and moved to both sides, clearing the way. Glowering, Hammerhand backed to the left side of the trail. Fat Ed had spoken, and he'd spoken straight: If Hammerhand tried to bar the Catheads, he would be in violation of the Law, and it would be the Society's duty to lay the hard arm on him forthwith.

Sheepishly, the Stormriders picked themselves up from the ground. Their weapons dangled futilely from their hands. Charger Charlie and his companions waited until the trail was entirely clear. Then they gunned their engines, spun their tires to spray dirt and grass over the nearer Folk—including Fat Ed—and rode across the Party Line.

8

To the wide-open heart of Rendezvous rode the three Catheads.
The wood was piled for the night's Fires. Beyond stood the long
wooden tables where the Diggers dished up grunt. The trio
halted alongside, dropped their kickstands, swung off their
bikes, swaggered to a table, and sat.

A cloud crossed the sun. Charger Charlie pounded a fist on
the pine and yelled, "How about some service here?"

Tying her apron, a little dishwater-haired Digger woman appeared from the cook tents. When she caught sight of the three
Catheads she stopped and her jaw fell. She looked at Fat Ed,
who had followed the three on foot, along with most of the rest
of Rendezvous.

"C-can you pay?" Custom demanded the question be asked.
She could barely speak it.

Charger Charlie tipped his head and studied her for thirty
heartbeats as she tried to melt into the bare trodden earth. Then
he pulled a pouch from his belt and laid it on the table with a
thunk. It was of a lightweight, pale hide. Tristan did not like the
looks of it.

Charger Charlie opened the drawstring, dug out an Osage Indian Head gold coin, and flipped it to the woman. "Here," he
said, as she fumbled it between her small breasts. "We can pay.
We're not mingy Walking Men like the Sidewinders, riding in
here with our asscheeks too scrawny to meet in the middle."

He dangled the pouch before her. "You like this, little lady?

Made it myself, from the left tit of the Sidewinder Prez's old lady, Suzie Cornsilk."

He flipped a brownish protrusion from the bag's bottom with his dirty-nailed thumb. "Had nice nips, didn't she?"

The Digger woman fainted. With a strangled bellow the Sidewinder road boss broke from the crowd and charged. With a sorrowful expression Fat Ed stuck out a hairy thick forearm and clotheslined him. He went down on his back in the dirt. Two Dog Soldiers stepped forward, grabbed him under the arms, and hauled him off. They glared over their shoulders at the Cats, and if looks could kill, the intruders would have burst into flame.

Diggers emerged to help their sister to her feet. Others brought soup and fruit, meat and bread, flasks of wine and Taos Lightning. Paying no attention to their hosts, the Catheads dug in.

A nomad broke from the crowd surrounding the table to approach the greedily feeding Catheads. Tristan locked a hand around Jovanne's wrist just in time to keep her knife in its sheath and a major breach of Law uncommitted; it was Pud, the Cathead turned Joker after the Burningskull fight.

The shorn-headed black woman paused in tearing at a barbecued chicken with strong yellow teeth to glare at Pud. "Say, I know you, don't I, pencil-neck?"

He nodded. "I'm Pud."

"I'm dipped," Charger Charlie said, and spat a piece of gristle on the ground. "Where your fuckin' colors?"

Pud turned slowly to show the Joker emblem sewn on the back of his jacket.

The black woman spat out a half-masticated mouthful and started to her feet. Without looking Charger Charlie reached across the table and hit her open-hand between the breasts, sitting her back down. "Don't give these jag-offs an excuse," he growled.

She subsided. Charger Charlie stood up to his full height, which was an inch or two better than Tristan's six-four. A head and more shorter, Pud held his ground.

"So what's the story, sag-nuts? Nobody jumps the Cats. Why aren't you off with Drago's mob?"

"Because they don't exist no more. Tristan Burningskull and the Jokers washed them away."

Charger Charlie looked more puzzled than angry. "The Jokers? That ain't right. They're a tiny little minge bunch."

"Tristan got his Sign, the Guest Star in Taurus—the Sign of the Burning Skull. He beat us under that Sign. And you know what? He's destined to wash the whole fucking Cathead Nation away. *It's the prophecy!*"

"What prophecy?"

"Our warlord weren't born named Burningskull. Birth name's Hardrider."

Charger Charlie went a shade paler beneath road-grime and tan. "Bulljive. City suckwads washed the last of those assholes away, ten years and more ago."

"Not all of them," said Jammer quietly, stepping forward.

" 'Prophecy'?" Jovanne said. "What prophecy? What are people talking about?"

Tristan chewed his lower lip. Jammer shook his head at the ignorance of the rising generation. "You mind how Anse the One-Eyed made his Hard Ride on WildFyre, girl, to rescue his clan from the Blackfeet and the Catheads?" he asked. Jovanne nodded.

"Well, after that, the Cats were in a mean mood at being cheated of their fun. At that time there was a witchy-woman living alone on the Powder, and the song says she was young and fair. Cats came upon her and burned her, just to be mean.

"Before she died, though, she uttered a prophecy: that one day the whole entire Cathead nation would be washed away by one of the Hardrider line."

"That's bullshit, man!" Charger Charlie bellowed, food spraying from his mouth and getting hung up in his beard. "That's bogus!"

Jammer pointed to Tristan. "Yonder stands the last of the Hardriders—and the first of the Burningskulls. You tell me why Earth and Sky preserved him, if not to make the prophecy come true."

Charger Charlie uttered a mighty bellow of rage. He brought his thick forearm down upon the table. It cracked with a sound like a rifle shot. Food went tumbling to the ground.

"Listen to me, sag-nuts and moldy minges who have the sand to call yourselves Stormriders!" he roared. "There's a new storm brewing out on the Plains, a Cathead storm—a Fusion storm. It's gonna wash away all the old ways, the old songs, the old laws.

"Stand up against us, it will wash you away too, like a twig dam caught in a gully-washer. And no horseshit prophecy will help you!"

He turned to his compadres, who stood on the other side of the wrecked table spread-legged and ready for trouble. The black woman looked as if she was ready to take on all John Hammerhand's army here and now. The redhead kept dropping regretful glances to the food.

"Catheads, we ride!" Charger Charlie declared. "We'll leave the fools to their fun and games."

As the black woman forked her bike she cast a last bloodshot glare around. "This is the last Rendezvous," she snarled. "Enjoy it while it lasts!" And the three roared away through the crowd that jostled and stumbled to get out of the way, then out past the Party Line and east along the valley.

Every head in camp, it seemed, turned to stare toward Tristan. The first drop of rain from the approaching storm struck him on the cheek as he turned his own eyes on a certain component of the mob. "I want to thank you for that little public service announcement, Pud," he said.

Pud smiled shyly and nodded. *Should've known. The outlaws aren't always real swift about irony.* Tristan noticed John Hammerhand standing with his arms folded, watching him in a thoughtful way, and some of his strapping young ManLodge followers clustered around, glaring at Tristan like a forest of pit bulls.

The skies broke open, and it was time to duck into cover.

The rain poured down. Clutching the youth by the front of his buckskin vest, Tristan slammed a right hard knee into his side, right below the short ribs. He followed it with a left, leaving the ground the way they'd learned in Empty, the brutal barracks martial art of the HDF, to add devastating power to the blow.

The boy's head lolled on its neck, and his hair hung in his eyes like wet straw. A trickle of blood ran from the corner of his mouth. Tristan judged he'd bitten his tongue; he hadn't kneed him hard enough to really bust him up inside, the way he had John Badheart. He was being merciful to the young fool. Wind and Water knew why.

Though the footing outside the Party Line was mud and treacherous, it was time to show a little flash. If you got hung with a rep—and couldn't keep your profile low—the only thing to do was embellish hell out of it. At least keep the amateurs otherwise occupied. He whirled clockwise and slammed a backfist into the boy's temple. The kid dropped as if shot.

Tristan stood a minute to make sure the boy wasn't faking. The kid just lay there and moaned. Tristan turned to face the silent crowd.

"Road that's traveled is road behind," he said in a ringing voice. "I was Outlaw One, and your foe. But I've made my peace with the High Free Folk, and taken up my rightful place among you by right of birth and Stormriding."

He bent down to grab the vanquished Seeker by the hair and raise his head from the mud. "This child'll live. The next man—or woman—to call me out won't be so lucky." He let the boy drop with a splat into the mud and stalked back toward the Party Line.

Jovanne tossed him his shirt without comment. He started to pull it on. Unusually subdued, the rest of the onlookers kept a respectful distance.

Most of them. One fell into step alongside Tristan. Tristan looked right, and into the slate-gray eyes of the tall dark-haired Brit.

"That was most impressive," he said in his soft alien accent. "Both the way you handled him and the way you spared him."

Tristan was just sour enough to tell the truth. "It was just a gesture. He wasn't much of a threat."

"*Any* opponent is a threat," the Brit said softly. "Sometimes an unskilled man most of all, I think."

Tristan stopped and looked him up and down. Though his elegant red coat was sodden with rain, the man looked not at all discomforted. Though the tightly tailored coat held him in an unnaturally stiff position, the way he held himself within it, the small cues of stance and balance and breathing, showed him a man who could handle himself.

"You're right." Tristan stuck out his hand. "I'm Tristan Burningskull. Sorry, but that's about as formal an introduction as we're likely to muster around here."

The Brit smiled faintly. "It's rare for your people to show such knowledge of our customs," he said, accepting Tristan's

hand in a grip just hard enough to show he could make himself
a real nuisance at the knuckle game if he chose. "I am John
Allanby, captain in the army of the Honourable Company. I'm
honored to meet you."

"Pleasure's mine. Now, if you don't mind, why don't we
walk toward where it's a little less wet?"

Allanby inclined his head slightly. He was very economical
in his movements. The two walked toward the camp.

A couple of ManLodge initiates stood in front of them, iden-
tifiable by the little toy drums hung around their necks on
thongs. Their arms were folded across their chests. Barely looking at them, Tristan increased his stride to go ahead of Allanby
and walked right through them. They glowered, but did nothing
as the Brit followed.

"If you'll forgive the intrusion," Allanby said, and if the
mini-confrontation had affected him his voice didn't show it,
"I'm curious as to your plans. The others all seem to feel you're
a man touched by Destiny."

"You mean am I going to call out Hammerhand? Everyone
thinks I'm going to." *And if his bun boys don't ease off, I'm going to have no choice. Not that I'm eager to ride to war under
command of a happy hero with a cinderblock for a head . . .*

"Nothing so immediate. I wondered what your intentions
were if your Star were truly on the rise."

"First, to beat the Cats so hard they'll never be a problem
again. After that . . ." He paused and glanced at the Brit as they
walked between the tents and the bikes parked outside them,
hung now with canvas for protection from the rain. "After that I
plan to back the Cities off the High Free Folk. Some of them are
looking to encroach on our territory. I don't like the idea."

"What of Quebec?" Allanby asked.

Tristan shrugged. "The Kaybeckers and the glaciers both are
far away to the north."

Allanby showed a tight, slight smile. "The Kaybeckers are
advancing somewhat more rapidly."

"I know they're pressing your cousins up in the Federation
hard, Captain. But that's no concern of ours until and unless
they start to squeeze the Plains. The Plains are ours—forever."

For the first time Allanby acted as if something had gotten to
him. He showed it only as a narrowing of the eyes, but Tristan
saw. "Don't you think that might prove rather a shortsighted—"

"Rider coming!" the cry went up. All around them hands went to hilts, and eyes began to flick in the direction of the tents, where the firearms were tucked away.

Tristan and Allanby turned to look back east along the valley. A lone rider rode his big Kiowa sled toward the Party Line. His ride was painted black, and he wore black from crown to boots—even over his face, it seemed at this distance. But something said he was no Cathead.

9

"It's the Black Avenger!" someone shouted.

Despite the rain, people came out of their tents to look at yet another Plains legend, come late to Rendezvous. To Tristan he was something of a surprise, and the next thing to a disappointment.

Tristan was not the first Stormrider to wage a one-man war against Homeland. For the past seven years the Black Avenger had stalked and killed City soldiers, though he hadn't waged such a concentrated terror campaign as Tristan had before winter shut him down. He was more a sometime menace. Nothing would be heard of him for months, and then a sentry would be taken, a message-rider would disappear, an officer would be cut down in his tent. The very sporadic nature of his attacks gave them a mysterious quality, almost supernatural.

With a reputation like that Tristan expected him to be a giant of a man who rode a bike the size of a bulldozer and used a power pole for a club. Yet as his sled—jet-black but for the legend *Vengeance* painted on the gas tank in gold-outlined red Gothic letters and gleaming with rain—growled toward the center of Rendezvous, Tristan had the impression its rider was distinctly on the small side.

"Ever seen this guy before?" he asked Jovanne out of the side of his mouth. She shook her head.

As the two of them, trailing half a dozen Jokers, reached the open area, the Black Avenger dismounted and walked over to

accept a handshake from Fat Ed. He wore a black hood pulled
up over his head and twin samurai swords crossed over his back
in their lacquered wood sheaths—black, of course. He seemed
to favor his right foot slightly.

"Welcome, Avenger," the Digger chief boomed. "It's always
an honor and a pleasure, both, to have you in our Circles." The
big bearded man looked around. "Too bad you got here just as
things was fixing to break up."

The Avenger looked around. "So it's true what they say,"
Tristan said from the corner of his mouth. "He's got a damned
mask on, doesn't he?"

"I didn't come to Rendezvous to party down," the Avenger
said, the words echoing slightly from inside the mask. "I came
for a purpose."

"What purpose is that, Avenger?"

"I came to call out Outlaw One. I heard he's here."

With his thumb Tristan flicked raindrops off the bridge of his
nose, where they were tickling. "I'm not trying to duck out on
this," he said, shifting on the balls of his feet, "but I'm really not
Outlaw One anymore."

His opponent faced him from a steady stance, side-on with
his feet two shoulder-widths apart, his right—forward—hand
down by the hip, his left cocked to his chin. His eyes were
steady behind the black mask, which was pierced with tiny
holes before the mouth and nose to facilitate breathing. Unlike
Tristan, who had stripped to the waist for the bare-hand bout out
beyond the Party Line, he still wore the clothes he'd ridden in,
including his pulled-up hood.

He said nothing.

Tristan had mixed feelings about facing the man. They had
been antagonists in fact over years, though their roads had never
crossed. Tristan would've been glad for it as Outlaw One; he
loved nothing more than a challenge, and the Avenger was
known to have killed two Strikers, call signs Oat Willy and
Bran Mak Morn.

But the Strikers, under Black Jack Masefield, didn't exist to
hunt down nomads for the sheer joy of letting their blood trickle
into the buffalo grass. They hunted the deadliest outlaws, two-
legged predators of human meat, the rapists and the raiders with
a taste for horror. Some of the men Tristan washed away were

admired by the outlaw fraternity, but as often they were feared
and hated by their own. The Black Avenger was as lethal and
merciless as a diamondback with full poison-sacs, but his vic-
tims of choice were those armed and theoretically ready for vio-
lence, the troopers of the City.

Tristan began to circle to the left, hoping to take advantage of
his opponent's curiously immobile stance. *This is bad medicine,*
he thought. To Tristan's knowledge the Avenger had done nothing that would make Tristan balk at taking his place beside him
at the Council Fire or on the firing line. If ever a season had
come when the High Free Folk needed all their heroes, that season was now. And here he was bound by his hasty-given word
to take the Black Avenger's life; and with the Avenger damned
near a foot shorter than he, the outcome couldn't be in a whole
lot of doubt.

Maybe if I put him down hard enough, they'll forget I said the
next to call me wouldn't be lucky enough to live.

The Avenger pivoted, keeping his right side toward Tristan.
Tristan shuffled forward, fired a left jab at his opponent's
masked face. It was by way of exploration, not to tag him
serious-wise—Tristan wasn't fond of busting his muscles on
bone, to say nothing of black-painted steel. Eel-lithe, the man
leaned back, so that Tristan ran out of arm before he could con-
nect.

At the same instant the masked man whipped up his right foot
and blasted it into Tristan's ribs in a side-kick.

Tristan *oofed* and staggered back a step. The crowd cheered.
There were a lot of people in camp who would not be unhappy
to see Outlaw One get his comeuppance. Or even Burningskull.

Tristan picked up his left foot for a stomp at the advanced ankle or knee. Empty emphasized striking at joints and general
dirty tricks, which fit well with Tristan's born allergy to fighting
fair. If the Folk didn't care for that against a small man, sod 'em.

But the leg wasn't there anymore. The Avenger had shifted
his weight back and cocked it up to hip level. Tristan turned the
low kick into a long step and whipped his right around in a
roundhouse kick to the solar plexus.

The Avenger pulled his knee up farther and blocked it with
his shin. He turned the block into another side-kick. The block
took Tristan by surprise but the counterstrike didn't; he danced

back out of harm's way, slapping the Avenger's foot down with his left hand as a sort of moral statement.

His fingers stung. *Damn, what's that boot made of, armor plate?*

The rain was picking up. He was cold and miserable and getting thoroughly pissed off. Tactics and technique had not worked against this cocky little bastard. It was time to make like John goddam Hammerhand and just *power* him down.

He charged again, leading with a jab. The scam was to grapple the Avenger any old how, get a grip so he could pound in those Empty elbows and flying knees with maximum effect. Fast the Avenger certainly was, and tough no doubt, but there was no way he could absorb what Tristan had to dish out for long.

The Avenger pulled his leading leg up high, his body tipping back till his down leg was straight and his right knee higher than his shoulder. Tristan's jab glanced off his thigh. Tristan had never seen this move before, but he snapped the left hand smartly back to block, aware that the leg was cocked like a rifle, ready to fire a kick. All he had to do was snap the leg straight, and that would bring a roundhouse into Tristan's head.

The Avenger's leg moved. Tristan's hand whipped up and back to block the anticipated kick.

Instead the leg straightened *in front* of his face. The heel snapped back into his temple.

He seemed to hit the ground floating like a feather. It knocked the wind from him anyway.

He was never really unconscious. As he knew well, a head blow that truly puts you under will generally implode your brain with a bleed inside the skull. His attention had merely wandered, and was having trouble finding its way back.

When it did he was lying on his back on a pallet in the tent he shared with Jovanne. He was aware of a presence beside him, someone sitting on a camp stool. "Water," he croaked.

His eyes wandered right. The first thing he saw was a black metal object lying right beside him. He stared at it for a dozen heartbeats before his mind made sense of it.

It was the Black Avenger's mask.

"If you think you'll hold it down," a half-familiar voice said, "then here."

He started up. A hammer punched out through the top of his skull and he sank down with a groan.

"You always were too damned hotheaded," the voice said. Water trickled into Tristan's mouth, blazed a cool trail down his throat. "That's how I beat you today, and that's how I beat you before."

He got his eyes to bear on the speaker's face, forced them into focus. What he saw convinced him that he was in Hematoma City and his brain was about to go.

"Ferret?" he croaked.

The Black Avenger lifted his sharp face and laughed. "I haven't heard that name in years. Since they dragged me out of Dorm C to be a slave."

Moving deliberately Tristan hauled himself onto his elbows. "Am I dead, or am I hallucinating?"

"You're definitely not dead. As to whether you're hallucinating or not, I can't say, but if you think I'm Ferret, you're right."

Tristan fell back down with tears in his eyes. He pressed the heels of his hands over his eyes. "What the fuck is going on?" he asked, half-laughing.

"A reunion of old friends," Ferret said. "And something more."

"Why did you challenge me?" Tristan asked. "Couldn't you have just said hi?"

"I heard you were thinking of taking on old Hammerhead. I didn't want to see you make a bad mistake."

"You don't think I could've taken him?" Tristan asked, outrage starting to rise in his veins.

"No. Though don't think a man's a pushover, just because he's a cripple." His legs were crossed; he held up his right boot.

"What's that damned boot made of anyway?" Tristan demanded. "Iron?"

"Steel. And it's not the boot; it's the foot. But back to Hammerhand—you could beat him, more than likely. And that's what I was afraid of."

"Why? You're not in the ManLodge, are you?"

"Oh, Christ, no." It was startling to hear a Citizen oath from the lips of a man regarded as a hero by the nomads. But the owner of those lips was City born and bred. "I've got no use for that, and not a lot of use for Hammerhand either."

"Then why did you have to kick my goddam head in to keep me from taking him down?"

"Because they wouldn't follow you. Yeah, a lot of them believe in this Sign-from-Heaven business. But they can't forget you were Outlaw One. As for Hammerhand—half the riders out there grew up hearing songs about him every time they lit a campfire. He's an *institution*. You don't have that kind of presence. Yet."

Tristan sank into the pallet, feeling defeated. It had been years since anyone had bested him in single combat. He didn't enjoy the sensation. He didn't enjoy what Ferret was telling him much more.

"So you think it's hopeless."

"I said *yet*. You need to prove yourself to them. Just like you proved yourself to the Jokers. But it'll take *time*."

Tristan got himself on his elbows again, and this time stayed there. "How come you know so much about what's going on in camp?" he demanded.

"Because I've *been* here all along. Why do you think I fool around with that silly mask? Most of the time I'm just a scrubby independent, who rides a scrambler and, aside from being small and having a bum right foot, bears no similarity to the Black Avenger at all. You grew up among these people, Tristan; you know the way they identify a man by his ride. And the Black Avenger would never stoop to forking a scrambler."

Tristan shook his head. "You always were a clever son of a bitch."

"You weren't too bad yourself. You just needed some education. That's still about the way things stand."

"What the hell are you talking about? I was just about to graduate high school when they busted me."

He thought about how lame that sounded, and laughed. "Well, okay. But I studied at the Library with old Bayliss. I really did pick up some education, not just the pap they dished us at school."

Ferret raised an eyebrow. "The Library, eh? I don't think I knew a person all my years in Homeland who'd seen the inside of it. But that's not what I mean. You need lessons of another sort."

"In what?" Tristan asked.

"The hero business."

"Oh," Tristan said.

10

"Whoa!" Jammer said, resting one foot propped on a crop of rock and a hand on his thigh. "I feel like I've walked so much I done all the walking there is."

Below them Star Lake glinted like a sheet of beaten silver. Above, Lew Wallace Peak raised its bald head high against a sky that had gone blue as though for one last time. This was the last day of what some gloomily predicted might be the last ever Ron D. Voo. Tomorrow the High Free Folk rode to meet the Cathead Nation.

"Oh, come on," Tristan chided. "We haven't gone that far, and you're not that old."

Jammer turned his silver shades toward him. The sun seemed to slide across them in a wake of glare. "I forgot, you were a Beastie for a while there, boy. Leading a pack mule all over them mountains."

"Got my legs even before that," Tristan said. "When I was with the Strikers we had to do a lot of roadwork."

"Roadwork? Of course you did. Every bro worth his oil puts in his time working on the Road. Not even Citizens are so dead from the neck up they don't realize what they owe the Holy Road."

"No, not repair work. *Roadwork*. Running."

Jammer lifted his shades and studied him keenly with his pale blue-gray eyes. "And nobody was chasing you?"

"Nobody."

"Whoa."

The old Hickory who was their guide turned his wrinkled boot-leather face back to them. "You wanna camp out on this mountain tonight, fine. I'll go home."

"Hey, man," Jammer protested, "it's morning yet."

"Takes time to climb a mountain. Takes time to go back down. You make up your mind yet, white-eyes?"

The old man's poker-faced threat had two barrels: He wasn't just their guide; he had a pass tucked inside his venerable flannel shirt, a scrap of pine bark with the mark of the War Chief of Taos Pueblo burned into it with a hot iron. This was the Sacred Ground. Without that pass the two Stormriders were in a potential world of hurt.

Jammer sighed. "All right, slave-driver, lead the way." He shook his head. "Shoot. That's the thing about these Indians. I mean, they see so many things, but then they go and overlook a little fact like I'm not *white*."

"You black white man," the Jicarilla said. "It's all the same."

Tristan laughed. After a moment Jammer did too. They recommenced their climb.

It was a tough haul, as the Steller's jays and the piñon jays quarreled over territorial rights in the trees that changed from Douglas firs to dense-packed spruce. They paused often, to the eloquently unspoken annoyance of their guide. They were glad of the excuse to gaze out along the spine of the mighty range of mountains that men long dead when the Star fell had named for the blood of a god-child worshiped now in Cities alone.

The Sangre de Cristos were green below and blade-gray at the crowns, or still capped in white. Away out east clouds floated at the same level as the puny climbing humans, dragging their shadows across the Staked Plains beneath them. Off north of east rose a column of smoke from Capulín, pale gray today and not so swollen. Caner-watchers claimed that was a good sign, that Old Cap had near puked himself dry. That was good news if true, for the road to the Catheads had to pass the mountain.

The unbounded vistas lifted their souls and trickled fresh energy to their limbs. As Stormriders they were born to the land, and the love of its beauty. Though of course no land was as beautiful as that which had a good smooth Road running through it.

The sun was well on the way to the quake-wracked wastes of

California, the bikers' Paradise Lost, when the trees fell away abruptly as if they'd been planed off by a giant hand. "Not far," puffed Jammer as Tristan gave him a hand up over a lichen-grown boulder. "Ol' hermit lives just above the tree line."

"What do I need a hermit for anyway?"

Jammer shook his head. "You young'uns. Always gotta *know* right away—when you don't think you know it all already."

"Tell me you weren't like that when you were young."

"Damn me, and I won't! I knew it all, and I had to know right now. It's your part to be that way when you're young, like it is to fuss about it when you're old."

"Are you through dodging my question?"

Jammer slapped the young man on the arm. "A part of your past is about to be revealed to you, and maybeso your future too. It's *supposed* to be mysterious."

Farther up the peak and a ways around they came on a man sitting on a rock in the sun, his hands upon his knees. A dog bounded toward them, barking, black-and-gray shaggy, with one blue eye and one yellow eye. A whistle stopped it short and turned it around to race back to its master.

Its master rose, stood waiting. As the party approached, Tristan decided he didn't look much like a hermit. Tristan's notion of hermits, formed by passing references in the Library's books, called for a scrawny ancient dressed in a sack, with a long nose and black mad eyes staring from a tangle of gray hair and beard.

This man, on the other hand, was compact and bandy-legged, dressed in use-darkened doeskin moccasins, jeans, and a red flannel shirt. His head was round, his cheeks not overgrown but grizzled, as if he was three days past shaving. Tristan wondered if maybe he was a visitor to the *real* hermit.

"Hail, hermit, and good afternoon," called Jammer, spoiling *that* conceit.

The hermit nodded to the Indian. "Afternoon, Hilario." The Hickory nodded back, unspeaking. The hermit squinted up his eyes at Jammer until they were all but lost in wrinkles. He was older than first squint made him.

"Is that Jammer?" he demanded.

"The very same." Jammer stepped forward to embrace the hermit.

"You're looking good, youngster."

"You too, old man. You still look the same."

The old man shrugged. "Like the mountain, I erode a little every day. But it's a slow process."

He turned to scan Tristan with a look of such dispassionate assessment that Tristan felt his hackles go up, as if he were a second-hand scrambler a bro was thinking of buying for his son. "What's this'at you brought me?"

"What's he look like?" Jammer asked with a grin.

The hermit looked back at Tristan, who fought a mad urge to stick fingers in the corners of his mouth and poke out his tongue at him. "Long drink of water, and trouble on the hoof. Got more'n a bit of the Devil in his eye . . . this ain't the get of old Anse, is it? Grandson, it must be, or I'm a Pawnee."

"Right again," Jammer said, laughing. "Both counts."

The old man tipped his head to one side and studied Tristan. "He ain't as dumb as his dad, is he?"

"Hey," Tristan said.

"He's here, ain't he?" Jammer said, all seriousness now.

The old man nodded, fingering his white-bristled chin. "So he's the one the Legacy fits. You sure of that?"

Legacy? Tristan thought.

"Takes two to reckon that, by the terms One-Eye laid down."

The hermit looked from Jammer to Tristan, and back again. "I won't say you're a better man than your pappy as Anse first trusted with his legacy. Then again, I'd lie to say you was a lesser." His shoulders rose and fell in a sigh. "I dunno. I ain't getting younger, that's sure, and no one to pass my burden on to. If you saw fit to bring him . . ."

He turned and started walking up the slope so abruptly Tristan thought he'd decided against him despite the seeming lean of his words. A few paces and the hermit turned back to gesture at them with fingers brown and gnarled as a mountain cedar. "Well, come on, then, unless you fancy a night on the mountain."

Without a word Hilario the Hickory sat down on the rock the old man had vacated. The dog sat down facing him six feet away. The others left them sitting there like that, staring at each other.

"You aren't from the Pueblo, are you?" Tristan asked, curiosity—or maybe years of City life—overcoming Plains reluctance to question a man about his backtrail.

"Oh, hell, no. I'm just an old *coyote*, half Mexican and half *gringo*."

"Why do they let you live up here in the middle of their Sacred Ground?"

"I got connections."

They came to a hole in the mountainside, covered with a heavy blanket which the hermit held open. A cave—a tunnel, rather, he thought, since Tristan's Library-gleaned knowledge of cave formation, which was sketchy, suggested no natural cave could form this near the top of a mountain. The old man gestured them inside.

Tristan halted with his foot upraised, the short hair rising at the nape of his neck beneath the ponytail he wore today. All the nomad's claustrophobic fear surged up around him like a pack of feral dogs. He had spent years between City walls, some in confinement. In all that time he had never totally relaxed.

"It's all right," Jammer said. "Mountain hasn't shaken down on the old man's head yet."

"Yet," Tristan said, but he went in.

Inside was dim, but lit by the yellow glow of a lamp. It was a round chamber, high enough that Tristan could stand upright. There was a heavy wood table, low, before a couch or bed framed from the same thick square timbers and covered with Indian blankets. A tall cabinet stood against the wall. Beside it hung a wool blanket in somber Navajo tones, gray and brown and black. To the other side of the couch a dark hole opened in the wall, leading further into the peak.

Tristan frowned. The furnishings were spare enough, weathered and rugged as their owner, but they didn't much match his picture of a hermitage either. The old man disappeared into the blackness, and Tristan lowered his voice to say, "I thought hermits weren't supposed to have anything but a wood bowl and maybe a couple goats," to Jammer.

"Don't want to be generalizing too much about hermits. Contrary breed, hermits."

"I suppose he doesn't spend all his time meditating either."

"No," the hermit said, emerging, with hands behind his back, "but I play a mess of solitaire. Grab yourselves some seats."

They did. The old man went to the cabinet. As he opened it Tristan noticed he was holding an oblong object, flat and black, an inch or so thick and perhaps a handspan long.

Inside the cabinet a black box sat on a shelf, wide rather than tall. The hermit touched the front. Lights glowed on.

"Hey!" Tristan exclaimed, outraged. "That's a VCR!"

Looking around he saw that the lamp, which he'd taken for a kerosene lantern, had an electric bulb within. He felt cheated.

"You can't play a videotape without one, youngster," the hermit said, backing away. He took down the blanket, revealing a flat television screen hung beneath. "Now hush up and listen, or you've wasted a hard climb."

Sulkily, Tristan turned his attention to the screen. And found himself staring into the one blue eye of his illustrious ancestor.

"Greetings, pilgrim," the man said in a rough and raspy voice. His face was long and gaunt and lined by hard life, but there were lines of laughter around the eyes. If there were more about the mouth, they were hidden by an excellent beard the color of iron and cut square at the bottom. "I'm Anse, knowed as the One-Eyed—if ye've the wit to be allowed to see this, you can see why, right off.

"Now, my boy Wyatt has all the sand in this wide world; he's a good boy, and he rides better'n any on these Plains, even me.

"But I'm gettin' old, and it's too late to change my habit of never shrinkin' from the truth, and the truth is this: He's dumb as a box of rocks.

"I leave him my band, with its prettied-up name of *Hardriders*. I wanted to call 'em *Iron Butts*, which is a true Plains name with hair on it, only Twelve-String Jake talked me out of it. I leave Wyatt the better part of my few traps, as laid out elsewhere. I leave him my love, and my best wishes.

"But I don't leave him my *everything*, 'cause deep in my gizzard I got me the fear the poor dumb sod's gonna blow his roll before his Star burns out. May Mother Sky grant he blaze a trail across her when he goes down, for I fear that's his fate.

"But while I never learnt to read nor write nor even sign my name, no man ever called me stupid and saw the next sunrise from beneath his hair. I don't think th' Iron Butt blood has got so thin. Got me a feelin' one of my good, dumb boy Wyatt's get will be greater'n all his fathers and mothers together—or some get of *his* mebbe. It's for you that I leave this message with one trusted of me: the 'foresaid Twelve-String Jake.

"So here's my legacy to you: none other than WildFyre itself."

Tristan's breath caught in his throat.

"Now, don't be goin' all fluttery on me," the face on the

screen went on. "I don't actually *have* WildFyre to give to ye. The songs say I handed it on to Amos Bad Water, Straw Boss of the Osage Manufactory and the first man of his Nation, and the songs don't lie, as they sometimes do—sorry, Jake, or your get as is seein' this too.

"But listen to me, and mark my every word: When I forked that ride, I rode somethin' bigger than me or you or anybody; I rode *legend*. The Destiny of the Plains is built into that bike, in her struts and forks and frame, writ into her engraving and enameled on her tank.

"Hear me now, young Hardrider—or whatever ye call yourself, for I got me a weirdin' feelin' here"—he touched himself on the breastbone between the flaps of his colors vest—"that you'll find a new name to carry with ya to greatness. WildFyre is yours by right, by right of me as stole her from the Kobold King whose people stole it from the ruins of the Carondelet plant in old St. Lou. Find her, take her, and the Plains will be yours. She's your ride to greatness. To immortality, even.

"Fail me . . ." He shook his head, and a haunting came into his eye. "Fail *her*, and the High Free life of the Plains goes down in blood and darkness. Don't ask me how I know, but know it I do.

"That's all my legacy, for as to worldly goods I'm poor as owl dung. May the Heavenly Bros and Sisters see that you heed my saying, and may they speed ye upon your Road.

"That's all she wrote." The image vanished into flicker and snow.

Tristan sat there feeling as if he'd been clipped between the eyes by a Thor's Hammer. "That's it?" he managed to squeak at last.

The other two looked at him, Jammer still wearing his shades despite the gloom. "What do you mean, 'That's it?' " the hermit demanded. "Yonder's none other than the Lost Legacy of Anse the One-Eyed. Many men have sought for it, and many men have died."

"They have?"

"He grew up a captive of the City of Homeland," Jammer explained apologetically. "He's been away from the Life a spell."

"If you say so," the old man said grumpily. He busied himself fussing with the furnishings, clicking off the television and re-

hanging the blanket over it. Jammer and Tristan took that as a
cue to leave without further speech.

"Such a crock I've never heard in my life!" Tristan burst out
as soon as the entryway blanket fell to behind them.

"Hush, now," Jammer said urgently. "You'll hurt the old
dude's feelings. He's spent his whole life guardin' that tape."

"Why? Who'd want to steal a tape of a one-eyed old fraud
running off at the mouth about Destiny being all tied up in this
wonderful bike, which he doesn't even have?"

"Plenty; and I tell you true."

"They'd be disappointed as hell once they got their hooks on
it, that's for damned sure. Jesus, what a raft of shit."

Shaking his head, he followed Jammer down the slope, too
pissed off to pick his way. "This whole *scene* is a shuck. I mean,
I climb this whole damned mountain, expecting some kind of
mystical revelation or gods know what—thinking sure I'd at
least get some kind of wizard dude to conjure me up visions in
magical smoke or something—and what do I get? A video!"

"You'll feel better about this after you cogitate on it a spell."

"I'm sure. Jesus." He closed his left eye as a thought hit him.
"Well, maybe there was a little magic here after all. I mean, how
the hell did he get power for his lamp and his VCR? He must
draw it out of the air."

"Manner of speaking," Jammer said back at him, deadpan.
"Has a windmill up, south face of the mountain. Trickles power
on into batteries."

"Augh!" Tristan cried in anguish. "I don't believe in magic
anyway, but can't I even have a few *illusions*?"

Jammer laughed, hoisted himself a few steps back up to pat
Tristan on the shoulder. "You're all right, man. You're the one
your grandfather had in mind."

"I'm so lucky I can't believe it."

Jammer took off his glasses. "Yes, you are. Come a time
when you'll believe it."

Tristan snorted and started thumping his booted feet down
the slope. Below them, their guide rose from his rock, and the
dog jumped up and commenced to bounce and wag.

The sound of two thousand engines turning over was like the
rumble of an earthquake. It was a sound to make the air itself
shiver. Sitting among the Jokers astride the cruiser he had won

from Badheart, Tristan could feel the noise beating on his cheeks like the slapping of small hands.

The sky was blue, for a wonder. It was as if Mother Sky was smiling down upon her sons and daughters as they readied to ride forth to war.

An obscure and complex rotation scheme ruled the all-important issue of precedence in peeling out from Ron D. Voo. Only the Diggers, who had charge of administering it, really understood its intricacies. But each club had a keen sense of where it belonged, and traffic monitors in yellow Digger vests ran back and forth, soothing tempers and trying to ready the outflow to run smoothly.

The honor of first departure fell to an obscure northeastern club called the Sand Kings. Their President was a young man with long yellow hair, whose sled had far-extended forks and a jagged design painted on the tank in yellow and blue. He waited on the Party Line, quivering with the power of his machine as he revved its engine to the max.

Fat Ed's ladle-staff came down. The Sand King Prez launched himself in a huge wave of earth and grass. He peeled so fast his rear wheel slewed wide right; just when he seemed on the verge of recovery his front wheel hit a round stone hidden by a clump of grass. Bike and rider went cartwheeling through the air.

The High Free Folk went silent. This was not a good omen.

As the honor of being first rider out of Rendezvous was extreme, so was the humiliation of having minged it up. The Sand King Prez righted his bike, hopped into the saddle, and rode straightaway up the valley's side slope and into the trees. He wasn't seen again.

Subdued—and more carefully—the remaining Sand Kings took off, one by one. Another club followed them, and another: the Angels of Death, the Red Dragons—an all-black club—the Diamondbacks, the Ghost Riders, the Latin Lovers, the Iron Vikings. The clans of the Plains were mustered for a Run, a Run such as Sun and Sky had never seen before.

As more and more clubs roared out into the wind, the run thunder rose in the veins like a drug. And so all of them, Tristan Burningskull among them, forgot the omen with which the Ride had begun.

11

The air reverberated to a crack as if Mother Sky's own lodge-pole had snapped clean through. As the aftershocks ran through Tristan's bones like impacts, the world of mud and rain and blackness lit with three cataclysmic white flashes. Thunder followed on their wheels, but its sound was almost benign to ears numbed by the first giant roar.

Zonker turned him a face made faceless by a kerchief mask and goggles. "Hell must look like this," he shouted. His words were almost lost in the rain and leftover ringing.

"We'll never find out," Thin Lizzy called, her voice similarly muffled. "We don't have to worry 'bout Hell, 'cause we've done our time in this."

Tristan knew better. First, he doubted the gods let you off from Hell so easily; the gods of the Plains were not particularly merciful, though they could be fun to party with. Not that he believed in them, any more than he believed in the lone God, gray and fun-hating, whom the Cities worshiped. Second, he *knew* what Hell looked like: The walls were hard and smooth and close, and all around, their gray weight pressing, pressing. The walls of the Man's institutions, in the belly of City, the cafeteria walls of Roosevelt Middle School no less than the blackness of the Hole in McGrory. Hell had many faces, and they were flat and none of them as kind as this.

This was bad enough, though. He stood with his boots in the mud, the engine of his yellow scrambler idling. He was not feel-

ing good. The three strobes of lightning had revealed the Gipsy
Jokers MC—they were very particular about the spelling, even
though not much more than half of the High Free Folk could
read well enough for it to make any nevermind. It wouldn't anymore, because every last man and woman of the clan lay dead,
covered so thick in ash that all the rain only turned it to thick
paste but couldn't wash it away.

The Plains' prevailing winds blew out of the east, and many
riders of the army wanted to cut straight north, once through the
Sangre passes, and not strike east until they hit the lower
reaches of the Purgatoire, or better still, the remnant Hard Road
that followed the course of the Arkansas. But John
Hammerhand and his advisors—the ones he listened to, from
the ManLodge and the Wanderers, who were the ones who
knew how to say what he wanted to hear—were hot for getting
at the Catheads. The northern route would delay too long, they
claimed, and require a transit of high Raton Pass, which was
frequently cut by weather or ambush.

So instead they dropped south, to another road that ran
straight into the Staked Plains, claimed by the Kiowa/
Comanche Nation but ruled in fact by the Kwahadi MC, who
rode now to war with the rest. That was surely safe enough; it
took them no nearer the erupting Capulín than forty miles or so.

It would, however, take them right through the plume of
Capulín's ejecta, unless they cared to ride closer than was com-
fortable or smart to Water Horse, the Kiowa/Comanche capital
on Palo Duro Canyon, in the region called the Panhandle.
Though "Water Horse" was simply the English for the name
Kwahadi—both meaning the pronghorn antelope who covered
the prairie like white and tawny wildflowers whenever the
Plains weather broke this time of year—the Kioway and
Comanch' had little use for their wild cousins who styled themselves a Motorcycle Clan. Though their own legends—and the
Western histories, true and otherwise, which Tristan had de-
voured in the Library—made them great raiders and riders
themselves, once upon a time, and though they were hard ones
in a fight, the Kiowa/Comanche had gotten stodgy and settled in
their ways, like most of the Indian nations of the Plains. Jealous
of their comfort as they were, too great a nearness of a biker
horde two thousand and more war-cruisers strong would bring

them from their houses like a yellowjacket swarm from a burning nest.

No sooner had the army cleared the Sangres, however, than the weather had turned savage with that suddenness that had always marked the Plains, and the more since StarFall. Mother Sky had announced that her benevolence was withdrawn with a stroke of lightning from clear blue, which struck the popular young warlord of the Outlaws square. His ride had gone up in a sudden yellow blossom of burning Mother's Milk, but he never fought the flames, and though the lower half of him was burned to thick black crust by the time anybody could reach him, his face showed no pain, just final surprise.

The omen of the mishap which began the ride, driven from the nomads' mind by the exhilarating drug of Run Thunder, had come flooding back. This was a worse omen still; the Outlaws MC held special status among the clans, for they shared a name with a legendary pre-StarFall band, which had given the Folk many of their mightiest songs. Not even Jammer could sing "Green Grass and High Tides" without his eyes brimming with tears; only "Free Bird" was more beloved, and "Born to Be Wild," perhaps.

As if to show she really meant it, Mother Sky had whipped her blackest cloak over the riders with dizzying speed, and poured the rain down like a waterfall.

The cavalcade had started out mighty and terrible, a Wheeled Nation of the Plains for true. It now bogged down quickly, with the Road gone slick where it was still Hard and to morass in between, and the inevitable accidents and malfunctions began to hit, made worse by weather. The advance slowed and stopped for the night almost due south of Old Cap, with barely a hundred road miles behind.

All that night Cappy made his presence known, with booms and flashes visible from forty miles away through dense cloud and rain. Though the Dog Soldiers, acting now as traffic controllers, tried to get the whole mob up and rolling with what they guessed was dawn, the army as a whole was not underway much before noon. Before that time several small bands were sent out ahead as scouts. They rode forth hooting and skidding their bikes through the slog, jeering their comrades for being bed-bound and losing out on the privilege of outriding.

At a little after ten Cappy gave a belch that caused the earth to shake and spilled riders from their sleds. The Gipsy Kings had not reported back, by radio or messenger. Hammerhand, who seemed unhappy at having Tristan too near, though he let the Jokers ride by his Wanderers near the head of the army, sent Jovanne's clan to investigate.

Now Tristan looked down. In the gray wet-cement mass by his boots a thick log with a round knob at one end was a body, and the raised branch with a cluster of bent twigs at the end was an arm, upflung in the final agony of asphyxiation. So swaddled in ash-mud were the Gipsy Kings that the Jokers were in the midst of them before Tooth gave a wild cry and laid his scrambler down, having bumped into a swelling in the mud which rolled over to reveal a mud-caked face.

Lightning flared again. You could tell in the snapshot glimpse it offered that something had happened, because Mother Earth did not reabsorb bikes as readily as she did her own children. Wheels and handlebars stuck up in the air, and the ash could not obscure their outlines.

"Pony," Tristan yelled, "have you got anything?"

She twirled the microphone by its cord to show futility. Radio transmission was a chancy thing, with all the energy that crackled in the post-StarFall atmosphere. Interference blacked them out.

"Damn," Jovanne said. She was drawn up knee-to-knee with Tristan. Since the night in their tent when they made love she had acted withdrawn and almost cool to him, as if regretting that she'd let her guard down—or he his. She did not seem to want to let him out of her sight for long, though. Just now she was as unhappy as the rest at having to double back to the main body in this storm, leaving the miles to be made good yet again.

She looked to Tristan, who shrugged. *No choice.* She stuck her hand in the air and whirled a finger in a horizontal circle, sign for *let's ride*!

"Old Hammerhand ain't gonna like this," Zonker understated, and put his ride in gear.

It was known to be true that a Caner, having spent its fury in a blast as great as the one that smothered the Gipsy Kings at a range of fifty miles, generally calmed down for a spell, or even ceased its uproar entirely. On the other hand, in the rare times that wasn't the case, the big blast was a mere tentative gesture, to be followed by a *real* temper tantrum. Such an eruption could put the whole mighty army in the dirt. Though that had never happened—if only because this gathering of the Motorcycle Nation was unprecedented—disasters of that scale were far from unknown. Cities had awakened happy and prosperous and people-swollen in the morning, and in the evening no soul remained in their bodies, after a Caner's wrath had struck.

Hammerhand insisted on his luck. Though some riders were beginning to grumble and trade glances, it was agreed to try to force a way along the same route despite the fate of the Gipsy Kings, with Hammerhand himself at the very point.

And the hero's luck of John Hammerhand held. This time.

No black deathcloud laid its heavy arms upon the rolling horde. There was ash aplenty, enough to blot the sun if the storm hadn't beaten it to the punch. Sulfurous grit worked its way into the eyes and nose and mouth, and forced the riders to mask themselves with bandannas to be able to draw breath at all. But there wasn't quite enough to choke the life from anybody, as the ash had from the Kings.

And then the riders were through the ash plume. They had reason to be grateful—for once—for Mother Sky's wet tantrums: The rain scrubbed the ash from the air, letting them breathe easily sooner than they otherwise might.

"Paradise, like," Zonker said, clutching his drawn-up knees with his arms and rocking back and forth on his skinny butt. Jammer was off, spreading himself among the whole vast horde—for all his friendship with Tristan and the Jokers, and the debt he owed them, he wasn't their exclusive property, as his soft voice had reminded them. Tonight the Jokers were making their own entertainment after a long and miserable day. "It's up in the FlameLands some'eres, so I hear tell. Chocolate grows on trees, and big old pools of Mother's Milk lie open to the sky, just waitin' for the bucket."

"Bullshit," Emilio said. Orange highlights glittered in his anthracite eyes as he stared into the heart of the fire. Mother Sky had relented of her weeping enough to let the army light up, in a hundred lonely islands of light scattered across the Plain, and try to get warm and dry. Or at least recapture the memory of what those things were like.

"If there was all this Mother's Milk lying open, wouldn't the

Caners just light it up, *carnal*? Then you got a bunch of big bonfires, not gas."

Zonker glared at him, his wide blue eyes possessed of less intelligence than usual. "Piece of shit," he gritted, and he dug at wetslick grass to propel him to his feet. "It's a magic place. Magic! And you can't spoil it, scumsuck—"

As if by more magic Jovanne was standing right there. She gave Zonker a straight heel-hand shot to the sternum. He went right back down on his ass.

"Cool your damn pipes," she said. Zonker stared up at her, measuring her with his mad eyes. He was probably stronger than she was—just about all men were stronger than just about all women, in Tristan's experience.

But strength isn't everything when it's get-down time. Jovanne's brown eyes pressed into Zonker's blue ones, squelching the flames that burned there. The fight went out of him in a sigh. His straggly blond head hung.

She reached down to tousle his stringy wet hair. "Save it for the Cats, baby," she said, gently now. "I have a feeling we'll need every ounce of everything we can muster. *Especially* fight."

She turned away to see Tristan watching her across the fire. Somewhat to his surprise, she came and sat down beside him. He noted that she didn't fully sit, but instead squatted to keep the well-packed seat of her jeans off the wet ground.

"You're good," he said in a soft voice. "Damn good."

She grunted. She didn't seem to have more talk in her just now, but he could feel satisfaction glowing from her. Maybe its heat was melting the barrier that had sprung up between them, just a bit.

Zonker had slumped into himself. Emilio was hunched in a little knot, staring into the flames harder than before, seeming to be shrunk out of the role of troublemaker. Not because he was afraid of Zonker. Because of what Jovanne had recalled to him—to them all. If he and Zonk mixed it up, the likeliest outcomes were one would wind up in the dirt, or they both would. Either way, it would mean fewer arms in the fight when the Cat-heads came. At this point, intramural combat would be one of those fights nobody ever won.

Jovanne's more the leader type than I am, Tristan thought. He could inspire men—and women—but that gift was more rabble-rousing than leadership. Though she would probably have laughed in his face if he suggested it, Jovanne was *responsible*. And she had the talent for instilling a sense of responsibility into a hairy-ass band of outlaws whose whole free-rolling culture was built upon denial that such a beast existed.

That's why I don't want to push her out as Prez, he realized with sudden clarity. In part, of course, it was because the Jokers were small potatoes to what he had in mind; and because, yeah, he didn't want to be hassled with responsibility for them.

But there was more than that. He needed her to do things he could not do, or do as well. Maybe he couldn't *take responsibility* as well as she could. But it seemed to him, if he played it right, she could do the job on his behalf. . . .

"The gods are pissed," Red Dog said. The red-haired man was looking straight at Tristan, the flamelight turning his point-bearded face to a mask of Satan. "I reckon I can see why. If they send a man a Sign, right out of Heaven, and he sees fit to ignore it—"

"Superstitious crap," said Jeremy, shuffling back to the fire from a trip to relieve himself. "The only signs an intelligent bro should read are 'Danger—Road Out Ahead' and 'No Dogs or Scooter Trash Allowed'—and they should only make him cautious or angry, not afraid."

Red Dog glowered at the small man, then turned his glare on Tristan. "You gonna let him talk that trash about your Power?"

"My Sign's in the sky, to be read or ignored as a brother or sister chooses," Tristan said evenly. "My Power doesn't depend on the stars, one way or another. And as far as I'm concerned any bro can speak his true mind beside the fire—especially when he's an old friend."

Red Dog looked a few more bullets at Jeremy, who sat down not very near to Tristan, as if to demonstrate he didn't need the bigger man's protection. Jeremy was accompanying the Jokers as just another unaffiliated rider who happened to be slight and somewhat gimpy. Vengeance rode in one of the Joker cages, identity swaddled in tarps, the Black Avenger drag stashed securely in her panniers. On the other hand, like the Ferret of McGrory days, Jeremy had a manner to him which suggested, despite his lack of inches, that it was particularly poor medicine to fuck with him.

Tristan accepted a bottle and took a pull, remembering not to wipe the mouth first and being silently grateful the Jokers, at Jovanne's insistence, were a relatively cleanly bunch. His years of City life had left their mark, no question.

Without seeming to he slipped his gaze toward Red Dog, whose trim head was hunched down into the open collar of his shirt. He had seemed to resent Tristan since the Burningskull battle. Maybe he blamed Tristan for the death of his saddlemate Sooz the Singer. Maybe it was Tristan's startling overnight rise from slave to de facto warlord. But he was only giving voice to sentiments that had been passed around the campfire before, and not just the Jokers' campfire either.

Tristan had punched out enough people that the High Free Folk were beginning to accept him as legitimately one of them, rather than a City spy—a hell of a way to run a polity, but there it was. Now the tales of how he had received his Sign—still burning away up there in Taurus's head, but invisible above the clouds—and led the Jokers to their surprising victory had percolated through the army. Instead of muttering, "There's that mingy Striker son of a bitch," when he passed, the bros were beginning to ask when he was going to take on Hammerhand and raise his Burning Skull at the head of the host.

Suddenly there was a growl of engines in the night. Eyes wide, Jokers jumped to their feet, clutching for knives and pistols at their belts or gazing wildly around for their long arms. Tristan sat and took another slug of wine. If the Catheads, supposedly concentrating hundreds of miles away on the western banks of the Mississippi, had the ability to infiltrate a raiding party mounted on big, loud outlaw cruisers past the army's pickets and sentries, then they *were* magic, no mistake, and Tristan would just as soon they cut his line now as later.

If wasn't the Catheads, though. Handsome—who had gotten himself accepted much sooner than his fellow ex-Cat Pud, mainly by keeping his yap shut—loomed up in the night beside a bearded young rider on a red and silver bike who had a bandanna wrapped around his head and a longhorn steer skull painted on the tank of his ride.

Tristan rose. "I'm Jesse," the newcomer said, "Prez of the Outlaws." Which was redundant since, by tradition, the Outlaws' Prez was *always* called Jesse.

With a certain overt deliberation, Jovanne stuck her pistol

back in its shoulder holster. "I'm Jovanne, President of the Jokers," she said formally. "You honor our campfire, brother."

Jesse nodded. "Honor's mine, sister. I'm lookin' for the one they call Burningskull."

Jovanne's eyes narrowed. Sighing, Tristan rose. "That's me."

Jesse dropped his kickstand, leaned his bike onto it, swung a skinny booted leg over, and walked up to Tristan. Tristan made himself relax, preparatory to reacting to sudden attack. For all his easy manner, Jesse might have just discovered that the man named Burningskull was the same as the Outlaw One who had scragged one or another of his blood brothers a few moons back.

Instead the Outlaw Prez stuck out his hand. Tristan was tuned enough to muscle movements to read the motion for what it was and not launch a preemptive assault. He took it and shook it.

"I wanted to ask you to join our band," Jesse said. "We need a new warlord. We'd be honored to have you."

In spite of the fact that inviting a bro to jump clubs could be considered an insult, Jovanne brightened visibly. Tristan could hear her thinking, very loudly: *If he hooks up with the Outlaws, then Jesse'll have to worry about his job instead of me.*

Her riders, on the other hand, were looking on with unconcealed scowls. Tristan had already declined to replace the man he'd killed, John Badheart, as Joker warlord. It would be a slap in the face to them for him to accept that position with another club. Of course, the Outlaws were a respected, powerful club on the Plains, while the Jokers were pretty much no-names nobody ever would have heard of but for their beating the Catheads. That didn't mean the Jokers wanted their noses rubbed in the fact.

Tristan, however, was not looking to be the mere warlord of any club, however influential. On the other hand, getting the Outlaws cranked at him big time wasn't part of his agenda. *My goals are so straightforward,* he thought. *Why does it have to be so complicated to get to them?*

"I've taken a vow," he said deliberately, "to join no club until we've paid off the Catheads. I ride with the Jokers because they're my friends, my blood brothers."

Jesse's handsome face started to crease in a frown. Inspiration hit Tristan in the head like the Black Avenger's loaded boot.

"Of course, there's no reason we can't all ride together now, is there? We can all use all the good blood bros and sisters we can get, when we face the Cats and their Fusion sorcerers."

The Outlaw boss blinked. Then he grinned. "You're right," he said. "Let me get my club, and we'll swear it here and now." He wheeled his flashy iron and roared off into the night.

The Jokers exchanged glances, then jumped to their feet, whooping and slapping Tristan on the back. "The Outlaws!" Tooth crowed toothlessly. "Imagine the Outlaws hookin' up with a bunch of low-down scooter tramps like *us*!"

Standing nearby, Jovanne put her head near Tristan's. "Hardrider," she said, and there was both bitterness and admiration in her voice, "you are one high-handed son of a bitch."

"They say it's better to be lucky than good," he said from the side of his mouth. "When you don't know if you're either one, I guess ballsy will do in a pinch."

12

The bridge over the North Canadian was out. Rumors ran
through the army that the Catheads had sabotaged it, an act of
blackest perfidy. Sitting astride his cruiser, looking at the stump
of bridge on the river's near side, Tristan thought earthquakes
and a river gorged beyond reason by storms and runoff were
more than enough to do the job. But the thought that the Catheads might be capable of such a stroke—morally as well as in
brute terms of getting the job done—sent a jolt of thrill through
the horde, along with a clammy black wave of apprehension.

Hammerhand reacted energetically. Standing beside the abut-
ment, the fierce rain-laden wind tossing his wheat-colored hair
heroically, he pointed this way and that and gave orders in that
bull baritone of his that seemed able to defeat the wind without
needing to be raised. He dispatched scouts from the Diamondbacks and the Seventh Sons to look for intact bridges or better
places to ford. He sent the Red Dragons and his own Wanderers
scavenging for timber to make rafts. That was a tough chore on
the mainly treeless Plains.

It seemed to Tristan that certain of Hammerhand's own cast
some ugly looks his way as they wheeled their irons and rode
off, in part at being harnessed together with blacks, whom not
all the High Free Folk comfortably accepted as brothers—the
status of Jammer notwithstanding—in part in resentment at
being asked to perform menial tasks, i.e., anything not directly
connected with hassling.

That left a cohort of a hundred or so strapping young men, mostly blond, hanging around Hammerhand and glowering pugnaciously at anyone who ventured too near. These were the hardest core of his ManLodge acolytes, wearing little drums slung on thongs around their thick necks.

"Those bucks're what really have the Wanderers cranked," said Jeremy from beside Tristan, pointing with his sharp chin at the muscular youths. "They're turning into his real club."

Tristan nodded. Jeremy was as sharp-eyed and sharp-witted as Tristan had known him back in Dorm C. He was glad for the reunion for more reasons than simple friendship.

Hammerhand stayed antsy after his various expeditions had gone booming off. His jaw set, he gimped around in a stiff-legged circle, trademark meathooks bunched to fists by his hips. Tristan ran the gauntlet of ManLodge glares to roll his sled up beside the war-chief.

"What's the trouble" he asked.

Hammerhand looked sharply at him, but then what seemed real affection came into his green eyes. He nodded. "Well y'might ask, my friend. Look at my army."

He turned and threw out an arm in a gesture that encompassed the horde, drawn up in masses by clan with their auxy vehicles looming among them, obscured or revealed by whims of the storm.

"Took me months to get 'em together and get 'em rolling. Wasn't for Rendezvous, I doubt me we'd ever been able to muster the strength to face down the Cats. And now I'm afraid."

His eyes searched Tristan's long dark face for a flicker at the word. None showed. "I'm afraid," Hammerhand repeated more softly. "Afraid that, if they stop too long, I'll never get 'em moving again."

Tristan nodded slowly. It was a damned good point. Even Hammerhand couldn't be wrong *all* the time.

The chieftain nodded with sudden decision. He turned to face his ManLodge boys. "I need a volunteer for a dangerous mission," he announced. "I'd do it myself, but . . ." He let the words trail off, unwilling to vocalize his disability, but smart enough to acknowledge it, at least to himself.

The ManLodge bucks all crowded forward, waving their fists, jostling each other, and shouting themselves red in the face. Tristan found himself envying Hammerhand ever so slightly. He had deliberately avoided cultivating this kind of devotion, selfless and mindless—the two seemed about the same to Tristan—in the Jokers. He wanted loyal men and women, not dogs. Now he saw the power inherent in getting your followers so drummed up that they lost themselves entirely in you.

"You, Strongheart." Hammerhand pointed to one, a youth as tall as Tristan with a downy beard and blond locks that flowed to his broad shoulders, or would have if the rain hadn't matted them down. His colors said he belonged to the Sons of Odin, a clan that had warmed conspicuously to Tristan since he'd knocked the dicks off their traditional rivals, the Sons of Thor, so decisively in the dirt. But where he was said maybe he didn't really belong to the Sons anymore, and the look he gave Tristan as he marched up front and center before his leader was anything but amiable.

"I want you to tie a rope to your waist, boy," Hammerhand said. "Swim across the river and hitch it up on the far side. We'll need something to guide our rafts across."

Tristan couldn't help glancing aside, down into the river. It frothed and roared like rapids around the pilings. It was high, fast, and nasty. What Hammerhand was asking sounded like suicide to him.

But the Son thrust his fists in the air and roared, "I'm your man!" Hammerhand embraced him.

Quickly the boy stripped down. A rope was brought and made fast to a remnant strip of railing. He tied it around himself with obvious reluctance, as if afraid securing himself like this was a blot on his manhood. Without a backward glance he ran down the bank and cast himself into the torrent.

It tumbled him at once, took him under, tossed him up again, arms and legs flailing. The river rolled him from view another time, and when he reappeared he was limp, limbs moving with the rhythm of the waters, not his will.

His brothers hauled him out again. The current must have slammed him against a sunken fragment of the fallen span. There was a blue dent in the side of his head you could have socketed your fist in, and his eyes were blank as painted porcelain. Gently Hammerhand shut them with thumb and forefinger, and the body was laid aside.

The volunteers were still clamoring around like hounds for the entrails of a slain mule deer. Hammerhand picked another.

With the same lack of hesitation this one went into the water too.

He was a better swimmer than the late Strongheart. He made it better than a third of the way across before a treacherous eddy from around a piling dragged him down. Urged on by Hammerhand's bellows, his mates began to haul on the rope. Still submerged, he started to come in—and then stuck fast on some unseen obstacle. For all their sweating and swearing the ManLodgers could not bring him to the surface or any nearer land. After ten long minutes Hammerhand, tears welling in his eyes, ordered that the rope be cut and reeled in for another try.

The ManLodge boys were plenty subdued by this time, but shamed by each other, all of them still stepped forward to volunteer. The third man, a Freebird named Ace, with lank brown hair and less of a crazy-dog gleam in his eye, was wiry instead of bulky. He was cagey too, refusing to oppose his strength to the river's—any good Stormrider should know in his nuts that it didn't matter a hoot how much you could bench-press; Laughing Girl was stronger. Especially when she had the wildness of storm and runoff upon her.

When the current got the better of him he rode it, trusting to his comrades playing out the line from the bank, keeping himself afloat, working his way slowly across the flow, knowing that a river is not a solid thing like an iron bar, all of a piece, but a myriad of streams running side by side, some faster, some slower. At last, a couple of hundred yards downstream, after his buddies had sent on a couple of extra coils of line, he made his way into the shallower, slower flow near the bank, stood up, waded ashore, and collapsed into the mud.

The watching army raised a mighty holler of triumph and acclaim. Tristan shouted loud as any. He knew heroism when he saw it.

After a time Ace hauled himself up, staggered back along the bank to the bridge, and made fast the line. Then he collapsed as if he'd been shot. Just because he'd declined to try to armwrestle the North Canadian into submission didn't mean the crossing hadn't taken everything he had, and then some.

"This'll make a king-hell song," said Jammer, who had come up to stand beside Tristan. His head was down, and he was visibly composing it in his mind as he spoke.

The jubilation didn't last long. "That rope's too long," somebody said. "It'll never take a raft."

The crowd looked at each other. "We need a steel cable," Hammerhand said, and Tristan was mildly surprised that anybody had thought to bring any. "Who'll swim it across?"

Though the deadliest task was done, the starch had gone out of the ManLodge boys. They hung back, not looking at their leader. Their hesitation lasted just a heartbeat, but Tristan jumped into the middle of it, stripping off his shirt and kicking off his boots.

"Give me the thing," he said. He took a turn around his waist and fastened the snap ring at cable's end back onto the cable. Then he called for a short length of rope, and used it to run a loose loop around his hips and the line Ace had strung.

Feet sideways for traction, he walked directly down the slick bank to the water. He didn't look back. He just didn't feel like seeing Jovanne hoping visibly he'd never come back.

Inside the small tent Tristan sat with his knees drawn up and a blanket wrapped against him. He took a slug from the big mug he held in his hand, grimaced, and drank again. The mug was filled with tea laced with Taos lightning. It was nasty but bracing.

"Damn," he said. "Haven't been able to get the chill out of my bones all day." He glanced up at his companion, and his eyes glinted in the lantern light. "Must be getting old."

Jeremy scowled. He was older than Tristan, which still left him in his late twenties. Tristan had found he was sensitive on the subject, though.

It was nice to know he could actually get the better of him, once in a while.

Tristan sipped his revitalizer. "So tell me how a skinny kid from McGrory wound up a Scooter Trash legend before me?"

Jeremy smiled. "Skill beats genes." The smile faded. "Or maybe luck does—and not necessarily good luck. You decide."

13

I was adopted out of McGrory to be a slave (Jeremy said). You know how the story goes. Guess you were luckier than I was. Course, that's what I mean about luck—my luck'd been better, I wouldn't have been out on the Plains the last ten years.

I won't bore you with details of the pit I wound up in. I was only in it a year and a half. Then I turned seventeen. That's when I cheated the fuckards: I joined the Homeland Defense Force. My fosters couldn't do one mingeing thing about it.

The HDF wasn't bad, if you don't mind life in a cage. I stuck it out for a while. Then I decided to take my destiny into my own hands. Release myself on my recognizance, as it were.

We were on patrol up north. Mobile squad, couple of armored cars, some Bison carriers. I see you nod—you know the drill. We laagered in for the night in a cottonwood stand on the Kiowa, maybe twenty miles south of where it hits the Platte.

It was oh-dark-hundred—three, three-thirty in the morning. I just got up and walked away. Walked off through the trees as if I was just going to drain the weasel.

Sentry didn't buy it. Piece-of-shit Civic First Class looking to cling to his stripe. He challenged me before I got out of the trees.

If I'd had any sense I would've shrugged and gone back. Stuck to my story about taking a leak, claim I was sleepwalking—wouldn't have mattered. I might've pulled some stockade time for it, but even that wasn't too likely. Squad leader thought the CFC was a sag-nuts too.

But I *couldn't*. I think you can feel it too. I'd been in a cage half my life—hell, all my life, considering where I came from, but leave it, leave it. I was all set to taste my very first breath of freedom. I couldn't turn back.

I bolted. The sentry was such a brown-nose that he actually followed the manual. Anybody else would just have lit me up, sprayed bullets clear up to Lodgepole Creek with damn-all chance of hitting me—I was a good thirty yards away at the time, and you know how I can move.

Could. Single aimed shot from the shoulder. Not well aimed, mind you. But well enough. Took me in the heel. Passed through my foot lengthwise, smashed all the bones to shit.

You know a bullet won't toss a man around like they used to back on TV. This was different. I tell you, the pain—I've taken two rounds since, and both times all I felt was numb. Not this time. That pain threw me up in the air, knocked me ass over breakfast—just *levitated* me. I landed on my back so hard I couldn't draw breath to start screaming again for what seemed like a minute and a half.

I heard everybody in camp jump up and start yelling at each other. Some fool started busting caps on the other side of camp—Brother Wind knows what he thought he was shouting at. And the CFC, the weenie, he was jumping up and down, yipping, "I got him! I got him!" in a voice like a run-over dog. And the squad leader keeps yelling, "You got *who*, you damnfool son of a bitch?"

It might almost have been a chance to get up and make a break for it. If I could run. Hell, I couldn't even stand—couldn't *move*. All I could do was lie there and holler, with tears fuzzing out the stars overhead—it was clear, I remember that.

They say luck evens out, over time. I couldn't say myself, but mine got better then. I mean, considering the alternative.

The first thing, I hear more shooting, and I wonder if my buddies've decided to use me for target practice, create a little object lesson in case anybody else's thinking of going over the hill. Then I see flashes through the tears, and for the craziest moment I think they're coming from *outside* our perimeter.

Right that instant the Hellbenders MC had decided to pull a razz on my squad. I hear engines revving up in the night, and then war whoops, and these shapes rushing past me with that buffalo-bull fart sound of outlaw iron. I didn't know whether to laugh or cut my throat with my belt knife.

I realize now that the timing of the actual attack, at least, wasn't coincidental. That they'd picked that very night to hit us was. But when I got my silly ass shot and woke up the camp, they realized it was now or never for that particular ambush—they could've just hunkered down and waited for another night too, same as I could. I wasn't the only one with buck fever that night.

They were screwed, of course. The mobile troopers had concealment in among the trees, and a fair amount of cover. Squad Leader, Vuharcic, he knew his business. He didn't miss a beat; got them down and firing before the lead raider was within ten yards.

The squad was green. They only dropped three Hellbenders, tagged another three. The 'Benders sobered up in a hurry then, the way these nomads will when their medicine's bad. Turned tail and rolled—which was the smart thing to do.

When they cut stick they took me along with 'em. Dragging a useless sack of mush at the end of my leg. I would have fought them—you remember, they must've told you the same stories in basic, what the bikers'd do to you if they took you alive. Of course, they're true sometimes too.

When I came too I was in a world of hurt, I tell you. A strong buck had me by each arm, another had me by the head, and they were cutting on me. I fought like a mad thing, but you know strength's never been my strength. Couldn't shake them.

They weren't torturing me, of course. Well, they were, but that wasn't actually the plan. They were amputating the foot. I'm not sure why. I don't know how your bike-tramp relatives worked it, but the usual rule is, a bro is cool if he can still ride, but a slave has to be able to hump it.

Maybe it was the little StarLodge healer, with the black eyes and hair and the sweet round ass. She took quite a shine to me later anyway. What she did right then was press a yellow-hot Bowie knife blade to my brand-new stump.

Even that didn't hurt quite as badly as the bullet. *Quite.*

When I woke up I was a slave. Again. Or still.

Huh. I've had worse gigs. Like all of them up till then. They didn't push me. They gave me some herbs, and made all those mystic StarLodge signs over me and whatnot. Nursed me for a few weeks like I was one of their own. Of course I know now you nomads don't reproduce like bunnies, the way they taught us in Civic Studies—just the opposite, so you're always on the lookout for new blood. So I suppose they were sizing me up from the outset as a recruit, shy a hoof though I was.

After they decided I wasn't going to up and die on them, they gave me a crutch and set me watching their herds up in the Medicine Bows up along the Cache la Poudre. I spent that summer with the toddlers and the grannies and the adolescents with enough hormones in 'em to take on the whole Siksika branch of the Blackfeet at once, and few enough brains to do it too. Then in the fall the riders came back, and we moved the herds to winter pasture, farther downriver in the foothills, and camped there. And you know what? Those were pretty good times. Maybe not quite as good as Dorm C, after you got yourself transferred in . . . but not bad.

Come next spring I was hopping around pretty good, and I talked a bored wrench with a few woodworking tools into making me a fake foot. Some of the women dressed it up in deer hide, quite pretty—you know how it goes; 'long about midwinter you'll do anything just to be doing *something*. Our Prez, Tito, decided to take me along when it came time for the riders to hit the road.

They set me doing shitwork around camp, and helping out Big Fat Phil, the wrench who made my foot. Didn't get to do any wrench-work on the rides myself, of course—I was still a slave. It was fetch, carry, and hold. But I'm a good listener, and I keep my eyes open. And I made sure to let them know I was learning things. Tried too hard a couple of times, and Phil backhanded me silly. But he wasn't a bad sort.

I'll tell you, he's the only grown-up ever to hit me that I've chosen to let live. There are plenty back in Homeland I haven't gotten at yet, but time's long, and so's my memory. I've squared more accounts than I've left outstanding, my friend.

So I rode the Hellbenders' fenders, and I was as content as ever I'd been in my life. But there was still that inside of me that wouldn't let go. I was freer than I'd ever been before, no question. But I still wasn't my own man. I was property.

I started getting friendly with the healer I told you about. Alpha, her name was. Beautiful little thing, had some Woods Cree in her. Skin like brown satin . . . She was smart too, for all the superstitious crap her head was stuffed with.

She was—how can I say this?—the first woman I'd ever really known to talk to in my life. Except for my mother, who hardly counts. Strung me on a line, she did. Not that she was trying, I'm pretty sure. I think I was the first man who ever really talked to her. Or listened, anyway.

There was a little problem with this, and his name was Frenchy. He was Alpha's old man, a renegade Kaybecker with mean eyes, a black beard, and a big old gut. Rode a blue-and-silver apehanger with a fleur-de-lis on the tank. He liked to get a major load on and pound on her. I know that's usually a risky proposition, because mumbo jumbo aside, the StarLodgers stick together, and they'll shank you right off if you mess with one of their own. And good for them. But Alpha was the only Lodge member in the clan. And she wouldn't do a thing to protect herself from him. Maybe she didn't know she could.

As you might imagine, old Frenchy was thrilled about her talking with me. Especially since I was always asking her why she didn't do something about where she was.

Right off I started that line, she'd ask me why *I* didn't do something about where *I* was. I said the situations were totally different. She said that was weak. Smart girl, like I said.

So . . . the inevitable happened. We were riding in the Sand Hills north of Plattesburg, looking to run a little razz on the trucking traffic. We had camped for the evening by a little stream. I was hauling water, and she was walking along with me. Just passing time.

Her old man turns up. Backhands me, knocks me ass over teakettle back into the creek. Then he starts to whale on her.

I come out of the water spitting mad—maybe a tooth or two too. He had his back turned, wasn't giving me a thought—reckoned he'd taken me down to stay. I was just a sag-nuts slave, and a half-pint cripple to boot.

I slammed that old bucket over his fat head from behind. I commenced to beating on him. He must have had a hundred pounds on me, so I wasn't doing him that much harm. But he was staggering around lashing out blindly at the air and hollering as if he'd just been branded.

I made a mistake then. I kicked him in the balls, hard as I

could. With my right foot. Doubled him up proper, but it also tore my damned fake foot halfway off. I fell down.

He managed to start breathing again and got the bucket off his head. We'd attracted a crowd by then, and the other 'Benders were hoorawing him, telling him they liked him better with it on. He started bellowing that I was a rebellious slave, that they had to kill me right away—do it real nasty too, skin me, burn me. Hell, maybe both.

So up I piped and said, "What? Are you afraid to fight me face-up, Lard-gut?"

The 'Benders broke up laughing. Frenchy was cranked; he knew he was screwed. I'd changed the whole scene from a slave revolt to a skinny little cripple challenging a gigantic loud-mouth to fight, one-on-one. There was no way the others were going to interfere at that point. They wanted to *see* it.

So Frenchy says okay, and comes lumbering after me, with those big old arms outstretched. I get up and start kind of hopping in a circle. And one of the riders—a sister, Mustang Sally her name was—says, "Let's make this interesting." She pulls out her Bowie and tosses it to me.

I see you grinning like a fool. I heard around Rendezvous that much the same thing happened to you. I figure it happens a lot. The clans do make an effort to work slaves and prisoners into their ranks. And every club has as asshole or two who's more an embarrassment to his bros than anyone else. If a slave wants a shot at him, the clan's liable to say, "Whaffuck? Whadda we got to lose?"

Well, you know how, unless they're real samurai, these damned bikers aren't half as good with a knife as they think they are. They all stamp and flail and posture like they're fencing or something, and when they run into somebody who knows better stuff they just figure, hey, he's into Mystic Fighting Arts. Well, at that time, all I was into was good old Dorm C down and dirty bladework.

And that was more than enough. I won't bore you with the details. But I will tell you ol' Frenchy had a while to think about the error of his ways before I let the fucker die.

Rode with the Hellbenders for two years after that. Alpha rode with me at first, but after a time we started to drift apart. I think she maybe stayed a little passive. Wanted me to give her shape. And after a while it just got to seem like too much bother.

What it took me a while to come to grips with was, finally, I was *free*. I belonged only to myself, for the first time in my life. It took, hell, a season or two before it finally came clear. I always thought when it happened, I'd feel different all at once. But it didn't work that way.

Well, eventually I decided to really use that freedom I'd won. I said "later" to the 'Benders—yeah, and Alpha too; it's not as if we weren't still friends—turned the former Frenchy's scrambler toward the rising sun, and putted.

And that's my story.

Tristan pursed his lips and blew out a long breath, fluttering the ends of his dramatic bandit mustache.

"What I don't understand," he said, stretching and rolling his head to loosen his neck muscles, "is how you went from there to this whole Black Avenger gig. I hope you don't mind my saying so, Fer—Jeremy. But it's just a bit, y'know, *weird*."

Jeremy laughed. It was a surprisingly full laugh to come out of such a small frame, but a touch shrill as well.

"You're the scooter-trash born and bred, not me," he said. He used the derogatory terms the Folk frequently used on themselves—and which no one else was advised to, unless they were tired of seeing the same old face in the mirror every morning—without apparent self-consciousness or fear of giving offense. As far as Tristan was concerned he had earned the right long before he had ever breathed the wild air of the Plains, back in McGrory, when the two had become bros in the truest sense. And of course, Jeremy was a member in good standing of the High Free Folk. With a slight shock, Tristan realized this born Citizen's credentials were stronger than *his* among much of the Stormrider confraternity.

"You know how the Folk love their heroes. Hell, that's why half the Stormriders in Creation are stringing along behind John Hammerhand, and him without a thought in his blond damned head.

"See, after I wasted Frenchy, the 'Benders decided I was a samurai of some sort myself, an arcane master of the blade. Well, I wasn't going to cry bullshit on that, especially since I could take any one of them, bro or sis, hopping on one foot. I went from apprentice wrench to knife instructor the same instant I went from slave to rider.

"I really enjoyed it. That can't be much of a surprise; I lived for the bouts back in the Dorms. That was all I had to live for. And all the time I was teaching them, I was learning from them, improving on my own licks. I left as much because the Hellbenders and I had run out of things to show each other as anything else."

He refilled his own mug with tea from an earthenware pot perched on a camp stove. "I spent the next few years looking up all the samurai teachers I could find. Knife, sword, nunchucks, barehand fighting—you name it, I studied it. I was stone fanatical about it. Masters loved me 'cause I was an ideal student— you hardly had to show me anything twice. Clans loved to have me around because, what the hell? You can't have too many samurai around if it comes to a rumble.

"And in time something came to me. I was *angry*. It was a deep abiding anger. I was righteously pissed off. Three quarters of my life had been stolen from me. I wanted *revenge*."

"So that's when you became the Black Avenger?"

Jeremy nodded. His eyes glistened like obsidian mirrors in the lantern light. The teeth in his grin looked very sharp.

"As I said, your nomads love their heroes. And their mystic wifty-drifty crap. So I decided to give them a megadose of both. I created a new persona right out of the comic books we used to get smuggled in from Broken Arrow and Iron City. And I went looking for vengeance."

"Whoo," Tristan said. "That's quite a story." He sat for a while, staring at nothing in particular and scraping at the inside of his lower lip with his teeth.

Finally the question welled up inside him like a belch that could no longer be contained. "What would you've done," he asked, "if you ran into me?"

Jeremy chuckled softly. "I always figured you'd follow me into the HDF. I just didn't stay around long enough. Out there on the Plains, I always figured I'd see you sooner or later. Especially when word started going round the tipis to be on the lookout for the Striker who called himself Outlaw One."

He looked Tristan in the eye, catching a look of surprise. "You think I didn't know? The Black Avenger was always on the hunt for Outlaw One, but he was damned careful never to actually *find* him. There was no way both of us could walk away from a meeting like that."

Morosely Tristan wrapped his arms around drawn-up knees. "You whupped my ass pretty handily back there."

"Yeah." Jeremy stood up, stretched. "Good thing we're bros, huh?"

He gimped toward the entry flap, stopped, and half-turned back. "Going to be a cold night. Why don't you ask that high-pockets Prez of yours in to help keep you warm?"

Tristan shook his head. "She's not too happy I exist right now."

"She's in love with you, you know."

Tristan snorted a laugh through his fine nose. "She thinks I'm dangerous to her."

Jeremy laughed. "Women always love what they think's dangerous to them," he said. "Weren't you listening to my little tale? That was the moral, brother."

He touched Tristan's shoulder. "Night."

14

Smoke rolled from the ground as if a fumarole had popped open in the Plains' wet grass-clad hide. Tristan's experienced nostrils picked out the smell of burning cloth and wood and meat.

He slewed the scrambler to a stop, raising a bow wave of mud and bits of grass. "What the fuck's going on here?" he demanded.

He realized he had almost rammed into the sprawled body of a woman, facedown, large and lumpy in sodbuster skirts. Without particularly thinking about it he broke his Bolo from its underarm holster and thumbed the selector to full rock'n'roll.

Jovanne reined her orange-and-brown-painted scrambler to a halt beside his. "What's the hassle?" she asked.

He frowned. "This." He waved his hand around, taking in the corpse and the smoke pouring from the subterranean farmhouse.

She shrugged. "Why sweat? It's just a bunch of Diggers."

It was another Plains contradiction—contradictions just naturally seemed to flourish on the Plains, like weeds and wildflowers. The Digger MC was well respected for their work on Rendezvous. They bore their name with pride. But in any other context the word *Digger* was the direst epithet of the Plains. It signified the lowest thing there was: somebody tied to a plot of ground, who grubbed around in the soil to make his miserable excuse for living, and could never possibly know the freedom of the Road. To call one of the High Free Folk a Digger—unless

97

they belonged to Fat Ed's clan—was an instant invitation to go round and round. Most of the Folk regarded Diggers as their natural-born prey, and it was safe to say that all viewed them with contempt.

Tristan was saved having to try to point out just what was wrong with that point of view when a couple of cruiser bikes appeared out of the smoke. Their blond young riders sported black T-shirts emblazoned with a stylized human skull in white. They'd managed to get the things silk-screened since departing Rendezvous—the gods knew what-all kind of stuff the army was dragging along with it now.

The hardest core of Hammerhand's ManLodge pals were traveling in packs and calling themselves Death Commandos now. They were highly impressed with themselves. These two stopped and eyed Tristan without friendship.

"What the hell do you think you're doing?" he demanded.

They passed each other *do you* believe *this asshole*? looks. "Requisitioning," one said, surprising Tristan that he could remember a word that long, much less pronounce it. "We need food. They had it." He shrugged.

"What happened to paying for it?"

"Are you crazy, man? We're *Stormriders*."

"I doubt that."

Half a dozen other Commandos came roaring up on their sleds. One of the first two started to swing off his iron. "You need to be taught some manners," he said.

Casually Tristan pointed the Bolo at him. "Too bad you won't be around to watch the lessons. You might learn something."

The man froze. His buddies glanced at each other, calculating the odds. The process took a while.

Just about the time the ManLodgers seemed to come up with a solution—*yup, four-to-one*—a gust of wind dissipated the ground-hugging smoke to reveal four more Death Commandos—and the rest of the Jokers, plus the Outlaws, drawn up left and right of Tristan and Jovanne.

Jesse putted forward. "What's the hang-up, here?" he inquired pleasantly.

"Trouble," Tristan said. "I think we all need to go talk to the Man."

Seeing Tristan holding down on one of the black Ts, the two

allied clubs had reflexively fallen back on the first law of Plains solidarity, *one for all and all on one*. They had therefore begun to point a motley but intimidating assortment of weapons at the twelve Death Commandos. Tristan thought he could almost see the smoke pouring from the Commandos' ears as they frantically tried to recalculate, but the best answer was one instantly obvious even to them: *There's more of them than there are of us.*

Sullenly the ManLodgers formed up under the Joker and Outlaw guns. As they began to roll back toward the body of the army, ahead of which the two clans had been performing a recon sweep, Jesse gave Tristan a puzzled look. "Hey, I got no problem seeing these dudes get their timing set a few clicks lower," he said. "They reckon they fart sweet perfume. But what'd they do?"

Tristan nodded at the dead woman. "This. Murder."

Jesse blinked. "So what's the shake? They're only Diggers."

The self-appointed boss of the Death Commandos was a kid with a downy reddish beard and a huge tawny tangled lion's mane of hair who'd once rode with the Nighthawks. His name was Tyree. He had a flat stomach, skinny legs, and wide heavy shoulders. His face at the moment was bright red.

"We're free men, ain't we?" he raged, pacing left and right before the folded-arm figure of John Hammerhand. "We're all bros, ain't we? We got the right to take what we want, don't we?"

"Too bad he's too young to stroke," Jeremy murmured at Tristan's side.

A Death Commando a head taller scowled at him. "Hey, no secret plotting here, ya little puke. Speak right up so's ever'bod' can hear."

"Shut the fuck up," Jeremy said, smiling, "or I'll kick you in the balls so hard they'll plug your nose, paste-eater."

Hammerhand raised one of his namesakes. "Peace," he said, "we're all brothers here."

"Is this guy nearsighted or what?" Jovanne stage-whispered from Tristan's other side. The ManLodgers glared at her, but kept their mouths shut.

"What are you saying, Brother Tyree?" Hammerhand asked in a mild voice.

"Look, we all know this puke who calls himself Burningskull

is really a City stooge. He's Outlaw One; he made a whole career of wasting bros."

"He's made his peace with the Folk," Hammerhand said. "He's one of us now."

Tyree's jaw muscles bunched as if his reflex was to shout *bullshit*! But he couldn't quite bring himself to pitch that word in his idol's face. His mouth worked for a moment soundlessly before he found words he dared utter.

"So he says. But he lies. He's still a pig. He's got a pig's moves. He's a mingy low-down spy!"

"What makes you say that?"

"He busted our fucking chops!" shouted one of the first pair of Death Commandos Tristan had confronted at the burning sod house—the one who'd offered the courtesy lessons. "We was just requisitioning supplies like you ordered, and him and his boys throw down on us."

Hammerhand turned lowered bushy brows on Tristan. "Is this so?"

"Yes."

For a heartbeat Hammerhand seemed taken aback that Tristan had answered so flatly. "Why?" he said after a moment.

"They murdered the householders in cold blood."

Hammerhand fingered his clean-shaven chin. "I won't jump to convict you of meanin' ill," he said, "but maybe you were in the City so long you forget the way it is out here. We're Lords of these Plains; we take what we need, and those who try to stand in our way get cut down. This is the Law."

Hammerhand had a point about his Citified values, Tristan realized. Freewheeling rape, pillage, and slaughter just didn't have that same old appeal anymore. "Maybe the Law needs to be changed," he said, "but that's not the point. The point is, best we know, the Cathead Nation matches our whole force sled for sled. We're going to have all we can handle without rousing the whole Plains against us as we ride."

"What a chickenshit," one of the ManLodgers scoffed.

"Yeah," agreed another. "Who's afraid of a passel of sag-nuts farmers?"

"Anyone who's been bushwhacked by a lot of them," Jeremy said. "You really eager to get hung on a wire?"

The ManLodger paled. A hand went to his thick unwashed throat. "Pukes wouldn't dare."

"They'd dare plenty, if they didn't reckon they had anything to lose."

"What would you have us do, my friend?" Hammerhand asked Tristan. "The army has to eat. Our herds can't keep up with us."

"Trade or pay for what we need." The ManLodgers hooted. "You know there's hardly a clan that doesn't trade regularly, with Citizens and Diggers alike—maybe SOTE and the Smoking Mirrors don't, but they're about all." The aptly named Scum of the Earth and the Mirrors—Tristan's mother's people—were Plains pariahs, outlaws too scabrous even for the outlaw brotherhood.

"We've just come off a long, hard winter," Hammerhand replied. "Our meat bags and money bags are both mighty thin."

"You want we should *work* our way to war?" sneered the ManLodger who'd called Tristan chickenshit.

"That'd be easier than fighting our way," Tristan said, choking down the urge to smash his face in. "But if we were smart we could stretch our gold plenty far. The sodbusters have as much stake in seeing the Catheads put down as we do. Maybe more, since we can ride off into the mountains or the BlackLands and hide out if we have to. They and the Citizens between here and the Big River might be willing to kick in some support."

"Do you *believe* this shit?" screamed Tyree. Hammerhand stepped forward and put his arm around Tristan's shoulder.

"Brother Tristan, I believe you're a true son of the Plains, and I don't care who knows it." He gave a significant look to his black-T-shirted followers, who looked sulky and shuffled their boots. "But your ideas ain't of this world.

"I tell you what, though. If the Diggers are willing to just give us what we want, why, we'll let them keep their miserable lives. But if they try to hold back . . ." A shrug of those massive shoulders. "Why, we can't let anything hold up the war effort now, can we?"

The army rolled northeastward. It crossed the Arkansas laboriously, in a thunder-shouting storm that lashed the horde with hailstones half the size of a man's fist, by means of an ancient bridge built for the long-extinct railway. More than twenty riders vanished into the greedy frothing waters, jostled from the narrow bridge by their brethren or stunned by the hailstones.

Since StarFall—as the legends of the Folk claimed, and as Tristan's Library studies had confirmed—the game had returned to the Plains in a crazy profusion, like nothing seen since Europeans reached the New World and maybe before. Herds of pronghorn, bison, and feral longhorn cattle flowed across the land like seas, feeding off grasses grown rank beneath two centuries of rain. That eased the army's commissary problems somewhat, though enforced contributions—which was to say *raids*—against the Diggers continued.

But the Divine Brothers and Sisters were contrary, like their children the High Free Folk. For every gift they bestowed, it seemed, they exacted some heavy payback. A buffalo stampede, touched off by lightning or maybe a hunting party, washed across the army's line of march like a tidal wave. Hemmed in by their brothers, many riders were unable to get out of the way in time. Over a hundred brothers and sisters vanished beneath the pounding hooves, with a score of cages loaded with vital ammunition, fuel, and food.

When the thunderstorms lifted, the Stalking Winds began to lash the land with their long black tentacles. Though a fair number of the riders had survived the risky rite of passage called Dancin' with Mr. D—playing chicken with tornadoes, thereby becoming true Stormriders—the size and cohesiveness of the army made it hard to maneuver out of the twisters' way. By ones and twos or half-dozens, the riders were plucked away by the funnels to be dashed to pieces, or have their lungs ruptured and die with their beards covered in pink foam.

Word of the army's advance spread faster than its wheels could roll. Armored patrols from Osagerie in the south began to shadow the force. Fort Hammond's City-owned radio station began broadcasting word to the horde that it would be attacked in force if it ventured within fifty miles of the settlement. A former colony of Missouri City, and recently liberated for about the third time by the Osage from its aggressive parent's grasp, Fort Hammond wasn't much of a much. But it had a City's complement of river guns—heavy machine guns—and City-sized stocks of ammo to keep them flowing. That disparity in supply, allowing Cities a decisive advantage in sustained full-auto firepower, had prevented any City's ever being overrun by a Plains horde. Numerous settlements had been trashed by the nomads, and many had vanished utterly as a consequence.

But not even Hammerhand was fool enough to try to tackle Fort Hammond armor and heavy weapons face-up. That did it for his intention to squeeze between Hammond and Misery City and thereby avoid having to cross the Missouri. In turn that meant the army had to detour well north, almost to the Platte; if it couldn't afford to tangle with small, insignificant Hammond, there was *no way* it wanted a piece of big, mean Misery.

Of course, the Platte route would take them near Plattesburg, where Tristan knew Omaha had once stood. Plattesburg, though, had a reputation for being friendly, or at least open-minded, where motorcycle nomads were concerned. The army stood a chance of passing through its territory unmolested. They might even pull down reinforcements; despite Fat Ed's enthusiasm, no more than a third to half the High Free Folk ever made a single Ron D. Voo, and this year's was no exception. The 'Burg was a favored wintering spot for the clans.

As the horde veered north morale rose, though the weather stayed filthy. With a little luck, the Folk might conceivably pick up support from the City itself. Maybe a shade better than mid-way between Fort Hammond and Misery City in size, Plattesburg was unlikely to feel threatened even by the large, cohesive Cathead Nation. But that didn't mean the 'Burgers were eager to see the Cats afforded unlimited access to their trade routes and the farm belt that surrounded the City and gave it sustenance.

Elation didn't last. The lead rider of a Slave Drivers foraging party rode between a pair of innocuous-looking fence posts only to have his head pop from his shoulders in a geyser of blood and roll back under the lead wheels of his bros. As they scattered to avoid the lethal wire strung across the road, hidden by the storm-filtered half-light, a volley of gunfire ripped them from the ditches to either side of the road. They fled, leaving six of their number lying on the blacktop.

The Diggers' vengeance had begun, just as Tristan and Jeremy had predicted.

From that point on the scavenger teams started coming back shy members, when they came back at all. Snipers emptied saddles from ranges that guaranteed retribution could never catch up with them. Point riders drove their machines at a nervous crawl, fearing the wire; armorers were kept busy hammering out throat-guards of various sorts. It was soon found that these tended to result in your face getting ripped off, but a lot of bros—and sisters—wore them anyway. There's something so *final* about decapitation.

Still, when the army hit the Platte and turned east again, the High Free Folk began to look at each other and shout that better times lay ahead, bro. The 'Burgers would help them out; their missing brothers would flock to the Cause.

And then a westbound band of Earthshakers ran into the horde's vanguard. Hollow of cheek and eye, they brought word of how a combined nomad/Plattesburger army had faced the Catheads.

And lost.

15

"It was magic," the Earthshaker told his audience of outlaw chieftains. He was a tall, rangy man with hair cut short beneath a flat cap, and a long, luxuriant beard. His beard was gray as lead, and his eyes held a faraway look. He was the ranking rider since the Prez, the warlord, and most of their right-handers had gone down. It was becoming a familiar tale.

"Black magic."

Tristan raised a brow at Jeremy. The small man made a circle of thumb and forefinger and sketched a jack-off gesture. It was lost to any eyes but Tristan's amid the shadows cast by the bodies hunched around a Council Fire that seemed to be trying to leap to touch the hanging bellies of the clouds.

Maybe not all eyes. Tristan caught Jovanne giving him a *gotcha!* look that slid into a half-smile as her eyes slid away.

The 'Shaker had most of his audience listening with slack-jawed fascination. For Plains warriors to beat City forces was no big deal; the Jokers had bested patrols out of Homeland and Fort Hammond often enough. When Tristan was in the regular HDF, only decisive action—not to mention insubordination—on his part had saved a mobile patrol from annihilation in a Cathead ambush.

But those were small-scale actions, involving squads, platoons, companies at the outside. Plattesburg had sent its main force against the Catheads and been defeated. What could that mean, but magic?

"Soon as the snow cleared off, the Cats rolled west from their wintering grounds north of St. Lou. They seemed to be lookin' to cross the Misery between P-Burg and Misery City. The 'Burgers mighta overlooked that, but the Cats' advance parties started hitting the 'Burg's big rigs and Diggers hard. More'n that. They started ridin' right up to the wire. Hide out where the pillboxes couldn't see 'em, snipe off Citizens long-range, right in their own backyards, or catch some Citizen and torch him off, so the local kiddies could watch their Uncle Buddy flop and burn. Then they'd ride off laughin' fit to bust.

"No way the 'Burgers were gonna take that. We wintered there, and the Flaming Arrows, and the Aliens. 'Burgers asked us, would we stand with 'em against the Cats. They always been square with us, and by that time we knew you boys was on the way, so we knew the cause was righteous. We said we would."

He paused to accept a skin of wine. He fired a long red stream that glittered in the flamelight in the direction of his mouth, not seeming to notice that much of it wound up matting his beard and slopping down his washboard belly.

"We crossed the Platte south from P-Burg, then took the old toll bridge 'cross the Misery, which was in a rare fury from the melt. We wasn't hearing squat from our scouts at that point, but nobody minded too much, 'cause we reckoned we was powerful enough to take down the Cats if they jumped us, what with our sleds and the City river guns an' all.

"Hardly we'd gone over when word come the Cats had double-crossed us. They did the Misery *north* of P-Burg, by th' old 80 bridge leads from the Bluffs through the Omaha rubble. They was bearin' right down on the 'Burg itself, with their sleds all shrouded in canvas and these shave-head yellowrobes ridin' along by the cageful.

"Well, our army turned right round on itself. Ever'thing just went to hell in a handbasket. The cages was runnin' into each other, and jostling each other off the bridges, and then when we got back to the west and headed north, it was like tryin' to swim up a waterfall, 'cause—would you believe it?—Citizens was streaming south *out of Plattesburg*."

He paused to shake his head and fortify himself with a hit of wine. He was obviously still shaken by the thought of Citizens, safe behind their wire tangles and minefields and pillboxes, fearing an outlaw army enough to hit the Road in flight.

It shook his listeners too. Faces turned toward one another, ashen behind their beards. Voices murmured in an uneasy cicada chorus until Hammerhand raised his huge scarred fists for silence.

"We managed to make our way through the City. Old Citizens, they was pleading with us to stay and fight behind the wire, keep the nasty old Catheads out. 'Burger big shots weren't havin' any o' that. King Billy's Catheads made 'em look like monkeys. They were looking to grind King Billy's fat face in the dirt for that one."

He faltered then, momentarily overcome. "'Cept it was our faces got ground. North of P-Burg we started seeing evidence that Cathead advance parties'd been there before us—folks nailed up on poles and sides of buildings, some by the hands, some by the feet, some by one of each. Some had their bellies slit so their guts sort of uncoiled over their faces. Some of them was still moanin'.

"Came down dark. We hunkered down for the night, feeling all eerie, clammy, and cold, like, from what we'd seen. I mean, all of us'd did our share of riding and raiding, y'know, and never shrank from hard deeds. But this . . . we'd never seen nothin' like it. Not ever.

"They hit us then, sometime after midnight." A murmur ran through his audience. Nocturnal raids were one thing, but the Plains riders as a general thing feared to engage in full-scale fights at night. "But it wasn't just them. There were *things*, out in the dark. Things black as Hell's deepest cell, with eyes that burned red like iron in a forge. Things could reach right down to the center of a man and rip his soul out."

He drew a breath that made his whole body shake, as if the air were chilled. "Cats hit us then, while we was half in the bag from stone fear. They came on their bikes, their yellow-robe buds came on foot. It was like trying to stop the wind. But . . . we held.

"Then a ruction started among those candy-ass Citizens. Cats had got in behind us. Said they was even hitting the wire at P-Burg.

"Them 'Burgers went ape-shit crazy. Started peelin' out of their positions like they was being washed off with a hose. We hung in 'long as we could, but they swarmed us, just swarmed us."

He hid his face in spidery hands. "At last we booked. We had to. Gods, there's just so much a body can take."

For a moment the chiefs just clustered around, those nearest reaching out to touch his sob-wracked shoulder. "How come they were able to get behind you?" asked Tommy Hawk, the Freebird warlord, who stood back from the crush with muscular arms crossed over his chest, bare but for a leather vest. He wore a hatchet stuck through his belt. As always, his handsome face was daubed with war paint, a yellow stripe that crossed his nose from cheek to cheek, right below the eyes. "What about your scouts? What about your pickets?"

The Earthshaker raised his hands. "I don't know, Brother Wind, I don't! Seemed like the night just swallowed them up."

There were more questions then. None of them amounted to much, as far as Tristan could see.

"They're talking to comfort themselves," said Jeremy, who stood hugging himself as if his fleece-lined leather jacket was not enough to keep out the nocturnal chill. Tristan nodded.

"All right," Hammerhand said, his voice as usual commanding without being raised, "let's break it up. Our brother here's had a hard time of it. We've all heard his story. Let's let the man rest."

A subdued crowd began to break up. As the clan leaders returned to their own campfires Tristan felt a hard, heavy hand upon his shoulder.

"Bide a minute, Brother Tristan," John Hammerhand said. "I'd like to share some words with you."

Jovanne flicked her eyes across his. They caught, briefly, like fingerprints on silk. Then she was gone, and Jeremy with her, and Tristan and Hammerhand were walking alone at the center of a circle of glowering burly youths.

"You heard the man," Hammerhand said. "What'er your thoughts?"

Tristan shrugged. "The Catheads can be beaten," he said. "We beat them."

Hammerhand laughed hugely. "I admire a man who believes in his medicine."

He sucked in a long breath, blew it out through distended lips. "I have my eye on you. You know that. You're a coming man. You're on the rise; everybody recognizes it, even if

Mother Sky won't always let us see your Sign through the lining of her cloak."

He stopped and squared to face Tristan. "Do you really think
it's fitting you should ride to war eating a woman's trail dust?"

Son of a bitch, Tristan thought. He wasn't actually part of
Jovanne's band; he'd tried to make that clear to all and sundry.
But I'm damned if I'll duck out that way.

"I'm willing to ride trail to anyone who's worthy," he said.

Hammerhand walked a few steps away and stood with his
back to Tristan. A few early-season crickets chirred.

"You'll need good scouts," Tristan said. "I'd like you to send
us out. We'll do a good job."

Hammerhand turned back shaking his head. "I want you with
me. Want your destiny nearby. Besides . . ."

He rolled his heavy shoulders. His brow creased in thought.
It cost him a lot of effort, Tristan reckoned.

"Now that you mention it, scouting would be good work for
the women—for the bands led by women, at least. Something
for them to do."

Tristan stared at him. It felt as if all the substance had been
teleported out from the middle of him, leaving nothing but a
thin, friable shell.

Good scouting was vital for war. To fight without the best
possible knowledge of your enemy's disposition and movements was like playing Russian roulette with five chambers
loaded. As a Striker for the Homeland Defense Force, Tristan
had been a scout first and foremost. Most people on both sides
of the Homeland wire thought of the Strikers as lone warriors of
the Plains, Hero Cops like something out of an old movie,
charged with hunting down and slaying the City's foes. That
image had deliberately been fostered by Black Jack Masefield,
the Strikers' founder and creator, to win support and intimidate
foes. But every Striker knew his main job was reconnaissance.

It was a dangerous job too. The Jokers knew very well what
an abrupt way the Catheads had with enemy scouts.

And here Hammerhand was blowing off scouting as *women's
work.* It was the old Plains refrain: If it didn't happen on a sled,
it wasn't war.

Hammerhand clapped him on the biceps. "Think about what
I said, son. It's your honor I'm thinking of, that and your mascu-
line essence."

Uh, yeah. "Think about what I said too," Tristan said, and walked away.

He had gone barely twenty paces when he felt looming presences hemming him in to either side. "We're watching you," hissed the Death Commando on Tristan's right. "Don't think we aren't."

"I hope I'm entertaining."

Both his flankers missed a step. *These boys have trouble walking and thinking at the same time, don't they?*

"You been bringing all this bad luck," said the one on the right.

"Oh?" Tristan said, hiking up his right eyebrow. "You mean, like volcanos, and floods, and bridges out, and tornadoes?"

The youth bobbed his shaggy head. "Yeah."

"And you been riding with chicks too," said the other one.

"We know you wanna push out Big John and take over for yourself, make yourself Maximum Lord."

Tristan spread his hands. "You got me," he said, shaking his head in feigned wonder. "I thought I was a pretty cagey son of a bitch, but you boys are just too smart for me. Yes, I caused all those *natural disasters*; nothing I like better than getting bashed around by a freezing cold river, and riding across the Staked Plains with my eyes all full of volcanic ash. And not only have I ridden *with* chicks, I've even, once in a while, ridden chicks, if you know what I mean—and you probably don't, do you?"

He noticed a figure hanging nearby in the darkness: Pud, the Cathead defector. Tristan looked at what he hoped was his eyes and shook his head microscopically.

"But you can tattoo this on your ass, so your buddy here can practice reading it while he's helping you out with all those man rituals: I wouldn't have Hammerhand's goddamned job if I was paid to take it."

"Hey, we got our eyes on you," the first one said. "You said we caught you—"

He cut off abruptly when Tristan slammed his right hand into the man's kidney in a three-inch punch. The Death Commando went to his knees with a strangled sound.

"Sorry," Tristan told the stricken man's gape-mouthed pal. "I must've tripped."

● ● ●

"Black things out of the night," Zonker said, hugging his knees. "Brrr. I don't fear no man, Cathead or not. But *magic . . .*"

"Magic, my left one," Jeremy said. "That wasn't anything more than fatigue, combat nerves, and a little chemical enhancement."

"You sound sure of yourself, loner," said Little Teal in the dead way she had since her man Big Jupe went down. Jeremy just gave her a lopsided grin and hitched his head knowingly to one side.

"What I don't dig," said Red Dog, poking the Jokers' fire with a stick of driftwood, "is why the Cats *bothered* to hit P-Burg. I mean, they had the City's main force outflanked. Why didn't they turn their wheels west and just call me the breeze?"

"They wanted to take P-Burg down hard to keep the 'Burgers and their scooter-trash pals from hitting them in the rear," said Jovanne, to her own obvious surprise. "They threaten the precious City, and then beat a real, live city army in the field, they'd put enough scare on the 'Burgers to keep 'em off their butts. Maybe help keep the other Cities' minds right too."

Tristan raised an eyebrow at her. Was it just his imagination, or was his little saddle pal talking like a strategist?

"How'd they manage to take the 'Burgers then?" Emilio demanded. "That's magic right there. Gotta be."

"No magic," Jeremy said, "strategy. Strategy—and terror."

Tristan nodded and rubbed his long chin. *Interestin'*, he thought. He was seeing his friends growing into something beyond themselves, it seemed, transforming from drag-ass refugees and outlaws into *chiefs*, strong voices in the councils of war. And suddenly he saw it clearly, as if the present had receded, and his foreseeing was momentarily more real: all of them, older, graver, a bit more worn, sitting around a fire as they sat tonight, only on every word the fate of entire armies, *nations*, hung.

Holy shit, he thought, *I'm having a vision.*

He grinned then, for his own benefit. *Or maybe it's just a trick of the light.* He had little more faith in mystic miracles than Jeremy.

And a tiny voice inside him whispered, *Aren't you forgetting the vision of the hawk, the stream, and the clear sky, that sus-*

*tained you when you were downed in the Man's hole? And how
it came to pass?*

"Huh," he grunted, rising. "It's late. Maybe we'd better get
some shut-eye, before we all start seeing red-eyed black
things."

16

"Nice heft," Tristan said, rotating his wrist left and right. Wan morning light slanting in beneath the cloud ran up and down the two straight edges of the broadsword's blade.

The weapon had a cross hilt with tapered, gently forward-curved wings. A stout knuckle-bow arced from hilt to pommel, to guard his fingers from swordcuts. A second bow similarly protected the back of his hand. The swept hilt was plain steel, unembellished. It matched the man.

He extended his arm in a slow-motion thrust. "Nice balance, too."

This morning the army had headed off due east from the point where the Platte veered north. It had almost immediately stopped. It had then begun a fitful inchworm progress, impeded by what no bro could say for sure, though plenty had opinions, some of which they thought carried the same weight as fact: The Cats had been contacted; the foraging parties sent out instead of the scouts Hammerhand disparaged had vanished; a new volcano had begun to rear up in their path; they were trying to hook up with fugitive remnants of P-Burg's Citizen army.

The smith stood by the rear of his van, taking advantage of the halt to deliver the weapon he'd been crafting to Tristan's order since Rendezvous. He was a wide-bodied specimen, who looked short unless he happened, as now, to be standing near enough to somebody like Tristan that it became apparent he cleared six feet. His nose was bulbous and great-pored. His gut

113

was prodigious even by nomad standards, and his mustard-colored hair and beard were to the same extent wild. His cage was black, its side painted with a shadowy axeman sitting astride a gigantic black horse. A thick-bodied dog, with short black and tan hair and a spiked collar around its bull neck, lay at his feet with its grizzled, scarred muzzle resting on its forepaws. It pretended sleep, but Tristan knew the beast was sizing him up for a takedown. It was well adjusted to StormLands life.

"Guns are all well and good," the smith said in a voice like pebbles rattled in a tin can. "But they're hungry puppies, and firestick fodder's mighty hard to come by, out under Mother Sky. One of these, now—" he nodded toward his latest creation—"they never need reloading."

He tipped his huge head to one side and gave Tristan a look that reminded him for some bizarre reason of an enormous baby bird. "Blade like this runs might thirsty, though," the smith said.

Tristan tossed a hide bag containing the balance due in gold coins bearing the likeness of an ancient Osage warrior to the smith, who caught it with a casual motion of one massive arm. Tristan then picked up the belt and scabbard from the black velvet display cloth unrolled on the van's bed.

"I have a feeling," Tristan said, slamming blade into scabbard, "that she'll drink her fill before too damned much longer."

A several-throated roar of engines made him look up. "New clan rolling in," the smith rumbled. It was true; a contingent of thirty riders threaded their machines through the stalled army, faces grim, weapons slung over backs. A few bros greeted them with happy familiar cries, ran forward to embrace them as they swung mud-spattered legs off their irons. The majority of onlookers acknowledged them with wary, weary nods and waves.

A tall, slat-lean rider walked over to a red van parked beside the smith's cage, its sides displaying a scene of boozy revelry replete with naked great-breasted babes, where a bandy-legged man with a squint and a bandanna tied around his head sold wine from the tailgate. The rider was obviously so tired he could barely manage to affect the obligatory outlaw swagger, but he held his black-bearded head defiantly high.

"How 'bout some good stuff for a thirsty bro?" he demanded in a voice rough from breathing trail dust laced with volcanic grit.

The wine seller gave him an appraising squint. "You got the ready?"

The rider's black eyebrows pressed down on the bridge of his nose like baby's fists. "Where's your damn hospitality?" he demanded. "I'd think a man'd be ready enough to share with a bro who'd ridden hard to pull his chestnuts out of the fire."

In the first eager rush from Rendezvous even the canny nomad hucksters' hands had been opened in generosity. Hardship, disillusionment, and several hundred weary miles of short commons had closed most fists. Now the wine seller replied, "You reckon this is the Big Rock Candy Mountain, where the Ripple runs down the slopes in happy red creeks? Get real."

The rider dropped fists whose knuckles were white and gorged with scar tissue and whose backs were furred black like an ape's in some City zoo on the top of the counter, which was a weather-warped plank propped across two oil drums, and leaned into them. "If you'd seen what was waiting for you a piece down the Road up close and personal, Shorty," he said into the merchant's face, "you'd change your damn tune pretty fast."

The squint-eyed man faced him without flinching, though the offended rider was a good head taller, and his bros were beginning to gather behind him, not exactly intruding on his affairs, but ready to enforce the ancient Plains law of *one for all and all on one* at need.

"We're strung out pretty thin here, cousin," the wine seller said. His tone was conciliatory, but his right hand was out of sight somewhere. That no doubt meant he was reaching for a sawed-off side-by-side, or some such fine Plains equalizer. "We been riding a long, hard Road ourselves. I poured for ever'body with a sad song to sing, I'd be flat and everybody else'd be thirsty."

Tristan stepped forward, noticing the newcomer bore an emblem of a skeleton riding an apchanger sled and the legend "Ghost Riders" on the back of his black vest. "I'll pay," he said, dropping a handful of Osage silver on the countertop. He was flush with the proceeds of the Cathead loot they'd sold at Ron D. Voo, where the Jokers had voted him a leader's share. Besides, he had that sinking, sizzling feeling in the pit of his flat belly that, one way or another, he might soon have no more need of it. "A round for everybody."

The newcomer rounded on him, eyes narrowed and red. Tristan faced him in an open, relaxed posture, but his right hand was ready to move on the Bolo in its break-open holster beneath his arm. The Ghost Riders were wired and tired and probably a little cranked off at not receiving a hero's welcome. Nomads in that state were always unpredictable, and might take offense at anything.

The Ghost Rider let the air out of him in an explosive breath. "Here's a man knows the meaning of brotherhood," he said. "Be honored to drink your health, man."

The rest of the pack would too, it seemed. As they gathered around to soak up Tristan's wine a crowd began to assemble. Since there wasn't going to be a rumble, those who had been riding with the army were hungry for news.

"You boys're the third clan to ride in today," said a wiry little Wanderer with a cast in one eye and gray in his beard. "Clans're gatherin', for true."

"Not only here," the first Ghost Rider said. "Clubs've commenced to join the Catheads too."

Shock ran the listeners like a gust of wind blowing high grass, with a visible ripple of expressions on bearded faces. "Who'd be that low-down mingy?" demanded a mean-eyed little redheaded woman in Nightranger colors.

A mountainous Ghost Rider guffawed so mightily his black T-shirt bearing the words "Ride to Live—Live to Ride" rode up his hairy belly. "Plenty," he said. "Scum of the Earth, for one. The Breed. Death Hogs. Skull Fuckers. Sons of Thor."

At this some of the onlookers glanced at Tristan, who smiled slow. "Some even say the Smoking Mirrors have hitched up with the Cats," a small Indian-featured Ghost Rider woman said.

That brought an excited apprehensive squall of comments from the onlookers. The Smoking Mirrors were the most feared necromancers on the Plains. They rode with *no one*. No one much wanted to ride with them.

If they had joined the Cathead Nation, the rumors of black magic had to be true.

Tristan felt a hot flush on the back of his neck. Nobody was giving him the fish eye this time. It might have been otherwise if people had recalled he was half Smoking Mirror himself.

"I hope we're not the last ones in," commented the first

Ghost Rider. "Talk is, the Cathead Nation mounts three thousand scooters, with at least a thousand yellow-robe cage-troopies and more rolling in each day."

"Mother Sky!" someone exclaimed. "Where'd they get that many?"

"You credit that number?" Tristan asked him quietly.

The rangy Ghost Rider nodded. He had been scrutinizing Tristan carefully as he drank. Tristan let him look. He didn't look to be sizing him for a sucker punch, and if he was, it was his funeral.

"I do."

"Where do they get that many?" an Iron Viking demanded. "At Ron D. Voo they told us they had fifteen hunnerd, two thousand max."

"Been recruitin' City scum from east of the Missus Hip," the Ghost Rider said. "Probably drawing down a thunderin' herd of independents too. Everybody loves a winner, and the Cats ain't been rolling many boxcars lately."

The crowd buzzed with outrage—and anxiety. The army had grown to somewhere upward of twenty-five hundred since leaving Rendezvous, even counting losses to death, desertion, and breakdown. They had counted on a comfortable edge over the formidable Cathead Nation. Now they were told the Cats outnumbered them—not even including the yellowrobes, who nobody reckoned of much account.

"You know how far off the Cats are?" Tristan asked his new friend quietly.

The man nodded. "Not more'n two days' ride north. I'd sleep with that pigsticker on one side of me and that broom handle t'other, if I was you. We whacked two Cat scouting parties on our way in. No way they don't know just where you are, and Cats bein' Cats, they may decide to open the festivities themselves."

"You speak true," Tristan said. "I'll heed your words."

He nodded to the wineskin the Ghost Rider was holding. "Enjoy," he said, and started off.

"Bide a moment, cousin," the Ghost Rider said. Tristan turned. "You're the one they call Tristan, ain't you? Last of the Hardriders?"

Tristan nodded. "I am that. Though I call myself Burning-skull now."

A smile spread across the Ghost Rider's grimy bearded face. "The whole Plains knows about your Sign by now, bro. We mind the Prophecy too. With you on our side, the Catheads don't have a chance."

Tristan smiled back. It was a tight kind of smile. "Thanks for the vote of confidence," he said, and left.

The Outlaw staggered out the farmhouse door, dropped to his knees, and puked volcanically. Zonker appeared behind him, his long pale face green beneath his beard and droopy mustache.

"Prez," he said, in a clotted voice that suggested he was having trouble keeping his breakfast from going on vacation. "Tristan. You better catch a look at this."

Despite—actually because of—the Catheads' reported proximity, Jovanne and Tristan had taken a mixed "foraging" party of twenty Jokers and Outlaws on a sweep northward ahead of the army after it began to move again in early afternoon. Though the Jokers knew better than most how risky scouting the Cats was, none of them was too eager to have the Catheads pop a surprise visit on them either.

Jovanne looked at Tristan, dropped the kickstand, and swung off her scrambler. Tristan drew his Bolo, dropped the short magazine, and clicked a thirty-rounder into the well. He set the selector for full-auto. The pistol wasn't real accurate that way, but it was nice for busting up close-range ambushes. Jovanne hauled her pet pump/semi-auto twelve-gauge Tallahassee Arsenal Renegade with fold-over stock and eight-round magazine out of its scabbard. It was even better for those intimate moments.

The first thing they noticed when they stepped inside the kitchen was the smell—not unexpected, but never exactly welcome. The kitchen itself was well lit, as could be expected, given the low rain-spitting sky. It had probably been spotless before what seemed like several gallons of blood got sloshed around.

The occupants had been your better class of Diggers, beings much higher on the nomad evolutionary scale than the wretched sodbusters farther west. The High Free Folk could never greatly admire those who accepted life between walls, but at least these settlers didn't burrow beneath the earth like moles.

Still, it took more than a little spilled Digger blood to turn an outlaw stomach. Jovanne and Tristan looked carefully around the room, then back at each other. Jovanne shrugged. *Nothing I can see.*

Zonker came back in behind them. "On the stove," he said.

Tristan and Jovanne both swiveled their weapons that way. Immediately Tristan felt like an idiot for acting as if the appliance was about to attack him. A large iron pot sat on one methane burner, half-filled with water.

"In there," Zonker said.

Tristan peered inside. There was a human brain floating in the water. About half-cooked, by the looks of it.

"Whoops," Jovanne said, and abruptly left.

Tristan looked at Zonker. "There's magic symbols in blood all over the living room," Zonker said, "and a naked dead teenage chick spread out on the floor. I think that's hers." He nodded toward the pot.

"Shit," Tristan said. "Get Pud in here."

After Pud finished tossing his cookies, Zonker said, "You know the Cats. What kind of magic were they working here?"

"I don't know," the little biker said, shaking his head compulsively. "I swear to Brother Wind and Mother Earth, we never did nothin' like this. I never *saw* nothing like this."

"The Smoking Mirrors?" Emilio suggested.

"Those aren't their signs in the living room," Tristan said by reflex, then regretted it. Nobody really liked to be thought of as knowing too much about the Mirrors.

"Then who the fuck did this?" Zonker demanded.

Jovanne and Tristan looked at each other. As one, they shrugged.

17

Black clouds danced like witches round the moon. The Council Fire roared to twice the height of a man. Those of the High Free Folk not required to stand watch were gathered around the fire, leaving a wide space clear. They were unusually subdued to-night.

John Hammerhand stood alone with his back to the fire and his big arms folded across his chest. A passage opened in the crowd, and three figures dressed in yellow robes walked down it, drawing a wake of mutters.

As they approached, the nomad leader held up his famous hand. "You have come to us beneath a flag of truce," he said in his rolling sonorous voice. "What's your business with us?"

"Surrender," said the apparent leader of the three. He wore the obligatory yellow robe, and wire-rimmed glasses perched on the front of an egg-bald head a size or two too large for his wizened little body.

Hammerhand nodded, as if it was what he'd expected all along. "I must consult the High Free Folk," he said, "but I'm minded to accept your offer. It's the Cathead Nation we have blood to settle with, not you."

Some of the Folk laughed. Others stood expectantly. The tall, dark man who stood behind the Fusion spokesman's right shoulder sneered. The woman—almost equally tall, with her head shaved like the others'—to his left gave him a look of black almond-shaped eyes. His face went blank.

"The bald bitch there," murmured Jovanne, standing near the front with Tristan, the Jokers, and the Outlaws. "Is it my imagination, or have we seen her somewhere before?"

Tristan had already been staring at the Fusion woman. It wasn't hard to do; the loose saffron robe did not conceal an aggressive jut of breasts and curve of rump, and the sculptured perfection of her face was such you didn't really mind the lack of hair. She was a totally memorable woman, and his memory was telling him he *had* seen her—riding with Drago's Cathead band, down before the Front Range.

"It is not our surrender we have come to discuss, friend Hammerhand," the big-headed spokesman said. "We have made ours. It's your surrender I am calling for."

Hammerhand shook his head. "I don't think so. We've come too far to toss in our hand now."

"But that is foolish ego talking," the yellowrobe said urgently. "That is what you must surrender. Your sense of uniqueness—of separation. *Individuality:* It warps you, sickens you."

He turned, raising hands at the ends of stick-skinny arms to the onlookers.

"We are all One: you, we, the Cathead Nation, the Earth. There are no barriers between us, only veils of illusion. You call yourselves the High Free Folk, but you are enslaved. You believe you live in harmony on the breast of your Mother Earth, but your ways are the legacy of the EarthRapers whom the Star was sent from Heaven to punish. You are held in bondage by your shiny machines—and by your selves.

"Hear me, O people of the Plains: King Billy is not your foe. The Cathead Nation is not your foe. We are not your foe. You have met the enemy—and he is you!"

"Bullshit!" somebody yelled. The crowd began to shift and rumble like pebbles shaken in a pan.

"It is not us you fight against. It is your selves, your fears, your drives. Abandon them! Give in to the peace. Give in to the love. Join with the future—join with the Fusion."

"I think the Fusion has kind of a different definition of peace and love from the rest of us," Jovanne said dryly.

Tristan grimaced. The scene at the farmhouse that afternoon had shaken even him.

The High Free Folk were not having any of it. They pressed

forward, growling. The Fusion emissaries stood with their backs to the fire, showing no fear.

When the crowd had halved the open space around the Council Fire, Hammerhand stepped forward and raised his arms again. "These folk came among us under a white flag of truce," he reminded them. "Only somebody as low-down as a Citizen would dishonor that."

Now that wasn't strictly true. Like most cultures that make a big deal of their honor the Stormriders had standards that were pretty resilient at need. Treachery was a longstanding StormLand tradition. But the force of John Hammerhand's personality stopped the mob like a wall.

"You will not taste my words, though they are sweet as honey, if only you will imbibe them," the spokesman said. "I am a stranger to you, and my appearance seems strange. Hear, now, one you *will* listen to—whom you've heard and heeded before."

A flash of light and a boom, from far back at the rear of the crowd. Heads turned.

A woman stood on top of a van. A puff of white dense smoke from a pyrotechnic device rolled skyward at her back. Her hair was long and wild, black shot through with silver. It flowed down around the shoulders of her simple white gown. She was not a young woman, nor was she slim, but her own personal force beat from her like heat waves from a lava pit, so that Tristan could feel it from a hundred yards away. She held a tall staff, crowned with a blue light brilliant as a star.

"Yolanna!" The name popped from the crowd like a volley of gunfire. "Yolanna Brightstar!"

She was commonly known as the Maximum Mama of the StarLodge. Initiates didn't think that was very dignified, but then initiates would never reveal her true title. Whatever she was called, she was far and away the most influential woman on the Plains.

"Hear me, my children!" she declaimed. Her voice rolled from concealed speakers. "Hear me, O Children of the Fallen Star. I bring you news of great joy!"

"So get it over with," muttered Jeremy, "and skip the mumbo jumbo."

"I have spoken with these devotees of the Fusion," Brightstar said, "up to the Obliterated himself, and I have come to tell you:

Theirs is a new Truth, one destined to sweep the Plains like a wild and cleansing storm. A Truth more potent than anything released by Mother Sky and Mother Earth since the Star fell.

"Sisters and brothers, listen to the words of the Most Effaced! Give up your struggles, your striving, your selfish desires to do and to be! It is time to surrender. To become one again with Earth and Sky and Running Water.

"The stars have shown us the way: We must join the Fusion!"

"Bullshit."

In the great bowl of silence the night had become, Jovanne's word seemed to roll around and around like a ball bearing in a steel bowl. The Jokers' Prez was abruptly standing in the midst of a cleared space, as if she'd gotten too hot to be near. Even Tristan felt a pulse of the urge to step away. Instead he moved close. But not too close. He didn't want to upstage her.

Yolanna Brightstar looked down from her van, her placid handsome face creasing with an expression more like concern than outrage or surprise. "I don't belong to your Lodge," Jovanne said, her head high, her voice clear, but a V between her eyebrows betraying that she couldn't believe she was actually doing this. "But I've always honored StarLodge, always given respect to your initiates. I've always thought you stood for wisdom and power.

"Now, I don't pretend to be wise, and I sure as shi—I'm not real powerful either. But I've seen what the Catheads are like, and what they do. And I've seen what these yellowrobes really stand for.

"To these Fusion buckos, people—us—we're no more than bugs. I don't know what they want with us, but it sure isn't anything good. They don't stand for love, or peace, or anything like that. They stand for destruction and pain."

Yolanna Brightstar shook her splendid head. "Daughter, daughter," she said sorrowfully. "Don't you see? As individuals we're not important—we don't truly exist. Our selfhood is only illusion. What the Fusion offers us is the only true reality."

"Cooking people's brains in a pot is reality?" Jovanne said. "If that's the way it is, then give me a good fucking fantasy any day! I say, fight!"

"Wait!" Hammerhand had to put everything he had into the word to draw attention from the two women. "Those are brave words, sister, and I thank you for them. But Mother Brightstar's

words have shown us one thing that's true, at least: We let ourselves be led into chasing skirts too damned long. It's time men
took back the doing of men's work.

"To my people, I say: Brothers, you can no longer let your
women ride to battle beside you, much less follow them into
battle. Sisters: return to your role as house mouse. We'll all rest
easier."

Many men were cheering, led by the ManLodge and its
Death Commando elite. Women were shouting back. Jovanne
spun and marched away toward the Joker encampment.

Hammerhand was on a roll. "To Mother Brightstar I say:
Your wisdom is women's wisdom. We're men. We fight.

"And to you . . ." He turned to face the Fusion ambassadors.
"I say the only peace between us and the Cats can only be when
we or they are every one dead!"

The shaven-headed woman smiled. "You called it," she said.

With the little egg-headed spokesman in the lead the three
walked away from the Council Fire, down an alley that opened
miraculously through the throng. The crowd's menacing shouts
and gestures did not dent their smug serenity.

Tristan didn't hang around to see whether or not the High
Free Folk decided to blow off honor and tear the Fusion emissaries to bits. He was elbowing his own way through the crowd in
pursuit of Jovanne.

He caught up with her walking between the dark untenanted
tents of the Joker/Outlaw camp. "Wait," he called. She kept
walking.

He ran after her, caught her by the arm. A tear fell like a drop
of hot rain on his hand as he whirled. "What the fuck do you
want with me?" she shouted. "I'm just a house mouse!"

"I wasn't the one who said that," he said in a dead-level
voice.

She pulled away, walked a few steps, and stood with her arms
crossed tightly beneath her breasts, as if to try to control the
heaving of her chest.

"You got it," she said, head down, not looking at him. "What
you wanted. The Jokers. Handed to you on a fucking platter by
that paste-eating fuckard Hammerhead!"

"I don't want them," Tristan said. "I won't take them."

"Oh, *yeah*!" she flared at him. "Right. You've been aiming for this all along."

Tristan laughed. "The Death Commandos think I made the rivers rise and the volcanos spit up. Now you reckon I arranged for Yolanna Dipstick to sell out to the Fusion and made John Hammerhand punt his brain and piss off every lady samurai who was fixing to ride to battle tomorrow with iron in her hand as well as between her legs." He shook his head. "I wish I could give myself half the gods-damned credit."

"Hey, bro, you heard the man. I can't fight, and Brother Wind knows I can't lead. Maybe I'll try to learn to fucking knit."

"If you don't lead the Jokers tomorrow," Tristan said quietly, "they won't ride at all."

"If you think they won't follow you, you're dumber than you look."

"Maybe they would, and maybe they wouldn't. But you're the Prez of the clan. If you don't lead, *I* won't ride."

"Bullshit."

"Is that your word for the evening?"

The moon had fought free of clouds and spilled a serumy yellow light down among the night-blackened tents. She raised tear-glittering eyes to his. "I don't believe it."

"Believe it."

"The Catheads are your traditional enemy."

"Reckon the tradition can keep on keepin' on. It's . . . traditional."

"But what about the Prophecy? What about your plans to unite the clans?"

"If the Prophecy's true, it'll still be true whether I ride tomorrow or not. If it isn't, I'm fucked anyway. As to my plans . . ."

He shrugged. "My heart is bad about tomorrow. Not riding might be the best thing that ever happened to me."

"You wouldn't sit out a fight."

"When my notion of what's right's at stake, I sure as Hell has four walls would."

She came to him, touched him on the chest. "You really mean it," she said wonderingly. "You'd stand up for me."

He said nothing.

She raised her head at him, looking into his eyes as if trying to see through to the back of his skull. "You don't want the Jokers, do you?"

He shook his head. "Not to be President of. I want the Jokers to follow you. And you to follow me."

She slid her arms around him, laid her head on his chest. "You got it, mister. Wherever the Road leads, we'll follow."

He stroked the short burnt-orange at the back of her head, and hoped it led somewhere other than straight into Hell.

18

"So," Zonker said, lying back against his sissy bar with one boot propped on his cruiser's tank, "are we going to sit here and wait for the Catheads all day, or go riding off into the storm to look for 'em?"

The clouds were mobile slate-gray curtains of rain squalls that masked and revealed the rolling land where King Billy and his allies awaited. Where the Stormrider army was drawn up in three long lines, it wasn't raining yet, though the air held a chill edge of moisture. Thunder growled sporadically, like a dyspeptic giant's stomach.

Thin Lizzy laughed and snapped her Leech & Rigdon .44 carbine forward and down. Her right hand was thrust through the guard of the lever, so that the weapon cocked itself and snapped back into her grasp.

"Hammerhand'll never be able to resist a straight-up charge," she sneered. "He's got balls bigger than his brain, that one. Oh, pardon me—I'm just a little house mouse. I oughta be waitin' back home for my man with my yap shut and my legs wide, oughtn't I?" She squinched her lips together in a ridiculous pout and batted her eyes.

The Jokers roared. Sly and Loco, white-blond Pony, Dip and Weevil, Tooth and Pud with their nervous titters, Handsome with a small smile that wouldn't disturb the perfection of his namesake face. Even Red Dog cracked a smile within the circle of his well-kept beard. They forked their cruisers and bristled with weapons. They were ready for war.

The clan hung loose and easy today. Everybody in the whole army seemed to, except for Tristan and his sense of foreboding. Even last night's dramatic firelight scene with the head of the StarLodge condemning the army as EarthRapers hadn't pulled down their spirits. Just the opposite; it was as if that was the crowning touch, as if at just that moment they had suffered as much bullshit as High Free Folk could possibly take.

Today held the joyous prospect of a righteous ass-kicking, the kind that made all the world new again, no matter which way it went. That their asses might be the recipients of that kicking didn't faze the Stormriders in the slightest. They were past that kind of calculation.

To the right Tristan could see John Hammerhand on his bike Influencer, surrounded by his Death Commandos. His clan, the Wanderers, flanked him at a greater distance, glum and disgruntled about having its President co-opted by the ManLodge. The clan and the self-styled Commandos would spearhead the assault.

The Outlaws and Jokers had been placed nearby on Hammerhand's left. Tristan cut his eyes farther back to his right to see Jovanne leaning defiantly between the buckhorn bars of her own ride. She grinned at him, and gave him a thumbs-up from a fingerless gauntlet. *Jesus, she's enjoying this more than anybody.*

He could read her reasoning, right enough. She had lived for the Jokers, and now she knew she wouldn't lose them. If she died, she'd die secure at the head of her clan.

Tristan stuck his thumb under the strap that held his fine new sword in its scabbard across his back, shifting the buckle where it chafed his chest. The hilt rode above his right shoulder, poised for a quick grab. His broom-handle Lakota Bolo rested beneath his left arm in its break-open holster. The buckskin scabbard of his Mk. V Saskatoon Scout carbine was strapped to the frame of the late John Badheart's flame-painted cruiser. His bear and other possibles rested in the panniers slung over the rear fender. He was ready to ride to war and not look back, as befitted a warrior of the Plains.

Part of Tristan's mind still hooted him for buying a thing as outmoded and silly as a sword. But that was the civilized part of him, conditioned by nearly two decades of City life removed from Plains reality. The City's television and newspapers and popular fiction—if there was really a distinction—portrayed the High Free Folk as hairy barbarians armed with archaic, ultimately futile weapons. But when those shaggy barbarians—that part Tristan didn't have any trouble with—broke through the firing line due to surprise, numbers, or command incompetence, the haughty City soldiers didn't find their swords, axes, maces, nunchakus, and spears so goddamned funny anymore. Face-up, a soldier with an empty carbine, even with a dagger stuck on one end of it, was as poor a match for an adrenaline-cranked nomad with a broadsword—or even a big club—as a nomad motorcycle charge was for interlocking fields of full-auto fire.

Though as a general rule Stormrider clans carried reloading gear—and frequently slaves to do the boring, repetitious work—that was mainly useful in replenishing ammunition expended in hunting. The brute uncompromising reality of StormLands life was that manufactured goods of all sorts were at a premium. And a battle consumed ammunition at an all but unimaginable rate. Even when, as among most clans, fully automatic weapons were scarce.

No mistake, guns ruled the Plains battlefield—until they ran dry. Then the fight was decided by muscle and iron, skill and grit, and just plain savagery.

A pair of men in orange Dog Soldier armbands rode along the line from the left, their eyes sunken, their faces haggard behind their beards. They were assigned to duty as couriers and traffic cops this day. Trying to keep order in this rowdy biker army was a task to age a man in his prime, but Tristan reflected they probably didn't have much time to brood about the Cats.

Zonker waved an arm at them. "Yo! How's it going, bros?"

They paused a moment to accept a squirt of water from a skin an Outlaw tossed them. "Could be better," said one, whose brow crowded down on the bridge of a mashed-flat nose until he almost resembled a kobold of the Quaking Lands east of the Big River. "We had three clans split on us so far this mornin'."

"Trolls, Cycle Savages, and them pusswad Slave Drivers," his partner said, and spat.

"Drivers was all het up about their stock," the first Dog Soldier said, "and I don't mean their wheels either. Well, thanks for the throat-wettin', gotta putt now." They roared off toward Hammerhand in the center of the line.

"Chickenshit," rumbled huge Stiff, who had strung a dozen scalps down his high apehanger handlebars. "Boogeying out on their bros before a fight. We oughta, like, *look 'em up* after this rumble's done."

"A bad sign, when brother deserts brother in the face of danger," Little Teal said.

With a grumble of engine noise a cruiser with long extended forks nosed into line next to Tristan. He glanced left. The word *Vengeance* was painted on the many layers of hand-rubbed black enamel on the bike's tank in gold-outlined Gothic letters.

Tristan looked up. Calm dark eyes met his from within the eyeholes of a black metal mask.

"Somebody's going to catch on who you really are," Tristan said softly. "We have Jeremy riding with us all this way, and then he drops out of sight and zango! The Black Avenger appears."

Thin shoulders shrugged. The cord-wrapped hilt of a katana protruded from behind each of them. They were his only armaments; the Black Avenger never carried guns.

"No gig lasts forever," the Black Avenger said. "Maybe it's time I retired the Avenger. Or even time I retired Jeremy. Besides"—an ironic chuckle—"odds're good the Catheads will retire us both."

"You're an optimist."

"We have a commander whose idea of tactics is to line us all up, turn our engines over high, and light out straight for the enemy. We're up against a foe that managed to beat a main-force City army with a posse of scooter trash. You'd have to be as big a half-wit as Hammerhead to be real *optimistic* about this."

"You could sit this out. Nobody knew the Black Avenger was here."

Another shrug. "It's a good day to die."

As if to confirm that, a veil of rain swept aside and the Cathead Nation appeared, strung out in a horizon-spanning line a thousand yards away. Cheering flew up from the nomad army; the High Free Folk appreciated a good entrance. It turned quickly to derisive hooting. These weren't supermen, or supernatural beings. These were just men on big irons. The assembled Stormriders were no less, and they were in their element.

They didn't just live their lives in the saddle; they lived for the saddle as well.

Shots were fired defiantly in the air. The outbreak was quickly stilled as presidents and sergeants at arms restored order. Weight shifted and magazines were checked as the army prepared itself for battle.

The Cathead line was advancing at a slow roll. Behind them lumbered trucks with high staked sides, presumably holding the yellowrobe infantry. You could hear the Nation's engines now, like a voice from deep in the earth. Even when the Stormrider army wound its own engines, you could still feel the vibration of the Cat sleds, down in the bones of your shins. Tristan drew his Bolo, set the selector to full rock'n'roll, and made the long lanyard fast about his wrist.

Some of the gloss had come off Jovanne's manic mood. "What's wrong with those fools," she said, winding up her engine a few revs in preparation for takeoff. "Why don't they dig in and wait for us?"

"Probably a trick to lure us into charging," the Black Avenger said.

She glanced at him, and did a take as she realized whose features had to lie behind that famous mask. Nobody in the clan had even thought to associate the small, scruffy, quiet-spoken old pal of Tristan's with a notorious Scourge of the StormLands.

"They have to know Hammerhand's fool enough to charge them," she said.

At that moment trumpets blared a fanfare, and with a thunderclap of engines Hammerhand and his retinue peeled away from the line.

"They're scooter trash too, Prez, just like us," Zonker said, pulling down his goggles and unslinging his semi-automatic Gabaldon Mini carbine. "And everybody knows we're all plain crazy!"

And then the moment came. With a wild yell the Jokers and their new friends the Outlaws lunged forward to take their place in the arrowhead-shaped attacking line. Despite himself, Tristan felt his heart race and then soar with a crazy exhilaration that left no room for fear. The smell of thunder, wet grass, hot grease, and gun oil filled his head like hash smoke. It was as if the fumes flushed the years of City life from his veins, and left him once again a pure child of the Plains, pristine and ferocious.

The big cruisers were not meant for extended cross-country action. But the land here south of Rock Creek was firm and not too broken. Even bashing the landscape at a good fifty per, the irons would at least hold together until contact.

Shots began to pop from the rolling horde. "Wait for it!" Jovanne yelled to her own troops. "Wait, dammit!"

The Catheads came on without shouting or shooting, their sleds swathed in canvas, aluminum poles tipped with catamount skulls held high. The Cathead standards had long yellow streamers tied around them today, apparently to signify the Nation's oneness with the Fusion. Tristan longed to hoist aloft his cow-skull symbol and torch it into defiant flame, but for better or worse this day belonged to Hammerhand, and on a lesser scale, Jovanne. Burningskull would have to await another day to lead the High Free Folk to war with the Cathead Nation—if such a day ever came.

At four hundred yards the Cathead army stopped. Tristan felt his scrotum retract into his guts. An aimed volley, even at this extreme range, could empty hundreds of saddles.

But no, the Catheads were leaving their renowned cunning behind today. Tristan saw the figure of King Billy like a mountain draped in black, dwarfing his big stock full-fendered Carondelet machine, which had rolled off the lines in the days of Bill Landrum, the legendary Boss Wrench who made WildFyre with his own black hands. The Cathead King reached down by his knees, and whipped a thick arm skyward. The canvas shroud covering his bike fell away, as did a thousand other shrouds to left and right of him.

The Cathead bikes were painted black. Every solitary one, hard and shiny as beetle carapaces.

The charging line of Hammerhand's army seemed to falter. The scene would mean little to City eyes; plenty of the Stormrider army's rides were just as black as the Cathead sleds, after all. But city eyes were blind. The High Free Folk were a wild, individualistic race, who painted their machines in all the colors of their souls. The sight of all that uniformity chilled their bones like a cold blue norther.

"So what?" the Black Avenger shouted to the riders around him. "Shows they've got good taste in color, that's all!"

The Cathead line stood a moment, to let the visual impact

sink in to the feathers. Then King Billy seized the hilt of his greatsword Headsplitter, strapped across his broad back. He held the weapon with its needle point threatening the clouds for a beat, then snapped it down toward the Stormrider army.

The Catheads rumbled forward like an avalanche.

19

Far gone on testosterone, the Death Commandos of the ManLodge opened fire almost at once, way the hell out of effective firing-on-the-roll range. All along the Stormrider line nomads followed suit, spurting their precious ammo futilely into the wet breeze. The Jokers and Outlaws held their fire, though, and so did the Cats.

A hundred yards, fifty. Jovanne engaged her throttle lock and dropped her combination semi-auto/pump-action Renegade between her handlebars. "Fire!" she shouted. To the left Jesse echoed her command.

Gunfire crackled from the two clans, though Jovanne, like Tristan, held fire. A the same instant the onrushing Cathead line sprouted flames like brief yellow blossoms on a vine.

Surprisingly little happened. Tristan heard screams as bullets found homes in meat, but nobody in his peripheral vision went down. He knew in his marrow that there's nothing easier than missing your man in combat, when the shithammer's coming down and bullets are cracking past your head. Hitting a target bouncing across the landscape from the saddle of a machine on the same crazy ride was more a matter of luck than skill. Still, he felt icy wind whistle over his teeth as his lips spread in a reflex grin of fury and fear.

At the edge of his eye he saw Hammerhand, golden hair flying, crash into the line near King Billy. Then he had his own problems to worry about. Right in front of him a rider in Cathead black snarled at him from a toothless mouth set in the midst of a rat's nest brown beard, tossing away an empty storm carbine to wrench free a double-bitted battle-axe taped to his handlebars. His own throttle locked wide-open, Tristan raised the Bolo and gave him a short burst the eyeblink before he would have come within range of the descending axe. Red spurted from the man's chest, and he went over his rear mud-guard.

Jeremy laughed shrilly as he whipped his big machine deftly around the riderless bike. He held a sword poised overhead in a gauntleted left hand. A Cathead passed him almost knee to knee, aiming a gigantic .50-caliber Saskatoon hammer revolver at his head. The katana whistled down. The Cathead cruised by, staring in wide-mouthed disbelief at the spurting black-sleeved stump of his arm . . .

They were through. Jovanne whipped her head left and right, seeking her people. All the Jokers seemed to have made it, though there were gaps in the Outlaw line.

Like the Stormriders, the Cathead Nation had deployed in several long lines of riders for successive shocks—the classic Plains battle plan when nomad armies met in force. Following a routine drilled into his very cells years ago as a Striker, Tristan dropped his mostly expended magazine from the Bolo's well, let the slim-barreled pistol hang on its lanyard as he pulled a fresh box from the breast pocket of his linen shirt, clasped the new magazine with his teeth, recovered the weapon, drew the well over the open end of the magazine far enough for friction to hold it, rapped the magazine's butt on his denim-clad thigh to seat it with a click, and raised the M96 again in time to shatter the face of a blond Cat in the second line who was blazing away one-handed at him with a Water Horse storm carbine.

They had passed the first line readily enough, but the Stormriders had been disordered enough that they crashed full into the second Cat line in a swirling melee. An impact knocked Tristan's rear tire askew. The sled went into a sidewise skid. He fought it, barely pulling up his leading right leg in time to keep it from being chewed up by the spinning front tire of a Cathead bike that struck his broadside. The Cat rider went flying over Tristan's rear tire. The collision got Tristan's ride straightened out again. Somehow he rode it through without going over the high side.

It was a general dogfight now, bikes snarling in circles as riders spattered with mud, blood, and shredded bits of grass jockeyed for advantage. Tristan let his Bolo go momentarily again to reset his throttle at the halfway mark. Full revs would make the big iron impossible to maneuver, and like as not squirt him all by his lonesome out of the fight and into the teeth and tires of the Cat third line he knew was bearing down.

He got the Bolo back, ripped a burst at a Cat going by to his left in a black blur, and saw no effect. He put a boot down, and torqued the sled right to face another foe his peripheral vision had caught charging him. This Cathead seemed all hair and black leather, and he took all the rest of Tristan's magazine before going down in a spray of reddish earth.

Tristan let the Bolo hang free and drew his sword. Reality became a tachistoscopic image-flicker.

Zonker, laughing, raising his Mini to slam a new magazine home. Rocking slightly; water-blue eyes bulging as they stare at the solid stream of red pulsing from the hole in his throat . . .

A rider dressed not in black but in conventional bike nomad clothes, grease-blackened jeans, long-sleeved shirt, denim colored vest, halting his long-forked ride nose-to-tail with Tristan's sled to cut at his head with a bell-hilt cavalry saber that had to be ancient when the Star fell. Tristan's blade parrying the cut in a rising block, wrist turning for a rattlesnake strike at bearded face when the saber withdrew for another blow. No power, but a red seam opening in the face, the rider swaying in shock and pain, the saber coming around too slow to catch Tristan's backhand killing stroke . . .

Jesse and bike wobbling, then toppling in seeming slow motion, his handsome face obliterated by a shotgun blast . . .

Red Dog tumbling from the saddle of his low-slung Black Mountain sled, a bullet through his head. He murmurs, *"Sooz,"* rolls over, and is gone . . .

Gigantic Stiff rocking back as a Cathead almost as huge as he drives a spear into his capacious belly. He breaks the shaft with a hammer blow of his hand and then, the weapon still inside him seizes its wielder by the throat and strangles him . . .

Vengeance's front tire exploding into shreds from another shotgun blast. The bare rim dropping into a slight grassy depression, bringing the sled to a sudden halt. Jeremy—the Black Avenger—hurtling forward between the bars, tucked into a ball, rolling in flight, hitting the ground, rolling yet, rolling to his feet right by the booted foot of the rider, waiting with his sled turned broadside, who had shot out Vengeance's tire. Japanese sword upraised for a two-hand downward blow; a sawed-off side-by-side hanging with one barrel unfired from disbelief-weakened fingers; a look of total stupefied disbelief, still in place when the halves of the shotgunner's head fall neatly away to either side . . .

Tristan, hypnotized by his friend's bravura performance, finding himself abruptly flanked by Cathead allies converging from either side. A frantic lean back from a machete blow that drives a great dent in the sled's flame-emblazoned fuel tank. A grab at a sweat-sodden armpit, a heave of effort, a hairy stinking body falling across the tank in front of him. From the other side a chain, whirling for his face. Action without intention: a handful of graying matted hair, yanking the fallen rider, whose colors read *Skull Fuckers MC*, up and into harm's way. The blow intended for Burningskull wrapping around the Skull Fucker's head and Tristan's left hand, drawing blood from both, shockingly bright in the corpse-colored light. Tristan's sword transfixing the chain-wielder's throat, then ripping free . . .

Another rider from the left. The man sprawled across his gas tank, face a mask of blood, blindly entangling him in his arms. Tristan bashes him with the heavy pommel of his sword, but he can't get free. The charging Cathead slews his cruiser to a halt beside Tristan's, raises a wood-chopping axe two-handed, taking his time, enjoying his opponent's doomed struggles. . . .

His rib cage exploding outward in a black shower of blood and chunks of bone, drenching Tristan and his wrestling partner. As he topples, Tristan hurls the chain-whipped man from him. He lands on the fallen cruiser. Tristan runs him through as he tries to rise.

Beyond the fallen bike Tristan sees Jovanne. She gives him a grin, raises her heavy shotgun in salute. He grins back. . . .

With a moment to breathe, time resumed its normal flow. He looked around. As far as he could see the grassland was covered with men on foot and on motorcycles, surging and struggling between splayed bodies and downed bikes. He had a sense that waves of other machines had joined the fight since he'd gone into his violent fugue.

He and Jovanne were momentarily in the clear. But most of

the bikes and bodies still up and moving seemed to be done up in black.

To the northeast, the direction the charge had carried the Stormriders, a line of men dressed in yellow was approaching on foot. There were shouts and songs, music of pipes and thumping of drums, drifting through the clashing uproar of battle. Some of the Fusion groundpounders seemed to be dancing as they came. All of them looked armed.

Somehow they didn't look too damned funny.

Jovanne met his eyes and matched his thought: "It's time to blow this pop stand. Army's gone to shit."

He nodded. Not even his dashing nitwit hero daddy Wyatt had any compunction about riding away and living to fight another day; when his life ended it was because Black Jack Masefield's mobile troopers left him no escape. Though the Cathead riders seemed just as disorganized as their opponents, when that yellow line rolled in it would be like a swarm of locusts hitting a ripe cornfield.

Jovanne turned away, shouting, "Jokers! Yo! To me, to me!" As he got ready to roll Tristan saw something that froze his blood.

The Black Avenger stood fifty yards away, surrounded by a heap of Catheads, some writhing, most motionless. He held one sword in guard position before him, the other cocked over his head, point forward and down. A pack of Skull Fuckers circled him like dogs.

A tall rider in a gray slouch hat faced him. "We're gonna gouge your eye out," he bellowed, "and skull-fuck you to death!"

Tristan heard the Black Avenger's laughter echo from within his mask.

As the outlaw chieftain orated a rider darted at Jeremy from the rear, swinging a sword in a looping horizontal cut at his back. "Jeremy, look out!" Tristan screamed, dropping his sword to claw his Scout rifle from its beaded scabbard. There was no way he'd have it in time.

Jeremy's right hand snapped behind him, slapping his blade upright between his shoulder blades. The outlaw sword struck it and rang like a bell. The small man lashed out with his left-hand weapon without looking. The Skull Fucker's head popped from his shoulders, went rolling away to be lost in the grass. The torso rode majestically on a few more yards, geysering blood, before it went over.

The outlaws swarmed the Black Avenger. Tristan saw blades flash in the grim light, saw saddles empty. He headed the bike that way, holding his Scout one-handed.

The plunging machines cleared his field of vision. He saw the Black Avenger standing there again, magnificent and alone, his blades a killing blur.

Then the Skull Fucker chieftain struck him in the back of his head with a ball-headed mace. He dropped.

"Jeremy!" Tristan screamed. He slewed his bike to a skidding broadside halt, dropping the kickstand, letting go of the handlebars to raise his rifle.

The Skull Fucker in the hat had only seconds to savor his downing of a Plains legend before the back of his own skull blew out.

The Saskatoon Mark V was a bolt-action rifle. Black Jack Masefield had wanted his Strikers to be able to aim their fire at need, and that meant a bolt gun. The Scout was not up to sniper standards, but was excellently accurate despite its short barrel. It was also extraordinarily quick to operate; skilled hands could fire it almost as fast as a semi-auto.

Tristan's hands were skilled. He emptied four more saddles with single shots before the startled Skull Fuckers broke and ran.

He stuck the rifle back into the scabbard, raised the kickstand, and prepared to go to his fallen friend's aid. The blast of a big sled being revved hard beside him made him turn.

It was Thin Lizzy, looking ghastly from the blood of a forehead cut that all but obscured her pointed features. "I got your fancy toadsticker," she said, holding up Tristan's sword. She pointed with it.

He looked around. Half a hundred black-clad Catheads were bearing down on them.

"Forget it," she said. "Time to get the fuck outta Dodge!"

He tossed a quick regretful glance at where his friend lay. Jeremy was hidden by the bodies of his slain. "Jammer will sing of your final fight, my friend. Your song'll be sung around campfires as long as the Plains lie under stars."

He turned his machine and followed Lizzy away, bouncing

and soaring across the land, at right angles to the Fusion troopers' inexorable advance.

His panniers packed, Tristan stood astride his cruiser and stared into yellow flame.

The fire was a small and fitful thing. Dry fuel was at a premium out under the unquiet clouds, and fugitives could not spare the Mother's Milk to build the fire higher. It would have taken a blaze fit to burn the world to warm the spirits of the hurt and haggard riders huddled around it.

It was lucky they'd topped their tanks off before riding into battle, because otherwise they never would've gotten far enough away to risk even a mingy little fire like this. Someone had hauled out a shortwave and was listening to the chatter sporadically audible between bursts of interference, which was mostly reports of triumphant Cathead patrols riding down bands of stragglers like this one.

John Hammerhand still lived. He had managed to pull together some scattered, shattered fragments of his army and withdraw to the west. He'd left upwards of a thousand Stormriders cooling in the light episodic rain. It was the worst disaster the High Free Folk had ever known.

The Catheads were letting him go. For now. Their victory had cost them plenty too; the Stormriders hadn't gone down easy. They might have been pausing to lick their wounds.

Or they might just have been letting Hammerhand stagger away, letting the survivors torture themselves with hope, knowing they could catch them up and finish the job any damned time they chose. It would suit the Cathead notion of fun.

Beside the fire Thin Lizzy and Little Teal were fussing over Pony. By chance the escaping Jokers had come upon half a dozen Cats who had caught the slim blond woman and were preparing to rape her. They'd had her jeans skinned off her thin shanks, and had been holding her arms and legs outspread while one of their number unzipped and unlimbered, ready for fun.

What he'd gotten was his face torn off by the front wheel of Jovanne's sled, which she had ridden off the lip of the depression that had sheltered the raping-party from view. By the time Jovanne's bike had landed, four of the others were down writhing in their own guts.

The last one had made the mistake of pleading for his life..

Lizzy and the normally subdued Teal had played keep-away
with his nut-sac until he'd collapsed from loss of blood.
Jovanne had put him under with a shot behind the ear from the
slender .40-caliber Dance Brothers & Park that had once belonged to Colonel Masefield, and told them playtime was over
and the time had come for riding hard.

Still, while the Jokers had suffered losses—Red Dog,
Zonker, Dip—most of them had survived and pulled together.
Tristan, too tired and hollow and fixed upon what he had to do
to let himself mourn his old friend Ferret, found himself thinking, wrestling with what that meant.

The Stormrider army had shattered on impact. Though sav-
agely mauled, the Cathead army hadn't. On the other hand,
while plenty of clans, like the Jokers and Outlaws, had been
scattered to Brother Wind by the battle, Hammerhand was obviously having some success pulling the survivors together, and
keeping the Cats off him for the moment. Maybe that was the
strength of the Plains folk; they seemed anarchic and disorganized, and mostly were. They came apart quickly enough when
the hammer came down. But what they fragmented into were
small groups of bros, bound by blood and many hard miles
shared, who knew and loved and trusted and stood by each
other. In defeat, they did not turn into a huge terrified herd the
way City soldiers usually did. They just dissolved back into
their component clans. . . .

"Let me go with you."

The quiet, almost timid voice broke him out of his reverie
like an open-hand blow. He looked up to see Pud standing beside him, gazing at him with his slightly popped blue eyes.

In the face of everybody's expectations Pud hadn't turned either his tail or his coat when it came down crunch time with his
former Cathead saddlemates. Neither, as it happened, had his
pal Handsome; Tristan had passed him on the way out, lying on
his side with the back of his head dished out from behind his un-
scathed namesake face by the blow of a cat mace.

"No," Tristan said quietly.

Pud shook his head. He seemed almost desperate. "Please. I
can help you. I won't get in the way."

Tristan was shaking his head when a shot cracked, off in the
night. A shudder ran through the Outlaws and Jokers by the fire.

A moment, and then Jovanne appeared out of the dark,

Masefield's old Vindicator still in her hand. Pud gave Tristan a last beseeching look and faded.

Tristan met her gaze. "Stiff?"

She nodded. "He hung on as long as he could. But there was nothing anybody could do for him. So he asked me to show him the way out."

He saw moisture shine in her brown eyes. "He'll be partying hearty in Heroes' Holm tonight."

"You don't believe that."

"No. But it helps to soften the blow. Lying to yourself isn't always bad."

"What about you? You're really going?"

He nodded. "You don't need me—like I've been telling you all along."

She looked away. "Maybe what I need isn't always the same as what I want," she said huskily. "Can't we at least go with you?"

"No. It's time to follow the Road my grandfather tried to point me down. I have to ride it alone."

"You're going after WildFyre."

"Yes."

"Will it do any good?"

He shrugged.

The others had risen, and came round to touch his shoulder and murmur quiet words of farewell. It was almost eerily quiet, as nomad leave-takings went. The survivors didn't have much left inside.

When the words of parting were said the Jokers drew back. Their Prez stepped up and hugged Tristan around the neck so hard his vertebrae squeaked.

"I love you," she said fiercely in his ear.

He kissed her. "Thanks," he said, and rode away.

20

"So you're the last of the Hardriders."

"That's right."

"We've heard a lot about you."

Tristan chewed the inside of his cheek and said nothing. The excellence of the Osage intelligence-gathering system was almost legendary. In fact, Tristan suspected it *was* legendary, to an extent, since nobody was really as good as rumor made the Osage spies. But they were good. They had to be, with the Plains tribes hungering after their rich shipping, and Dallas sullenly determined to remove the main stumbling block to its northward expansion.

Randy Firecloud, Straw Boss and CEO of the Osage Manufactory, tipped his head to one side and regarded Tristan across the expanse of his hardwood desk. It was a long, narrow, high-forehead kind of head. It was shaved on both sides up to a long scalplock on the crown, which was dyed red. It hung almost to the shoulder strap of his blue overalls.

"You've come to steal WildFyre," the Osage said. It wasn't a question.

Tristan looked him in the eye and nodded.

Firecloud raised his chin till his scalplock hung down his back and began to laugh.

Three days on the road, dodging storms and far-ranging Cathead patrols, and Tristan was rolling through well-tended farm

143

country around the Osage capital of Broken Arrow. The houses were built defiantly aboveground, and solid. The farm folk and the drivers he met on the road eyed the scruffy, battered nomad on his distinctive outlaw cruiser with plenty of curiosity, but neither animosity nor fear.

You had your Diggers, pathetic creatures burrowing under Mother Earth's hide and groveling for survival. You had your usual farmers from the ag belts surrounding the Cities— overworked and downtrodden, deprived of the right to own fire- arms except for single-shot shotguns and .22 rifles to keep down the pests, lest they get ideas about resisting taxes or want- ing to charge more money for the food they produced. To the High Free Folk they seemed like natural prey.

The Osage yeoman farmers were anything but. They were proud, free, and well-armed. An Osage farmer thought of him- self as a warrior first and foremost. Reality had a way of repeat- edly proving them correct. The Osage militia was a major reason neither would-be imperialists from Dallas nor nomad raiders ever made much headway against them.

The Osage family unit was another. The womenfolk learned how to fight, just the way nomad women did, and the kids grew up with guns in their hands. And under attack, those squat blocky farmhouses turned into miniature fortresses.

When the locals eyeballed Tristan, they weren't seeing any threat they didn't think they could handle.

There were wire tangles on the outskirts of Broken Arrow, and cement hardpoints on either side of the road. There were young men with red paint on their hard brown faces to bar his way. There were no demands for papers; they just wanted to know his business. Just because it was open didn't mean Osagerie was lax.

"I want to talk to the Straw Boss at the Manufactory," he said.

"Firecloud? Randy Firecloud?"

"That's the one."

Maybe they really bought that as legit, that this scooter tramp off the prairie had actual honestgod business with one of the most powerful men in the Osage Nation. Or maybe they figured anybody that ballsy deserved to be rewarded. You never could tell. The Osage had a pretty damned arch sense of humor, some- times. They waved Tristan right on through.

The City felt spacious and clean. The streets weren't crowded, and the people who were on them were mostly tall copper-skinned folk, all of them dressed like day-laborers, but spotless. Like the countrymen they seemed mainly intrigued by the visitor from the Plains. Most everyone was armed, some with holstered handguns, most with large knives worn on the belt in scabbards sporting fine—and pricey—Crow beadwork.

He had thought about trying to sneak in. It didn't fly. Broken Arrow was an open society, but it was also close-knit. A visitor would go unremarked and unmolested, unless he made trouble. An intruder was liable to be spotted, and then he'd be in a world of hurt.

It was a paradox. Homeland was officially paranoid, and bent every effort to keeping its citizens under strict control. Yet criminals and spies passed in and out every day. Somebody had to see them, as a general thing. But almost nobody ever got around to mentioning the fact to the authorities.

Here in the Arrow government was so loose most outsiders didn't have a clue what it really was: There was a Council of Elders, who seemed mostly concerned with safeguarding the traditions of the People, and an informal standing committee that from Tristan's reading seemed like a cross between a Chamber of Commerce and an ancient-days Syndics' Guild. But when it came to danger, the whole Nation snapped together like fingers in a fist.

If Homeland had one-tenth the Osage cohesiveness, his dream of one-day conquest would be even remoter than it already was. Fortunately the ruling Purity Party confused *strength* with *control*.

Even if he felt optimistic about his chances of busting into Broken Arrow on the sly, there was the little matter of the Manufactory. It was a huge operation, producing machinery from firearms to heavy-hauler tractors. There were a number of plants dotted around Broken Arrow, most of them large—and all of them well-guarded.

He had no clue as to which facility WildFyre might be kept in, or where within it. If he could locate the machine, there was still the problem of getting in, finding her, and getting out again. Tristan had a high estimation of his own abilities, but he wasn't delusional. He wasn't Electric Bill, who legend said could walk through walls.

On the whole, he decided, *there's no harm in asking.*

• • •

"Stealing isn't necessarily what I had in mind," Tristan said when his host had settled down. "That's why I came to talk to you."

It was warm and close in the office despite the open window. No wind stirred the overcast afternoon outside. Except for the splendid desk, the room might just as easily have been a dispatcher's office for a trucking line. The Osage were so big on informality they virtually made a ritual of it.

"Do you have enough money to buy her back?" the Osage said. He had a glitter in his obsidian-black eye. He might not be as young as Tristan first thought he was, closer to his forties than his mid-twenties. Again, you could never tell.

Tristan rubbed his jaw. "Figures we might negotiate. I, uh—I need the bike. Might just be in your interest to let me have it."

"You think the Catheads threaten us? Broken Arrow isn't Plattesburg. And the *Wazhazhe* aren't led by John Hammerhand."

"It's not just the Cats. They have allies."

Firecloud's wide thin-lipped mouth smiled. "Supernatural allies?"

"I can't really speak to that. They sure didn't need magic to beat us at Rock Creek. But the Fusion's got numbers, and they seem to have a plan. What else they might have . . ." He shrugged.

"You don't believe their plan is to have us all joined together in one big universal love?"

Tristan smelled again the stench of spilled blood and cooked brains. "They have some weird notions about love," he said, paraphrasing Jovanne.

"We have some of their missionaries here in Broken Arrow. They talk a good line. Not many of the People listen."

He turned sideways in his swivel chair. He was a rangy man, with big hands. His manner left no doubt he was in charge, even if he did dress like a hick farmer.

"What the Fusion says doesn't seem to fit what they do," Firecloud said. "If all they want is to spread peace, what do they need with an army of the most vicious bastards on the Plains?"

He leaned forward and laid interlinked hands on the green blotter on his desktop. "The Manufactory has been very proud of WildFyre since your grandfather gave her to my grandfather.

It was a great honor he did us. But we see the Catheads as a threat to our Nation. We could stand to make a sacrifice to counter that threat."

Tristan sat up a little straighter.

"But there's a problem."

"Uh, what's that?"

"We no longer *have* WildFyre. The kobolds stole her back five years ago."

Tristan blinked. "I, uh, I beg your pardon?"

Firecloud laughed again. "It's true. We don't have her anymore."

"Why didn't I hear about this?"

"To be honest, we were stone embarrassed by it. Didn't make us look real swift."

"The kobolds?"

"Anse the One-Eyed stole it from them. Guess they felt entitled to steal it back."

That made Tristan feel just great. There he was, Outlaw One, Tristan Burningskull, last of the Hardriders, afraid to risk Osage security to steal back his birthright. And the kobolds had just waltzed in and snagged her back. That really burned his ass.

But that was nothing to what the future had in store. Because if the kobolds had WildFyre, he was going to have to go and steal it from them all over again. And the kobolds lived across the Cherokee in the Shaking Lands, a place that made Hell seem like a high-rent district.

But it was sweet compared to the people who lived there.

21

The ferryboat was little more than a layer of planks slapped
onto some oil drums, with a desperate little one-lung two-stroke
engine to inch it across the Cherokee River, which daisy-
chained the great lake system that separated the peaceful Osage
realm from the Shaking Lands of the Ozark Plateau. It seemed
that every little wave that lapped against it threatened to pitch
Tristan and his sled right over the waist-high rail.

The Cherokee looked like a mile-wide mudflat. But mudflats
held *still*.

"Be a shitload cheaper to run a rope across and just haul the
boat over," said the ferryman. He was a starved-looking specimen of youth, with bad teeth and a beard that looked as if it had
been drawn on his inadequate chin and damp upper lip with a
felt-tip pen. The High Free Folk had it that these river-rats' parents were all related before they were married. They were, however, children of Laughing Girl, and guardians of one piece of
the Sacred Road, so they were immune to harm. Even if they
did have that cockroach way with nomad nerves—that trait
which makes a body want to squash them with savage righteous
joy even though they do no actual harm.

"Why don't you do that then?" asked Tristan, since it seemed
expected. Also, concentrating on the youth's natter meant not
concentrating on the heave of the water and the matching motion in his belly.

The boy squeezed a shrill laugh through his thin, crooked nose. "'Cause the tsunamis'd wash 'em away!"

Tristan cocked a brow at him. " 'Tsunamis'?"

The boy gave one of those infuriatingly superior *don't you know nothin'?* hoots. "Sure! Ever' time the ol' New Madrid fault uncorks one, we get a real mommyhumper wave up 'long the lakes. Anything fixet, it jest wash right away. Stuff what floats jest rides up and down. We maybe have to fetch it back down the bank a ways to float again, but it comes through good as gold."

He scratched beneath his chin and belched softly. "River teaches us a power o' lessons 'bout life. We river men've learned not to try to fight things. Thet way lies disaster. We jest ride 'em out, ride 'em out, and ever'thing come out fine."

He beamed at Tristan, full of his own profundity. Tristan wondered if every bucktooth hick you met had been a philosopher *before* the Star fell.

The raft gave a lurch. He clutched the splintery wood rail so hard he was sure he'd leave dents. Mother Earth never intended Stormriders to leave her broad bosom. Laughing Girl was great in the mountains, bright, happy, fresh, and pretty, ideal for drinking or skinny-dipping. Like most women, she was a lot better young and slim than old and wide.

At least Mother Sky was giving him a break today; overhead was almost clear, and after so long the blue almost hurt his eyes. He just hoped Mother Earth didn't decide to give him a ride. He glanced nervously south, expecting to see a wall of water rushing down upon them.

"You Plains boys're real sissies when it comes to open water, ain't ye?" the boy asked. The river-rats were well aware of their protected status. Also, most Stormriders had no clue as to how to steer a raft.

"Shit," the kid said. "Ol' River ain't nothin', once you know how to take her. But you, heading' off into the Shakin' Lands . . ." He shook his head. *"Brrr.* Now, *that's* spooky."

Thank you so much, Tristan thought.

"Yep. I tell you. Oncet you get over, 'tween here an' the Missus Hip, them lands was never meant for human folk, if you catch my drift. Allatime mountains bein' shaken down, new ones thrustin' up, never know when a big ol' crack'll open up beneath you and swaller ya right down. And the *things* there . . ."

He shook his head. "Monsters walk them lands. Gods' truth. Body never like to overnight over t' the east side, for fear of what might come creepin' round your window. I ferried some critters west, it'd make your blood flow cold to know was on the other side of the world. All wrapped up in black, they was, with eyes like live coals. Red eyes on 'em, and mounts to match."

He was watching Tristan with keen kingfisher eyes for a response. Tristan suspected he'd gotten that last grace note from *Lord of the Rings*. It was popular among the Skalds and singers, so even an illiterate barnacle like this kid was probably familiar with it.

A shiver ran mouselike down Tristan's spine, all the same.

"Course, the kobolds are bad enough," the boy said, a note of disappointment creeping into the whine of his voice. Evidently Tristan had successfully kept his face impassive. "Strange damn critters, they are. No two alike, and not many much like real men like you or me neither."

He tittered. Tristan gave him an eye.

"They hate us true men, and that's a fact. They stay down there in the bowels of th' earth, making their bombs and war-machines and black magics, and River Mother help your sorry ass should you fall into their claws. They'll strip the skin off you and make you dance before they let you die. And that's iff'n they *like* you."

I can't tell you how comforting this all is, Tristan thought, repressing the urge to throttle him.

"The Kobold King, old Jubal, there's a sly one. But what you really got to watch for are them kobold womenfolk. What they do to a man makes your nut sack suck right up into your belly. Worst of all's the twins. The King's Power-Liftin' Daughters. Tall as trees, wide as semis, mean as a catamount with mites of the asshole. Eat a man right up, if you know what I mean and I think you do."

"Ever get any of them as passengers? Kobolds, I mean, not the King's daughters."

The boy's head bobbed up and down above his prominent Adam's apple. It made him look like a cormorant trying to swallow a big fish. "Sure enough. Code o' the River says we got to ferry anyone as has the fare, or sore need, so we takes 'em as they comes. And none come stranger than them kobolds, I can tell you.

"Why, I mind the time a few years back—I was but a minnow then, learnint the trade from me pappy, River give his soul rest as swallowed him down one day. We carried half a dozen of the twisted little devils east. They had 'em a big old panel truck with 'em. Damn near swamped the boat. I tell you, they weren't so dad-gummed small, we'da had to take 'em in shifts. And you know what they told me was in that there truck?"

Tristan felt his heart descending rapidly toward his boots. "Let me guess."

"It was *WildFyre*," the boy whispered reverently, as though there were ears that could hear within a thousand yards either way. Then again, Tristan thought, casting another glance at the greasy brown slog, maybe the boy knew something he didn't.

"The bikest of the bikes," the river-rat said. "The last ride outta the Carondelet plant upriver 'fore the quakes shut her down, wrenched together by Bill Landrum's own black hands. Wouldn't scooter trash like you give a purty penny to get her back again, hunh?"

He suddenly scrunched his head down on his skinny neck and gave Tristan a knowing squint. It made him look like a turtle that had somehow slipped its shell. "Say, I bet I know why you're headed into them Shakin' Lands! You're gonna try an' steal WildFyre back from them old kobolds, you sly ol' catfish you!"

"Never crossed my mind," Tristan said through set jaws.

The boy slapped him on his back. "Whoo-*ee!* I reckoned you weren't crazy enough to head into the Shakin' Lands jest for a vacation. No, sir! You're *even crazier*! I knew it right off." He shook his head. "But shitfire, maybe you're just crazy enough to pull it off. And I kin say I ferried you acrost! They'll put me in the song right with you."

He bit the black-nailed tip of one finger. "Course, they did that, the kobolds might come a-lookin' for *me* . . ."

He broke off to point away downstream. "Whoa! Lookie there! Now, that's a *big* mama!"

At first Tristan thought it was one of those river farts, when gases trapped in the sediment suddenly let go. But the disturbance was no bubble. A shining sinuous arc appeared, several times the girth of a man, shining like a week-old corpse in the sun. It seemed to roll on and on, and finally the brown water swallowed it again, leaving a whitewater roil.

"What the fuck," Tristan breathed, "was *that*?"

"Only the reason ain't no river-runners know how to swim," the boy said reverently. "Whoo, *doggies*. Musta been a seventy-footer easy!"

He gazed up at Tristan with watery blue eyes. "Bare onc't a blue moon do them big mamas surface, and then usual by night. One thing, sure, mister—you're tetched by Destiny, better or worse. That 'ere was a Sign, sure enough as the Guest Star up in Mother Sky's skirt tails is. You're bound to make one helluva big splash." He shrugged. "Course, sign don't say whether or not you'll *surface* again . . ."

"That's nice, but *what the fuck was it*?" Sacrosanct or not, Tristan grabbed a handful of his well-holed T-shirt and lifted him on tiptoe.

"Easy, there, partner," the boy said nervously. Tristan let him go. He stepped back and dusted at himself. Tristan wiped his fingers on his pants.

"That was a river-cat, sure enough," the boy said. "Anybody'd know that."

"A *cat*?"

The boy laughed. "Cat*fish*. You Plains boys're sure bone-ignorant. Bottom feeders. Jest lie down in the silt, and eat, and grow. And grow. Still and all, though, ain't nothin' to what they got in the Missus Hip. Them babies're *big*."

He slapped the rail. "Make sure you don't go fallin' overboard, friend. That baby'd swallow you right up—and your fancy ride as well, was you astride her."

"Thanks for the warning," Tristan took a step backwards from the rail, deciding he didn't need the support after all. He had a good sense of balance.

"Yup," the boy said. "I know it sure now. You're a Hero. Like ol' Duke Shaftoe or Electric Bill."

"Or John Hammerhand," Tristan said glumly.

"Sure 'nough. Man's gotta be braver'n smart, to head into the Shakin' Lands without a noose around his neck and a shotgun to his jaw. Kobolds ain't even the worst thing in them mountains anymore!"

"Do tell."

"Word is now—" his voice dropped low again "—that

there's a *dragon*. Even that old Kobold King shits his drawers when the dragon roars."

"I'll just bet," Tristan said, not bothering to keep the skepticism from his voice.

"Hey, partner, I'm just tryin' to help. But, hey, you don't want me to, I know how to let a man sink or swim on his own."

"I thought you said you river-rats didn't know how to swim."

"You got that right." He retreated sullenly to the left side of the raft. Was that port, or starboard?

Tristan gazed off toward the eastern shore. Khaki bluffs rose from the olive-drab water, crowned with thick green trees. Safety seemed a watery continent away. If you could call the Shaking Lands *safe*.

"This hero business isn't what it was cut out to be," Tristan muttered under his breath.

"What say?"

"Nothing," Tristan said. "Nothing at all."

22

The country across the Cherokee was almost anticlimactic in its normality, at least in appearance. The land was fairly broken, but suitably flat areas were green with cultivation, and there were farmhouses dotted around, usually in folds of the land or behind screens of trees so planted as to seem natural—as cover, in other words, instead of as a windbreak as they generally were out on the Plains. The few people he saw were wary to the point of furtiveness, ducking quickly out of sight, no doubt to arm themselves. The horses didn't have six legs or anything, though he didn't get close enough to any to see if their eyes glowed red. And the farmhouses he did glimpse looked if anything more fortresslike than the ones in Osagerie across the Lakes.

But on the whole, it was a normal scene, if paranoid. Stood to reason, Tristan reckoned. The ferrymen would not stay in business for the sole purpose of transporting monsters and the odd kobold raiding party out to steal a legendary gimcrack.

As he was thinking that, though, a noise sounded, like three shots of the old-timey muzzle-loader cannon kept by the gazebo in Homeland's central square, which they fired off on festive occasions like the Mayor's birthday. The red clay road he was following twitched beneath the wheels of his bike like the flank of a mare trying to shake off a horsefly. However normal it looked, it was the Shaking Land for true, rocked by the internal turmoil of a New Madrid fault system hugely expanded by

154

the crust-busting impact of a chunk of the Star. Even without supernatural menace it was plenty dangerous.

He was inclined to blow off most of what the river-rat kid had told him—at least about the Shaking Lands. The river-cat stuff he kind of had to buy, since he wasn't such a knee-jerk skeptic that he disbelieved what his own eyes plainly saw, unless he was stoned. He didn't really think mountains were constantly being raised and shaken down in there, for example, unless it was on the very slow time scale of geologic activity. A lot of the Earth's surface features had been altered by the hammer blows of the Star as it calved on hitting Earth's atmosphere—at least so the theorists had written in old books Tristan had viewed in the Library, though by his time few Citizens had interest in such matters. He knew from Plains tales substantiated by his reading that volcanoes could rise up fairly quickly, in a matter of months sometimes. There were Caners farther east, in fact, around the confluence of the Ohio and the Missus Hip. But he had heard no stories of vulcanism in the Shaking Lands.

As for the weird and horrible creatures—he was inclined to reserve judgment, though the apparition of the monster catfish had shaken his City-imbued sense of the order of things between Father Sun and Mother Earth. On the other hand, he doubted he'd encounter vultures with human faces, or shaggy jack-o'-lantern-headed monsters nine feet tall. And as for dragons, he reckoned that was the silliest thing he'd ever heard in his life.

The farmland began to play out, and the land to contort itself into steep, thickly wooded ridges. Tristan stopped at a roadside trading post to top off his tank and fill his spare fuel containers. He wanted to ask the proprietor what hard dope he had on conditions within the Shaking Lands, but a look at the man's dead face and blank eyes convinced him he really didn't want to know what the man might have to say—provided he could even talk, since he uttered not a word throughout the transaction. Tristan found himself chattering along like a sparrow on a branch about the weather, which was clear and bright. Then he roared off on his cruiser, leaving the man standing, staring after him as if he never intended to move again.

As the road rose into the hills it began to fade. Somehow, the day did too. No more clouds appeared in the sky; the whole scene just got a tad darker, a bit more chill. *You're letting your imagination get the better of you here, big fella*, he told himself.

To guide him Tristan had the accounts of his grandfather's exploit, family tradition as well as Plains song and legend. Anse One-Eye had come into the Shaking Lands pretty much the same way *he* had. Story was he had ridden half a day into the Shaking Lands to a valley of dead trees. He'd turned southeast up that and ridden two more days, until he'd come in sight of a mountain that looked as if it had been split by the blow of an axe. He'd then dismounted and hiked to the vicinity of the mountain. Somehow—the stories grew pretty fuzzy here—he had found a little-used secret entrance to the kobolds' underground realm.

One problem was that Tristan reckoned songs and traditions alike to be highly embellished, after the manner of such things. Another was that even if the landmarks were authentic, they might not still be there, or recognizable, at any rate. They didn't call this the Shaking Land for nothing, as he could already testify.

Oh, well. Old Anse had to play it by ear. Reckon his grandson can do the same. I'm his chosen heir, after all, even if he wouldn't know me from Vicky Three.

The sun was getting uncomfortably close to the hills that had closed behind his back when he looked right up a steep-sided draw to see the trees standing all white-boled and straight, stripped of lesser limbs and leaves by some long-ago conflagration. It would do for a Vale of Dead Trees such as the songs spoke of.

He decided to camp on a ridge overlooking the burned-over forest—spending the night among the ghosts of trees was a little much even for him. He found a spot that gave him good visibility in all directions. At first he intended to make it a cold camp. His primary concern was the various two-legged monsters that might be roaming the hills. Even if you didn't buy the campfire tales you had to be on the watch for the kobolds, of course, and the hill people, fierce and distrustful of strangers. The Shaking Lands were also a refuge for outlaws too scabrous and vile for even the High Free Folk to shelter. He didn't want to risk attracting anybody's attention by building a fire. He unrolled his bedroll, and gnawed some jerky and ate some biscuits as he watched the sun set. He drank some water and lay down.

A few hours after sunset he came awake with Bolo in hand. *Something* was rustling in the underbrush, just down the ridge from his lie-up. He came up to a crouch, ready to fire.

The moon was rising east over the peaks. It was distended and green, three-quarters full. It made the dead trees seem to glow. •

As it came upon the sky he saw its light reflected in several pairs of yellow-green eyes.

He fired a shot into the air. The eyes vanished. He heard more rustling as whatever had been watching him beat cheeks.

Another thing his reading told him was that, before StarFall, either the wildlife was a damn sight more tractable or people were just so far removed from nature they thought all creatures were animated stuffed toys or noble beasts. In the world Tristan had been raised in, animals tended to be mean as hell, as if they figured Man had blown his chance on top of the heap and it was time to crowd him some. He busied himself gathering wood, stumbling and swearing in the blackness, and didn't go back to sleep until he had a blaze he was sure would burn for hours unattended.

He was shaken awake. For a moment he rolled back and forth, making whining protests, imagining himself in his adolescent's bed at the Tomlinsons' house, resisting being gotten up for another day of school.

Then he realized it wasn't his bed that was shaking, it was the *Earth*. He rolled onto his belly and hung on until the spasm passed.

He made slow progress that day. He saw no game, which was surprising. Life was usually plentiful in the post-StarFall world. But there had to be some, because he followed the trails through dark, twisted woods.

The clouds came in again, though it didn't rain. When the branches parted overhead he frequently saw birds kiting on the thermals over the valleys. They all seemed to be big, black bastards, and it was easy for him to see how, after a few days riding through the dismal forests, being stalked by night-beasts, and getting your brain rattled half out of your skull every hour on the hour, you could start thinking they had human faces.

They were the only birds he saw, their lonely haunted cries the only bird sounds he heard. The woods were oddly quiet, without the usual chatter of jays and the hard rapping of flickers probing for grubs. There weren't even the crowds of little guys, sparrows and chickadees and what have you, that usually swarmed everywhere there were trees.

There was something, though. Motion off to his side kept catching at the corners of his peripheral vision. Whether it was the wolves or feral dog pack that had watched him last night, or something else again, he could not tell.

It was getting on toward sunset, and the woods were growing chill as well as still, when he rounded a bend and had to set his bike broadside to the trail to keep it from slamming into a big log that lay across it.

Apparently this was not the way somebody planned things. Two somebodies, bone-white bodies wrapped in rags, popped up from behind the log, brandishing tree-limb clubs. He heard a ruckus in the limbs above, and looked up to see a third pale form dropping on him, arms outstretched.

He stiff-armed the being, who fell on its back across his rear fender with an ugly crack of bone. A fourth figure had stepped out onto the trail from behind a black oak and stood with club upraised.

It seemed shocked to find Tristan still on his ride and staring at him. The eyes that met Tristan's were red as fresh blood. By this time Tristan's Bolo was in his hand. He shot the thing between those red eyes.

The first two, after a moment's dithering, had begun to scramble over the log after their prey. The sound of the gunshot froze them halfway over. Tristan whirled, still in the saddle with a leg down to hold the bike upright, and shot one.

The other dropped immediately from view. A heartbeat later and it was up and running for all it was worth, crashing the underbrush, bouncing off trees, screaming in a horrible grating voice and shitting down its pallid legs. Tristan followed the thing in his sights for a ways, but couldn't get a clear shot. Regretfully he let it go; he somehow had the feeling he didn't want to be wasting ammunition on wild shots at fleeing foes.

The one who had pounced from the tree was writhing around in the road, making weeping sounds and bleeding profusely from the mouth. Its back was obviously broken, plus it was clearly all busted to shit inside. Its mouth was strange, a muzzle almost, and the teeth were pointed like arrowheads.

The teeth, anyway, he guessed were art, not nature, the product of loving labor with a file. As for the red eyes and almost animal features—he shrugged. There *were* strange damned things in these hills, no question, though these particular specimens seemed more pathetic than supernatural. He thought he had a clue as to where some of the "burning red eye" stories had come from.

He put the beast-man out of his misery with a thrust of his sword. When he went to pull the one slumped over the log away so he could clear his path he was startled to discover it was female, with shrunken dugs and gray nipples. Like the other, she exuded a disgusting sour smell.

With a lot of effort, not unaided by the adrenaline jangling in his veins like a fire alarm, he got the log dragged far enough to the side that he could clear it with the Diablo. Then he rode like hell. To the extent he thought about it at all, he reckoned reinforcements were a lot more likely threat than another trap. Mostly, he just had to get back up to the openness and comparative safety of the ridge line.

That night he slept in the crotch of an oak tree, strapped in place with his belt, with his panniers hung over a limb and his various weapons all within reach. Tonight was as lively with screeches, hoots, and wails as the last night had been quiet. It was all punctuated, of course, by periodic tremors.

During the more violent quakes Tristan clung white-knuckled to the tree. "It's an old sumbitch," he said aloud. "It's made it this far; it ain't likely to go over tonight." He could almost talk himself into it.

Though the adrenal rush of combat had passed, leaving him wasted and depressed, he could not get to sleep for hours, what with the noise, discomfort, and tremors. Finally, when the moon went down, the animal sounds eased off. His lids drooped.

A sound the like of which he had never heard in his life snapped them open again. It was part bellow, part roar, and part scream. It sounded like a cross between a lion and a locomotive airhorn, and it seemed to make the ridges shake.

"What the *fuck* was that?" he demanded of the night. It had been too damned loud for a hallucination.

He listened for a repetition. It didn't come again. He consoled himself with the thought that anything capable of making a god-awful noise like that stood no chance of sneaking up on him without being heard. On that encouraging note he slid into sleep.

The road into the Shaking Lands—to the extent there was anything you'd dignify with the sacred name of *road*—was far from easy. True to its name the land quaked incessantly. Tristan frequently had to detour around landslides, and three times had to do some fancy riding to avoid getting swept away by one. Twice while he was riding through woods the tremors dropped forest giants, trying for the brushcut crown of his head.

Johnny Badheart's cruiser was poorly suited for the work even as sleds went, what with its flashy long extension up front. But Tristan was more than just his father's son. He had also grown up under the tutelage of Quicksilver Messenger, who some said was the finest rider the Plains had ever produced, and was certainly the best off-road rider of his day. He also had his years of riding with the Strikers under his belt. Unlike the motorized nomads whom they emulated in so many ways, Homeland's elite scouts disdained the Road, regarding it as a crutch. By preference they bashed brush whenever they could, which of course gave them certain advantages over the outlaws, who tended to flow along the highways.

Tristan had the tools, and he needed them all.

Oftentimes his keen Plains senses, honed by his years of over-the-edge life in the Strikers, told him he was being watched. Sometimes he sensed something pacing him as he made his slow progress through the thick forests of black and white oak. He couldn't hear much, what with the constant bass grumble of his engine. But he caught occasional flickers of motion, just at vision's edge. And he had a *feeling*.

The Albino Mutant Cannibal Vampires, as he thought of them, stayed well clear of him, if indeed it was they who shadowed him. Tristan felt that it was not. He had no rational reason for the feeling, but he didn't need one. For all his City schooling, there were times when *sensation* was enough. He had learned this the hard way, when he was one of Masefield's merry men.

The kobolds, then. Almost certainly they were watching him, tracking his progress into their domain. He had no idea how to avoid their being aware of his presence, and suspected there was no way. That had been part of Anse's song too, how the kobolds had spied on him as he infiltrated their stronghold. They still hadn't stopped him, for what that was worth. Still, Tristan could not shake the sensation that they were toying with him, amusing themselves by watching his perilous journey.

Hell, the bastards are probably laying bets on what'll get me, the rockslides or the Cannibal Mutants. The only thing he could see to do about that was to turn tail and flee the Shaking Lands. That he would not do. He had no problems with tactical retreat, as a rule, but this was different. He had set his mind upon a quest, and to turn away would be to fail himself.

And there was the little matter of WildFyre, besides. He was not so broken to the City's halter that his pulse didn't quicken at the thought of forking the greatest bike ever made. And even if he couldn't entirely see how, his heart told him that, yes, that machine was key to the survival of the high free life of the Plains, and more than that besides.

To go back without WildFyre was to concede the fight to the Catheads—and worse, to the Fusion, and a dark day it was when a Hardrider came face-up to something he had to grant was worse than the Cats.

He rode on.

The peaks rose higher and sharper, darker and more threatening. He rode down a valley where it was already dark as late twilight, though it was no later than three in the afternoon. The grim mountains shut out the light of Father Sun.

Unless the songs were way off—in which case he was up Shit Creek—he should within a few hours be getting into sight of the Big Split Mountain, beneath which lay the Hall of the Mountain King. It was chill, and he was glad he'd paused to pull on a wolfskin vest. He followed a more or less clear path through brush that grew dense and prickly despite the long hours the valley lay in darkness, along a creek whose water seemed to have a blackish cast to it. That was probably his imagination; it smelled sweet enough. Nonetheless, he was glad the bottles in his panniers, replenished that morning from a healthier-looking stream, were still fairly full.

He became aware of a cloud, rushing into the sky above the ridge line ahead and to his left. He halted the bike, dropped his boots to the muddy banks, hands lightly holding throttle and clutch, keeping the engine revved and ready to bolt. He had seen no sign of volcanic activity since entering the Lands. But he knew the swift and lethal things that could come from Caners, and preferred to take no chances.

The cloud swept over the ridge, down into the valley. He sucked his nuts up, poised to bolt. Something held him. Something about the way it moved—

And then the cloud was upon him, around him. It was alive. Bats, thousands of them, fluttering around him in a gray, squeaking swarm. He let his sled rev down, and sat and watched, feeling eerie, until the horde passed on.

The sun was about to set on the second day since he left the valley of dead trees when he nursed his bike, whose engine was beginning to miss now and then, to the top of a ridge. He looked out across a deep and desolate valley, already so sunken in shadow it seemed to be flooded with ink.

Across it rose a craggy peak, higher and sharper than those around it. Or maybe two peaks, for the mountain seemed split just down from the top, as though by the blow of a giant axe.

23

He heard them long before he saw them: the growl of outlaw bikes, winding up a grueling grade. At first he thought it was after shocks of the most recent tremor that had set the black oak limbs to rattling overhead. But the vibration from the rocks underfoot tailed away quickly enough, and the sound persisted, assuming unmistakable outlines in Tristan's ears.

Quick as thought he was up, scooping up his little grizz from its place of honor by the fire, stuffing him into his panniers as he scattered the coals with his boot. Moving quickly but without rushing, he kicked earth over the embers. Then he pulled his Bolo from his holster, which he had taken off, and faded into the rocks above his campsite to wait. He had racked out on the ground tonight. He just couldn't face another night up a tree.

The bikes came closer, protesting the labor they were being put to. Kiowa sleds were beasts of the open Plains, and even more the open road, out of place as elephants up here in the mountains. Scramblers would've been better suited by far. Even they would have made a power of noise. That was one disadvantage that motorized nomads faced: To be stealthy, they had to forsake their beloved rides, and either shag it afoot or entrust their butts to the saddles of horses, something many of your haughtier Pure Engine People declined to do. If it wasn't powered by internal by-god combustion they disdained to fork it. That tended to circumscribe the tactics open to many of the clans.

That the riders—half a dozen or so, by subtle differences in engine tone, to which Tristan's ears had been attuned before he was weaned—were approaching openly on their bikes meant they were either unaware of Tristan's presence or stone confident. Tristan guessed the latter. It was a little too coincidental to believe a party of Folk had just wandered into these legend-haunted mountains the same time Tristan did; the last Stormrider to dare the Shaking Lands to Tristan's knowledge was Anse Hardrider his one-eyed self.

He heard the rustle of brush on steel flanks and thumbed the Lakota's selector to full-auto. In the wild mountain dark, with no moon showing and underbrush crowded round the rock outcroppings, hitting the target was more a matter of the gods' favor than skill. A quick bullet-spray might give him a better chance of planting a couple of rounds in meat at close range. It might also freak his opponents out, convince them to leave him alone or at least to keep their heads down.

A crackle of limbs breaking, right by the dead campfire. A gleam of light from somewhere skittering like a squirrel along a chromed front fork. A voice said, "Tristan?"

He sucked in his breath, held it. He knew that voice. The question was, would he answer by word or by increased pressure on the Bolo's trigger? Or maybe not at all.

What the fuck, over. The fact was he was curious.

"What the hell are you doing on my back trail, Pud?" he called, making sure he had hard rock between him and the intruders.

"I just couldn't stay behind, Tristan. You don't know how dangerous it is up here."

"And you do? Who are your pals there?"

"Bros from the Chosen Few. Their Prez made 'em swear an oath to follow you and aid you on your quest."

Tristan slipped off the safety, quietly as he could. "Bullshit."

"I tell you true. Word of your sign is spreading, man. People saw what a fuck-up Hammerhand made of things. They wanna follow your Star, man."

Tristan sighed. "Make some light and let me have a look at you," he called.

A click of a lighter. A torch made from a wad of dried Spanish moss wound around a tree limb flared to life.

There were four of them with Pud. Chosen Few, all right, to

judge by the silver chains hung around the shoulders of their leather jackets and the insteps of their boots.

"This is Ernie," Pud said, nodding at a tall, dark-bearded man with a pockmarked face.

"That's Aardvark." A round pale-looking dude nodded his bandanna'd head.

"Mad Dog." A flash of silver tooth from the middle of a mass of hair and scar tissue. Thick black-furred fingers drummed restlessly on the high apehanger bars of his machine.

"And that's Ozone," A skinny, clean-shaven character with a faraway look in his eyes grinned and bobbed his head.

Tristan let the standoff just breathe while he thought about things. If this little pack had ill intentions, they also possessed balls of milled brass. Pud knew Tristan packed a full-auto-capable piece in his long-stemmed Bolo broom handle; with the group packed together like this, a couple of good slashing bursts and a little smear of luck would put them all in the dirt if Tristan got edgy.

That was the smart thing to do, of course. Tristan's ass was controversial, to say the least. And treachery of the blackest stripe had gone down time and again over a prize far less sought after than WildFyre, the Holy Grail of bikes. The Chosen Few had no more low-down a rep than any other Motorcycle Clan, but they had no special reason to love Tristan, the Jokers, or the long-lost Hardrider club.

Still, everybody loves a winner. Tristan had a victory over the Cats and his own personal Guest Star in Taurus. Hammerhand had the worst battle catastrophe in the history of the High Free Folk. The Chosen Few's Prez might've decided Tristan was the man to save the Plains from the unholy Cathead-Fusion alliance.

Tristan had trouble with cold-blooded gundowns under most circumstances—the Catheads he'd executed after the Burning Skull fight didn't count; they had it coming. He'd feel especially bad about it if these boys really *had* sworn to help him on his quest. Of course, he always could just send them on their way. Maybe put a couple in the fallen leaves at their feet if they dawdled.

But Tristan had been riding solo for the better part of a year now. He had made his one-man war on Homeland until winter clamped its white jaws down, then spent the snow months in the tiny cabin he'd built himself, talking to nobody but his mule, Dr. Johnson. He had been back among other humans beings for a few scarce weeks.

And here he was, riding alone again. The fact was, he was starved for company. Especially after two nights spent alone with earthquakes, strange sounds, and glowing eyes.

He stood slowly, and leapt lightly down to the flat place where his fire had been. He bent to pick up some of the dry sticks he had gathered for his fire. He kept his Bolo in his hand. From the corner of his eye he sized the newcomers up, an old Plains reflex.

The hairless-looking dude in the bandanna seemed slow as he swung off his iron. The shaggy one was too twitchy—you could draw him with a feint easy. The smiling skinny one was a space cadet. He might surprise you if you didn't watch him, but it would probably take him a few key milliseconds to respond. . . .

The tall man with the acne scars and the beards, who seemed to be the leader, showed no obvious weaknesses. Best to take him down first then.

It wasn't as if Tristan really figured he could go four-on-one face-up and come out walking. But in a situation like this, you seldom had to take everybody down. If you put authoritative hurt on one or two, the others generally got their minds right in a hell of a hurry.

Tristan accepted the torch, set the rebuilt fire alight again. Then he squatted with his wrists on his thighs and shook his head across the blaze at the Cathead defector.

"Pud, Pud, what am I going to do with you?"

Pud looked at him with puppy-dog eyes. "I only want to help you, Tristan."

Tristan stared into those bulging eyes, trying to read the mind behind. He had a feeling there were a lot of snakes twisting around in there. Since coming over, Pud had acted as if he were in love with Tristan. It might simply have been that Tristan had saved him from Joker vengeance.

The Chosen Few swung off their rides and swaggered to the fire. Tristan noticed they were careful not to flank him left or right. That was wise on their part.

They settled with Pud to Tristan's right—sticking close, of course. Then Ozone, Ernie across the fire, Mad Dog, and finally roly-poly Aardvark on Tristan's left. *I'll let them hang awhile and chew the fat,* he resolved. *Then I'll send them on their little way.* He didn't want five loose wheels rolling around while he slept. He was lonely, not stupid.

Somewhere an owl hooted. "What's happening with the army?" he asked.

A look was passed around the crackling fire. "Well," Ernie said, running his fingers around his collar where sweaty leather chafed his neck and drawing the word out long, "nothing too damned good, y'know? Catheads got us on the run, and that's a fact."

"Never seen nothin' like it," Aardvark said. He had an unusually high-pitched voice and soft-looking hands. "Cats come on like a storm front, just a rollin' and rollin', nothin' a body can do to stop 'em."

Mad Dog was digging into a nostril of his tomato nose with one black-nailed thumb. Intermittent grunts were his contribution to the discourse. "An' magic," Ozone said. "Don't forget magic."

"They come more like Citizen soldiers than bros," Aardvark continued, ignoring his partner. "Regular, like. You got anything to eat?"

Tristan slipped his Bolo back in its holster and laid it back on the ground beside him. Digging in his pack he came up with a couple of sticks of jerked antelope. He tossed these to Aardvark.

"Anybody else feeling peckish?" Tristan asked, a slight ironic edge to his voice.

"No, thank you, cousin," Ernie said in all seriousness. "We just et a few mile back."

"Why'd the Cats change their game plan, meet us face-up, line to line?" Tristan asked, looking at Pud.

"Reckon they wanted to show they could whip us on our own terms," Ernie said. "Really grind old Hammerhand's nose in it."

"We laid some righteous hurt on 'em, we purely did," Pud said eagerly.

"They sure ain't comin' at us straight anymore," Ernie said. "They're hittin' us with combinations, left-right, left-right. Just keep flankin' us, flankin' us. Drive us on back."

"Dunno if they'll stop shy of the Front Range," said Ozone with a slack-lipped grin. Tristan guessed he wasn't actually *pleased* with the current drift of events; he was likely always that way.

"So whaddaya think?" Ozone asked. "The Catheads DemonCallers, or what?"

Pud flushed and started to sputter denial. Tristan thought about the brain in the pot.

"I don't know about the Cats," Tristan said slowly. "They've been a lot of things, but never that. The Fusion, now . . ."

He shrugged. "I wonder if they're maybe not something worse."

Ozone whinnied laughter. "Worse'n DemonCallers," he hooted. "Feature that. You're a pretty funny dude, Burning-skull."

Ernie rubbed his pocked and bearded face. "Don't reckon he's shittin' us," he said thoughtfully. "Don't know but that he's right. Something mighty overworldly 'bout them Fusion pukes."

"Well, folks," Tristan said, stretching, "it's been real. But I got to think about catching some winks, and while I do appreciate your kind offer of aid, this is still a trail I have to ride alone—"

For all his laid-back careless air Tristan had his senses stretched wide and tight as tent canvas. Now the half-expected bounced off them: a quick purposeful dive of Aardvark's left hand beneath his jacket, way around to the left.

Tristan grabbed the broom handle of his M96, whipped it cross-body, and shot the fat man right through the holster as a pudgy hand came out with a snub-nosed revolver.

A boom like the New Madrid slipping major, a world full of light. A sledgehammer blow to the ribs spun Tristan half around, driving the breath from his body and white spikes through his brain.

He fell back, catching himself with a left hand on hard cool rock, twisted left on his haunches. He held the Bolo up right-handed and just jacked it, unable to aim, trying desperately to stand the bastards off while he recovered.

Ernie was sitting back on his lean butt, holding up the piece he'd nailed Tristan with—a big ass revolver from Shawk & McLanahan, holding five .60-caliber shots in its fat cylinder. The Shocker pushed the big bullets out slow, so the recoil didn't bust the shooter's wrist. But if they connected, they fucked you *up*.

The glancing hit hadn't been enough to put Tristan down,

which spoke well for his chances of surviving—if, impossibly, he could keep the others from drilling him. The odds were not good.

Ernie went over backwards with a shrill curse. *Score one for the good guys* flashed through Tristan's brain. It was a moral victory, anyway.

And then Pud was on his feet, scattering the fire, lips skinned back from bad teeth, holding a Dallas Micro machine pistol in both hands and blazing away for all he was worth.

24

Stroboscopic flashes filled Tristan's brain. He turned and threw himself into the darkness.

Plates of loose shale slid away beneath his feet. He tumbled forward down the steep slope, crashing through bushes, bouncing off sharp-edged rocks. At last he fetched against the bole of a tree with an impact that jarred loose the slight amount of air he'd managed to claw into his lungs.

He lay there a moment, stunned. The moment called for violent, decisive action to survive. Tristan had nothing in him but pain.

From the hilltop he heard Ernie's voice raging: "You brain-dead son of a *bitch*, Pud! What the *fuck* made you get in the way like that?" The Chosen Few leader's voice was edged with something more than anger. With a certain detached satisfaction Tristan realized he must have tagged him one with his wild shooting. Unfortunately he hadn't killed the bastard.

"But I hit him! I hit him!" Pud came back. He managed to bubble and whine at one and the same time. "Didn't you see him go down?"

He was also a lying sack of shit, unless Tristan had caught another one without noticing. This was possible.

Ozone tittered. "Well, let's go finish him then!" A shrill animal scream of bloodlust must have come from Mad Dog.

Gotta get it in gear, or cash it in here, Tristan thought, and was vaguely pleased at the rhyme. He rolled over. It felt as if somebody had jammed a Comanche war-lance into his side and busted it off.

He heard the crunching of boot soles in the loose rock at the top of the mountain, the curses as the pursuers slipped and battled for balance. Tristan stood. He swayed. His brain seemed to be revolving slowly inside his head.

"Sumbitch is up!" A weird, wild scream in a voice he hadn't heard. *So Mad Dog can talk after all.*

Miraculously Tristan still had hold of his Bolo. He raised it, fired twice. He missed.

"I got him! I got him! Lemme get him!" Pud came bounding in front of the others, Micro held up before his chest as if he were praying down the muzzle.

"You dumb fuck!" roared Ernie. "Get out of our line of fire!"

Another burst flashed from the Micro. Tristan could hear the rounds crack overhead. He turned and stumbled off down the incline.

More shots cracked from behind, individual shots. Ahead of him a gnarled tree rose painfully from a jumble of boulders. Pud fired again, his bullets gouging the trunk, baring swatches of orange underbark.

Tristan juked left, reacting to the near miss. He ran straight into nothing. The ground just dropped right from beneath the soles of his boots.

He fell.

He didn't lose consciousness. It was too bad. He lay wedged between rocks, wondering which of his bones weren't broken. If any.

"Got him again!" he heard Pud exult shrilly from up the mountainside. He longed to get his hands around the scrawny neck. Squeezing the life from that filthy little traitor would see him off happy to Heroes' Holm. "Didja see that?"

"Should we go down and make sure of him?" Ozone asked.

"Wait!" Pud yelped. "Sister Moon, you're hurt!"

"Owww! *Shit*!" It was Ernie's voice. "Watch that! Don't go sticking your fucking fingers in the *hole*, dammit!"

Tristan heard the slide of loose debris underfoot. Someone was coming down the slope, up to the lip of rock Tristan had run off of.

"Let me help you, Ernie," he heard Pud plead. "You don't wanna be bleeding all over the place if the kobolds turn up."

"The kobolds," echoed Ozone, and he wasn't laughing any-more. "Gee, Ernie, maybe we shouldn't, like, hang around too long."

Ernie bellowed in pain. Tristan heard a patter of quick foot-steps, and then an angry growl from the hair-mass that was Mad Dog's head.

He rolled his eyes—about the only part of him that didn't hurt—upwards to see the familiar skinny silhouette of Pud lean-ing over into space above him, hanging onto Mad Dog's arm.

"I see him," the traitor shouted. "He's history. You fucked him up big time, Ernie! You really paid him back for putting that hole in you."

"Ernie, can we *go*?" It was Ozone's turn to whine.

Tristan was real interested in the course of the debate. But he didn't get to hear any more. He passed out instead.

He woke in a world of hurt. His first response was to chuckle, which hurt too—everything did. He had heard that expression all his life.

Now he knew what it meant. The world—the whole gods-damned *universe*—was full of pain. It spilled into him every-where it touched him, every unyielding edge or surface of cold rock, every molecule of air.

He was still stuck in a crack. It was still night. The sky had cleared. The stars seemed to be rotating above him, leaving trails, like some time-lapse photograph he'd seen in a book once.

The night sounds of insects and birds—and less indentifiable things—had commenced again. That might mean that the Cho-sen Few had set up camp and settled down. That didn't seem likely. They hadn't appeared eager to spend a second longer than necessary in the heart of kobold-land. Smart of them.

That meant they had gone and left him for dead. That wasn't so smart. Because he *wasn't* dead, not yet anyway. And if by some miracle he stayed that way, that meant that one fine day he would hunt down Ernie, Ozone, and Mad Dog—and Aardvark, if his shot hadn't done for him—and make them wish their mommies had drowned them at birth.

And Pud . . . Tristan gritted his teeth until they creaked. He had spared Pud's worthless life. He would correct that error too. And he would not be gentle about it.

It came to him that if he wanted to live to take his vengeance on those who had tried to kill him and had stolen his ride and his bear, lying forever wedged between a couple of rocks in the Shaking Lands was no way to go about it. He stirred, tried to force himself up.

The action set off various explosions within his chest and head. They blew his consciousness to pieces.

Another night, or the same night. Something roused him from unconsciousness. He opened his eyes and looked up.

Standing on the larger of the rocks he was stuck between was a tall figure, a deeper blackness against the black sky. Its eyes were flaming slits of red.

His left hand clutched at his throat. He was rewarded by fresh pain, as the obsidian arrowhead he wore on a thong sliced his fingers. The thunderstone amulet was the luck of the Hardriders, passed to him by his father on the day he died. It supposedly kept the wearer safe from harm. It had fallen down on the job tonight, of course . . . unless it was what had saved his life from his attackers.

His right hand reached out, groping like a blind arthritic spider across rough rock. The fingers found cold familiar metal. They closed around the round handle of his Lakota M96. Ignoring the scarlet spears of pain it sent through him, he whipped the pistol up and fired three times. He would have emptied his magazine, but his strength failed him. Still holding the weapon, his hand dropped back to the rock.

When the dazzle of the muzzle flashes had left his eyes, the red-eyed horror was gone. Tristan resolved to sleep no more, but as he formed the thought the world slipped away from him again. . . .

His parents were there, Wyatt Hardrider and Jen Morningstar, looking solemn and sad. It shamed him that they should see him like this.

"Mom, Dad, I'm sorry," he said. "I'll try to do better."

Wyatt shook his head. His hair and splendid mustache had gone almost totally the color of lead. He wore a braid to the right of his face, among the hair that hung to both broad shoulders. His face was heavier than Tristan had known it in life, sagging by the jowls.

"Son, son," he said. "You turned your back on us. Now look where you are."

Afrit Jenny laid a hand on his arm. She was still beautiful, though her face was lined and her hair was the color of fine wood ash. She wore a buckskin dress, fine Piegan work.

"He stayed true to us, in the end," she said. "Remember that. He killed the man who stole our lives."

"After serving him as a City trooper for a mess of years," her husband countered irritably. Tristan's heart sank. Then he saw his father begin to tug the end of his mustache, and he felt better. Wyatt Hardrider always did that when he was about to back down from laying down the law too hard to his son.

"All right. Shit. I never could stay mad at you, boy. You've made me proud, son. You've grown into a real warrior. Damn near brave as I was."

"But considerably smarter," Jen said.

Wyatt colored. Then he laughed. "Hell. Never had much horsepower of the head. But what the hell. I always had you around."

He slid his thick arm around her shoulders. "Maybe he got the best parts outta both of us."

"Gee, this is nice and all," Tristan said, "but I seem to sort of have my butt in a crack, here, and—"

"Never you mind, son," Wyatt said. "It's your destiny to win back the ride your grandfather stole. Anything else'd be cheatin' old Jammer out of a damned fine song."

"Now, Wyatt," Jen chided, "you know destiny's something we make for ourselves. Don't give Tristan the idea this will be easy."

"Well, hell, I was just trying to let him know I believed in him. You're always ragging on me 'cause I don't give him enough credit. Can't a body catch a break even in th' afterlife? I mean—"

She put a slim finger on his lips in a gesture that brought so many childhood memories flooding back it was all Tristan could do not to bust out crying. "Hush, dear."

"All right, all right." He looked at Tristan, and his bushy brows knotted. "Be strong. There's more at stake here than your own hide. The Catheads and their pals are up to some powerful bad medicine. Somethin' so evil it puts the wind up me to think about it, even now."

"What are they up to, Dad? What's the Fusion? What does it want?"

Wyatt shook his head firmly. "I can't give you those answers. The World Behind the World ain't got many rules, but them as it has can't lightly be broke. You're ridin' solo on this one."

"But we're here for you, dear," his mother said, "always. We love you."

"I love you too," he said, and he was crying now. "Both of you."

They started to fade. "Remember Bro Weasel," his father said. "And Trickster Charlie too."

"Follow your heart, dear," Jen Morningstar said. "And remember, true courage doesn't always lie in striking without thinking."

They were gone. A great emptiness yawned within Tristan, great sadness came upon him. Yet happiness swelled to fill that void.

He had thought his parents lost to him, the day he took service with Black Jack Masefield. They had not come into his dreams for many long years. But now they were back with him.

Part of him knew they weren't really there, that this was all just a wish-fantasy, product of the strain his current fix had put on his body and mind. He was glad to have them back all the same.

He woke again to find himself staring into a glittering black eye, set in a strange, gray, wizened face. He screamed. The hunched shape stirred irritably, raised black wings.

A vulture. A mingy vulture. "Fuck—" he hawked and spat "*—you.*" It hit the bird smack between its beady eyes. The creature's wings boomed out from its sides, and uttering a dismal, resentful cry it flew away.

His little victory elated him almost to the point of tears. *Catch a grip*, he told himself sternly. *You've got work to do.*

His hands, to start with. Both were free, both worked. That seemed like a pretty good beginning.

He was lying on his side with his left arm pinned to the rock by his body. Slowly he began levering himself up, out of the crack.

The effort hurt worse than anything he'd known in his life. He'd thought he hurt before, just lying there. He realized now

that had been sheer downy comfort. *This* was pain, triple-
distilled and shot straight into the mainline.

He fought the pain. He would not let it control him. He was in
charge. He was the master.

No, he thought, slumping back. *No, Jesus, I can't do it. It just
hurts too damned much.*

A vision came behind his eyes: the Burning Skull on its pole,
lighting up the lava waste with its glare. The other vision that
had persisted through all his years of captivity—that had not de-
serted him even when his parents forsook him. The vision that
had teased and tantalized him for half his life and more, and
only come clear when he lay in chains in the Joker camp, waiting for daylight and the inevitable Cathead assault. The Guest
Star had blazed alight in Taurus, and set off a sympathetic flame
within his mind.

You thought to be Lord of the Plains. The voice tolled in his
skull like a great and ancient bell. *Yet you cannot even master
yourself. You make a mockery of your aspirations, Tristan.*

Great. This was just great. He didn't just have his mom and
dad; he had a whole new supernatural entity looking over his
shoulder now. And bitching.

"Bull-fucking-*shit*," he gritted. He braced his abraded palms
on the stone and hauled himself up out of the crevice, inch by
agonizing inch. After an infinity of effort and pain he rolled free
of the crack, to lie gasping on his back on the mountainside,
drenched in sweat.

"Now," he said, when he had air to talk, "will you all kindly
go away and leave me the hell *alone*?"

"Do you mean us?" a mild voice asked.

He blinked away the stinging sweat that clouded his vision.

They were all around him. Big ones, little ones, one-eyed
ones, three-eyed ones. Anything, it seemed, but normal human-
looking ones. All bristling with warts, fangs, and automatic
weapons.

He slammed a fist into the ground. "Oh, well, *hell*!" he cried
in exasperation, and consciousness failed him again.

25

Someone was tugging at his sleeve. He murmured and rolled away, unwilling to awaken.

"Tristan, come *on*," the voice said. "You're just so darned *lazy* sometimes."

The voice was familiar, though he hadn't heard it in nigh onto fifteen years. "Jamie?" he said fuzzily.

"Who else? Come on. Get out of bed. We've got plenty of things to do."

Jamie. It was so good to have her back. She was his only true friend in life, except for Ferret. Her dad had pulled out of camp before the ill-fated attack on the Homeland convoy, and taken her with him. Tristan hadn't seen her since, and had long been reconciled to never seeing her again.

Sudden panic seized him: What if he'd found her again only to lose her right away, the way he had Ferret. He sat bolt upright and opened his eyes.

It wasn't Jamie standing there. It was a slender young woman with a pointed-oval face. Despite the boyish-short cut of her brown hair she was strikingly beautiful. She was dressed in a cammie blouse and tights, and she had, of all things, a bow slung over her shoulder.

"What's the matter," she asked, and her voice was Jamie's but all grown up. "Don't you know me?"

He licked his lips. "Jamie, I—"

Her head snapped suddenly around. "Uh-oh," she said, "gotta go."

She darted away from him. "Wait!" he called. "Come back! Don't leave me again!"

She paused, looked back. "It's up to you to follow me, Tristan," she said, and ran away into the mist.

He tried to follow then, but something held him back. A great weight pressed him down. He fought it as long as he could, but it bore him down to blackness. . . .

She was dressed as he had last seen her, in an off-the-shoulder evening gown of emerald green that matched her eyes. Her hair was blond, that kind of blond that seems to have silver in it. Not the silver of age, for she was young. And beautiful enough that it sometimes hurt to look at her.

Like a figure cast of silver, she was. Flawless, but cold. With a shock he realized she was the woman he loved.

"Elinor?" he said. "Ellie?"

He reached a hand to touch her arm. His fingers passed her bare skin without making contact.

"Ellie!" he shouted. "Oh, God, Ellie, can't you hear me?"

For a moment she turned her perfect head and looked him right in the eye. And then her gaze passed through him as his hand had passed through her arm. She turned and raised her arm for a man who appeared from the candlelight haze of the ballroom of her father's house. He seemed to be dressed all in white, the white of Purity, the faction that had murdered her father and hunted Tristan from Homeland like a rabid animal.

He took her by the arm. She smiled that ironic half-smile of hers in response to something he said, and then she glanced back at Tristan.

With a bellow of rage he tried to hurl himself forward, to tear her away from the man in white. The scene vanished before his eyes.

"Oh, baby," a voice murmured. "There, baby, there. It's okay."

He was aware of great enfolding warmth and softness. He opened his eyes.

His head was cradled between two dark-skinned breasts. They were well-suited for the work; each was easily as big as his head. The skin was smooth and soft, the nipples large and chocolate brown.

He was not your usual bro, in that he didn't find truly humongous tits to his taste, though he didn't think that more than a mouthful was wasted either. On the other hand, compared to the naked female body lying pressed against his, these tits weren't really large. Just about right was more like it; the owner of these astonishing breasts dwarfed him as if he were a child. He could feel her coarse pubic bush brushing his knees.

Now, this *is something I didn't expect*, he thought. This wasn't the Heaven of the Church of Christ, Citizen, that was for damned sure. And the babes in Heroes' Holm were supposed to be red-skinned, not like Comanch' or Kiowa, but really red.

Logically, that meant he was in Hell. It looked like the City had lied to him again. They said it wasn't a nice place to be. . . .

He looked up from between the enormous breasts. A face was looking down at him. It was quite a pretty face, if a bit on the round side, with full lips and huge long-lashed brown eyes.

The face lit when it saw him looking. "Oh, you're awake, baby! You had me so worried there for a while."

She hugged him. Pain stabbed through his chest and made him cry out. The unfairness of it devastated him. *It's not supposed to hurt in Heaven. Or Heroes' Holm either. Maybe I really* am *in Hell.*

"Oh!" the woman exclaimed. Or maybe girl; the voice sounded teenaged, but the body was definitely grown-up. "I'm sorry, I forgot. I have to be careful not to hurt you. Here."

She rolled onto her back, pulling him gingerly on top of her. He felt as if he were lying on a nicely padded ridge.

She put her vast hands under his armpits and drew him up that magnificent body. "Now you come on along up here, you adorable little critter," she said, "and Stormy'll kiss you and make it *all better*."

Part of me, he thought, as her lips enfolded his, *feels much better already*.

"Feeling better?"

It was a raspy kind of voice, though its tone was solicitous enough. Tristan levered an eye open.

A man three feet tall was sitting beside his bed in a simple wooden chair big enough to accommodate a giant. He had a pointy head, bald as a bottle except for a fringe of white hair. He gripped a gigantic cigar unlit in his teeth.

"Huh," Tristan grunted. "Another dream. The last one was a whole lot nicer."

The little guy hiked up a bushy brow. " 'Last one'? You'll have to tell me about it, if I decide to let you live. Because I'm not a dream, buddy boy. I'm real."

"Yeah, right. Then who the hell are you?"

The little man took the cigar out of his mouth. "I'm Jubal," he said cheerfully. "The one and only King of the Kobolds."

As if to emphasize his words the room shook. Tristan tried to sit up. His wrists were fastened to the bed by something that clinked.

"Where the hell am I?" he demanded.

"In the Hall of the Mountain King, of course," chortled the kobold. "Where else?"

Frantically, Tristan looked around. The room might have been in any clinic or hospital in Homeland, with plain white walls and furnishings. But there were two important differences.

First, his hosts weren't human medical personnel, but inhuman monsters legendary for their cruelty and hatred of true humans. Of course, that didn't make them all that much different from some of Homeland's Therapeutic types.

Of more visceral immediacy was the fact that he was *underground*. To the High Free Folk it was no accident that Hell was buried deep. Worse than that, he was *under the Shaking Lands*.

The worst fate imaginable, for a Homeland Citizen no less than any bro who happened to stray near the Front Range, was to be caught and immured in the living death of the Hellville mines, where a quake could shake the mountain down on your head at any old time. The Shaking Lands were *much* more seismically active than the post-StarFall Rockies.

He struggled, though it felt as if somebody was stirring a redhot poker around inside his rib cage. *Gotta get out! I can't stay here! I can't mingein' breathe. . . .*

The tiny man put a tiny hand on Tristan's sternum and pushed. He found himself pressed inexorably back as though Buffalo Bull, the outsized Kiowa strongman who rode with the Kwahadi, was leaning into him with all his beef.

"Now, just settle yourself down," the King said. "You took a crack at belly-cutting range from some kinda big-ass Coman-che, a Shocker or a Thunder Dog." *Comanche* was Plains lingo for a big-bore rifle or pistol; the Comanches were consistently poor marksmen, and believed in overcompensating. "Didn't pop a lung, but it knocked hell out of you, and you took a couple of good cracks when you fell in those rocks. You had a hell of a fever when they dragged you in here. Antibiotics got that down; you'll probably live, least until I say different. Still, won't do you any good rolling your eyes and snorting like a frightened horse."

That was true. Tristan sucked down a huge breath, and let it slide out slow beneath his bandit mustache. It was shameful to let an enemy see you fall to pieces. Bad tactics too.

"All right," he said. "What now, Your Majesty?"

King Jubal hooted laughter through his big hooked nose. "That's the spirit, boy. I'd hate to think any pussies had come to steal WildFyre."

"What?" Tristan said, aggrieved. "Does everybody in the whole damned world know what I'm doing? They having nightly updates on me on the Evening News, or what?"

"Cool your engines, boy. Think about this. Why *else* would a cycle nomad risk his buns in the dreaded Shaking Lands? Especially one with your illustrious antecedents."

"You know who I am."

Jubal put the cigar back in his mouth, took it out again, and brandished it. "My little girls won't let me light this in a sick-room. They'd have my nuts. Lemme tell you, son, uneasy lies the head that wears the crown. You can sit all high and mighty on your throne of gold, with a gaudy purple velvet cushion with gold tassels to pad your royal butt, but if you think you're gonna get any respect from your offspring, you got another think comin'."

"Yeah, I know who you are. You haven't exactly been keep-ing a low profile."

"Maybe I should rethink that."

"Naw. Never change your coat to suit the times, son. Keep your throttle wide. You scooter tramps are kinda boneheaded in a lot of ways, but you got some good ideas."

"Well, I don't want to give offense, Your Majesty, but I'm still kind of curious: What's going to happen to me?"

"Now, that depends on you. You've violated our territorial

integrity with intent, as they used to say. In spite of our cunning and carefully orchestrated PR campaign to make sure you surface-crawlers are too afraid to get up to hijinks like that."

He lifted his cigar again as if to take a deep draw, then raised his shaggy eyebrows and glared at it in mock exasperation.

"Appearances gotta be maintained; when you live like we do, that's of utmost importance. So here's the drill: You get dragged in chains to the footstool of my royal throne. Then you get subjected to trial by ordeal." He gestured with the cigar. "Sound fair?"

Tristan sucked on his lower lip. "Better deal than I expected," he acknowledged. "What happens if I pass."

"Wealth beyond your wildest dreams. Or a reasonable facsimile thereof."

"And if I fail?"

The Kobold King shrugged. "You die hideously. Natch."

"I knew that," Tristan said.

26

"Look well, smooth-skin," the head of Tristan's guard detail hissed in his ear from behind. "See what hatred the True Folk have for you and your kind."

He pulled his head back a fraction to avoid a glob of mucus intended for Tristan's cheek. After it found its target he leaned close again.

"Much would I give to open your throat with my claws. I shall beg the King for permission to. You should beg him too, soft white thing; I am far kinder than *them*."

The walls of the throne chamber soared upward until they were lost beyond reach of the light of smoky torches and oil lamps. They had the gloss and melted-wax look of a natural cave formation. They were perhaps sixty yards apart. The space between them was tight-packed with a vocal, angry throng of—well, maybe *humanity* was too strong a word. Or not strong enough . . .

Where the hell do these people come *from anyway?* Tristan wondered. Most of the throng were fairly normal-looking, if generally on the small side, except for little off-touches—pointed ears, say, or green hair.

Some of them, though, amply fulfilled expectations engendered around a thousand campfires and grown to maturity in nightmares. The man with the tusked boar's head, glaring at him with red eyes—not self-luminous, thank Bro Wind—the three-eyed woman, the dude with four arms and a green and or-

183

ange Quad Cities gimme cap, the snub-nosed girl with the cute little devil horns sticking out of her blue hair—they didn't seem to fit anywhere within the confines of the orderly if violent world he'd read about in the Library.

They did not, by and large, seem as if they were big fans of Tristan's.

The chains on his wrists were gold. By their heft, they were actual gold, not plated steel. The kobolds were giving their captive VIP treatment. *Gee, it's so nice to be appreciated.*

Besides the chain, his captors had dressed him in his jeans and boots, scrubbed and shined respectively. A bandage wrapped around his chest completed the ensemble.

They had also left his heirloom thunderstone amulet on its thong about his neck. For what that was worth. He was definitely beginning to have his doubts about its protective potency.

Away at the chamber's far wall, down an all-too-narrow passage between solid blocks of hostile bodies, was set a throne. King Jubal hadn't been by-God kidding when he said it was gaudy. A good seven feet its back must have risen, glittering painful gold in the light of a strategically placed—and obviously electric—spotlight. Monstrous twining figures had been engraved into it. The elevated dais was carpeted in purple, and purple was the cushion beneath the royal rump.

The King himself was dwarfed, so to speak, by the throne, as well as by the enormous golden crown he wore at a jaunty angle on his mostly hairless head. The royal robe of state was many sizes too large for him, and looked suspiciously like a bathrobe trimmed with cat fur.

With unhurried, unfriendly efficiency his guards herded him toward the throne. Fists and claws were shaken in his face, but the crowd stopped short of laying touch on the prized prisoner. He had an uneasy feeling it was fear of spoiling the fun to come rather than respect for his guards that kept the crowd from just grabbing parts and pulling them off him.

Thirty feet shy of the throne a black-taloned hand on his biceps hauled Tristan up short. His chief escort, a tall guy who could have passed in polite society anywhere as long as people overlooked his reptilian head and scales, stalked past him and approached the Presence.

"Your Majesty," he said in a sonorous baritone, "we have brought the prisoner, obedient to your command."

Jubal gestured with his scepter, which appeared to consist of the bones of a human forearm and hand fastened together into a rigid structure. It came to Tristan that, in terms of what he *could* have been, King Jubal's physical appearance was boringly normal.

"Well, bring him on ahead," Jubal said.

Tristan was hauled forward and dumped on his knees at the foot of the dais. His guards seemed reluctant to leave him until Jubal waved them irritably off with his skeletal scepter.

A strange little creature squatted next to the throne. He was hairless, and naked, and seemed to consist mainly of a gigantic head that, in turn, consisted mainly of bulging frog eyes and an enormous mouth. Tristan tried not to stare too hard. For all he knew it might be the King's favorite wife.

Jubal fixed Tristan with a stern eye. "You have trespassed upon the lands of the kobolds," he declared. "That ain't good."

The strange squatty creature opened its mouth. *"Mighty are the kobolds!"* it announced in a bull-fiddle voice so loud it seemed to shake the cavern. Tristan jumped.

"You have violated our law, and risked the hideous retribution for which we kobolds are so justly famous," Jubal continued.

"Terrible are the kobolds!" the frog-mouthed herald boomed.

Jubal jumped down from his throne and raised his arms. "Let me hear you, O my people," he cried. "What's the penalty for those who mess with the kobold kind?"

"Death!" the crowd shouted enthusiastically. Some of them tossed hats in the air.

Jubal turned his head sideways and cupped a hand by one ear. "What'd you say?"

"Death!" The force of the collective cry almost knocked Tristan on his nose.

"I can't *hear* you."

"DEATH! DeathdeathdeathdeathDEATH!"

Jubal made a quick cutting gesture of finger across throat. The crowd fell silent.

"I love this job," he said to Tristan behind his hand. He hopped back up on the throne.

"Nevertheless—I'm always looking for a shot at using the word in a sentence—nevertheless, you display exemplary bravery for a surface-dweller. Also, you have found favor in the eye of Our royal daughters, horny little bitches that they are. Therefore, even though you have come among us to steal the greatest of our treasures, it may be that We will find it in Our royal heart—shouldn't that be 'hearts,' if I'm gonna use the royal we?—anyway, We might just extend mercy to your miserable butt. Even if it's just the mercy of a quick death."

"Merciful is King Jubal," the herald declaimed.

Jubal whacked him on the head with his scepter. "Shut the hell up," he said. "Enough's enough."

He gazed around the cavern. "Speaking of the royal daughters," he said, "they seem to be late again, as usual."

"I'm right here, Daddy," a voice said from behind the throne.

Though Tristan hadn't seen any opening back there, a hidden door must have existed, because a young woman stepped forth to stand on the dais at the King's right elbow. Tristan's jaw dropped.

She was nothing but a knockout. She had that East Plains farm look that made so many bros rethink their thoughts on Diggers: corn-fed, fresh, and pert. Blond hair swept down in bangs to just above big blue eyes. She wore a cloak over shoulders that were a bit broad for Tristan's taste, and beneath that a white fur bikini kind of thing. High-top Apache moccasins completed the ensemble. Her waist was also a trifle wide, but it wasn't fat; she wasn't carrying any excess anywhere that Tristan could see, just the hint of padding that added a delightful roundness here and there.

She was also a good eight feet tall.

She gave him a dazzling toothpaste-ad smile. "Hi, I'm Sandy," she said. "You probably don't remember me. You were in pretty poor shape when the patrol brought you in."

"I must've been at death's door," he said, "for I have to confess I have no memory of you. And I don't think you're anyone I'm in any danger of forgetting."

The truth was, there was something familiar about her. She reminded him of the woman of his fever-dream. That woman had been outrageously tall and lovely too. But she had been a distinctly black babe, whereas Sandy was about as white as you get shy of albino.

Sandy turned to twinkle at Jubal. "See, Daddy? Isn't he nice? I told you you should let him live. He's a Hero."

"Gimme a break," the King said peevishly. "Haven't I given you my lecture on Heroes."

"Not *today*, Daddy."

"Yeah, yeah. Well, later. And what's the big idea here? I wish you wouldn't wear clothes like that in the throne room. How dignified is that?"

"But, Daddy, it shows off my exceptional abdominal development." She sucked in her belly and rippled her six-pack.

"It shows off a shitload more than that, daughter."

Sandy pouted. "A warrior should be proud of her body."

"Honey, we're kobolds. We're supposed to be *butt-ugly*."

"I know I'm a freak," she said, "but I refuse to be ashamed of the way I am."

Jubal rested his big head on his palm and looked at Tristan. "Spoken like a true kobold," he said, "worse luck."

"Would you mind if I stood up now, Your Majesty?" Tristan said. "My knees are starting to hurt."

"Silence, surface-dweller!" shouted the scaly guard behind him.

"It's okay, Elvis," the King said. "Lighten up. Yes, boy, you may stand."

As he got to his feet Tristan heard a commotion in the crowd behind him. Jubal looked over his shoulder. "I see my other wayward child has seen fit to grace us with her presence," he said.

Tristan looked back. The crowd parted. Into the flood of light from the wall-mounted spot bounced a young woman dressed in pink sweats. With her dark hair done up in pigtails to either side of a broad, cute, black face with great chocolate-colored eyes, she looked almost like a little girl. But there was nothing little about her. She was perhaps an inch shorter than her sister and a shade or two plumper.

Tristan goggled. It was the woman from his dream. The one he'd . . .

She popped up onto the dais and curtsied. "Sorry I'm late, Daddy," she said.

"Allow me to introduce my famous Power-Lifting Daughters, O stranger," Jubal said, "Stormy and Sandy."

Stormy curtsied again, to Tristan this time. She also flashed him a wink her sibling and father couldn't see.

"I'm, ahh, charmed," Tristan said. "I've never seen such overwhelming beauty in all my life."

"Isn't he *cute*," Stormy said.

"I saw him first," Sandy said warningly.

The Kobold King sighed thunderously. "You see how it is?" he said to his people, holding his hands out imploringly. "Everybody knows what a softhearted, indulgent old fool I am when it comes to these daughters of mine. Their eyes have fallen on this funny-looking character from Above, God knows why, but the King who can rule the heart of even one of his daughters ain't yet been born."

The crowd made sympathetic noises. "Does this mean we can't kill him?" somebody shouted from the rear.

"Not necessarily," the King said, using his scepter to scratch himself behind the shoulder blades.

"Daddy!" Sandy and Stormy wailed in unison.

"We have to keep up appearances, daughters," Jubal said firmly. "He's an intruder. A surface-dweller. The enemy of our kind. Don't you know the fear and loathing the surface-dwellers have for us? They call us monsters, and hunt us down like animals."

"He hasn't treated me like a monster," Stormy said ingenuously.

Tristan tried to give her a surreptitious glare. *Shut the fuck up,* he thought. *Please.*

"We didn't find our laws in a Cracker Jack box," Jubal said. "There's *reasons* for 'em. And the law says your pet here has to die."

The crowd cheered happily. "But he's a Hero," Sandy said.

"Think of the design pointers he can give us," Stormy said.

Design pointers? A certain part of Tristan's mind leered. *I got your design pointer right here, baby.* He squashed that thought in a hurry.

Jubal looked at Tristan. "I'm not a total wimp, junior. It's not just a matter of law; we got a reputation to uphold. I can toss you to the slavering mob just as easily as I can give you to the girls. Strictly between you and me, boy, I'm not so sure I wouldn't take the mob."

"What can I do to affect the decision, Your Majesty?"

Jubal settled himself back on the throne. "So you claim to be a Hero?"

"I didn't use the word, Your Majesty."

Jubal shook his head. "Wrong answer. You can be only one of two things. One, a Hero on a mighty quest. Two, a low-down plain-vanilla Surface scumbag come to swipe our hard-earned treasure. Heroes we might cut some slack. The other . . ." He shrugged. "We just cut."

"I've never been one to contradict a lady," Tristan admitted.

"All right, then," Jubal said. "Then show us all she's right. Show me some class, bike trash."

Tristan took a deep breath. He could only think of one thing to do. No, that wasn't true—he *could* think of another thing. He could leap forward, try to wrap his chain around the King's throat, and hold him hostage.

At which point the King's demure daughters would each grab him by an arm and make a wish.

Of course, what he was *going* to do didn't offer a much better hope of success . . . oh, well. There was a great liberation in having exactly nothing to lose.

Slowly he raised his hands before his face. The light danced along the golden links of the chain. He spread his arms outward to the fullest extent of the chain. Then he pulled with all his might.

The veins popped out on his forearms and forehead. Tendons popped out upon his neck like pillars. Sweat poured down his face. The cavern fell so quiet you could hear a frog fart.

Tristan felt his trapezius muscle begin to tear. Pain pulsed in his chest as if Osage Oil drillers were sinking a shaft in there. Blood pressure was setting skyrockets off behind his eyes. *The good news is, I don't pull this off, I'm liable to pop an A and die. . .*

With a ringing musical tone the chain snapped.

The crowd went crazy, stamping, hooting, cheering, throwing the same hats in the air they'd thrown when they were crying for his blood. Tristan fell to his knees.

"All right, boy," the Kobold King said. "You've won the right to live. For now."

"I—thank—Your Majesty," Tristan choked out.

Jubal smiled. "Don't thank me until you know what you're letting yourself in for."

27

"So when does this Ordeal kick in?" Tristan asked. His voice echoed softly down the low passageway. It wasn't *that* low—six-four Tristan could walk upright without bumping the top of his brushcut on the fluorescent panels—and he and the Kobold King could walk shoulder-to-hip comfortably. But it was still claustrophobia time, with the smoothed irregular walls threatening to close in at any old moment, and quivering periodically to a tremor to put a little edge on that threat.

"I'd think you'd be eager to put it off as long as possible," Jubal said, drawing contentedly on his now-lit stogie. "Given that it might turn out bad and all."

Tristan shook his head. He was keeping it high and his shoulders back, though the effort cost him constant pain from his busted ribs. Like many another Plainsman before him, he was seeking refuge from fear in the sound of his own bantering voice.

"Huh-uh. Rather get it the hell over with. Anticipation's worse than reality any old day."

The Kobold King cocked a bushy white brow. "Don't be too sure of that, boy. I got a few tricks up my sleeve. . . ." He shook his head. "Don't know why I waste my air. Sandy's got one thing right: You're a Hero, and that's for damned sure. It'll be a relief to see the last of you. One way or another."

Despite the ominous cast of Jubal's words Tristan grinned. He couldn't help liking the outlandish little monarch. Any more than His Majesty couldn't help liking *him*.

He had awakened to find the gnarled little man sitting in the chair next to his bed in his hospital room-*cum*-jail cell. It had given him a start. When he was raving with fever it was one thing, but he wasn't used to *anybody* being able to creep up on him when he was asleep. There was no way anybody, no matter how stealthy-crafty they were, could have worked the massive locks that kept Tristan in—and prospective ill-wishers out, as Jubal had repeatedly reminded his captive—without snapping Tristan instantly awake. *The place has got to be honeycombed with secret passages*, Tristan thought; that was the only possible explanation.

Today the King was taking Tristan on a tour of his domains. As Tristan had guessed, the kobolds had started with an extensive natural cave system and systematically expanded it into a three-dimensional labyrinth of tunnels and chambers. It was an impressive feat of engineering. It was not the kind Tristan was prepared to appreciate in more than an academic way.

The floor shook beneath his boot soles. The walls gave a little twitch, like the shoulder of a mare trying to lose a horsefly. Tristan set his jaw. He didn't flinch.

"Looking a little pale there, boy," Jubal said. Both solicitude and malicious amusement were in his gravel-truck voice. These kobolds were even bigger on contradictions than the High Free Folk were.

"I just keep waiting for the roof to come down on our heads."

Jubal shook his bald, pointy head. "Never happen. Or, *probably* never. See, one thing about the Shaking Lands, we have near-constant small tremors. But that means the fault system is constantly bleeding off stress, rather than letting it build up to a big-ass bust-out. So we never get anything but minor shakes."

"New Madrid goes off pretty much all the time," Tristan said, "and *its* quakes come in two sizes: big and cataclysmic."

Jubal chuckled. "An optimist, aren't you, boy? New Madrid's got bigger problems than our little StarFall fracture. And if these hills ever *really* let rip . . ."

He reached out to touch the wall. The limestone had that slick but lumpy cave look. "These caves've endured for millions of years. Nature builds to last, and we've given her some help here and there. We do get the occasional cave-in, but it would take the mother of all quakes to drop the roof on our pointy heads."

"What happens if it comes?"

Jubal shrugged. "Then we die. This is our home, boy. Out on the Plains you have your rains and your hailstorms and your lightning and your Stalking Winds. You still live out there in all that shit, Lord knows how, and you're proud of the doing of it, in your stiff-necked half-savage way.

"You nomads like to think of yourselves as outlaws, outcasts. But you're the Surface world's spoiled and pampered darlings, compared to us kobolds. You're outsiders by free choice. We don't have the choice. We're freaks, abominations to the eyes of the straight. This place . . ."

He raised his hands as if to cup his vast hidden realm in the horny palms. Like his head, they were disproportionately large for his body. "This is where we make our stand against a world that would exterminate us all with fire and sword in six seconds flat if we weren't so damned cunning and just plain mean. If our refuge fails us, us freaks and monsters know how to die just as well as you outlaws. We've had millennia of practice."

Tristan nodded. It was a good saying. There was a part of his soul a decade and a half of City life had never touched. The Kobold King had spoken to it.

"Where do you people come from anyway?" Tristan asked.

Jubal took his cigar from his mouth. "None of your beeswax. You're an honored guest, even though liable to be shortened by a head should I take it in my mind. But we gotta have some secrets."

"Oh," Tristan said. They walked a while in silence. Just when Tristan felt the walls pressing intolerably in again Jubal turned him into a side door with an expansive gesture.

They were in a little glass-fronted cell that overlooked a cavern almost as big as the throne room. Dozens of kobolds scurried between brightly lit workbenches where others hunched over gleaming big machines.

"Mortar tubes?" Tristan asked.

Jubal nodded. "Right here, yeah. And a ways further over, you can seem 'em machining and assembling our excellent break-open grenade launchers. Just a part of our line of fine explosives and the devices to hurl 'em at the bad guys. Most of the Cities of the central Plains buy from us, not to mention the Osage. Osage put their name on 'em and remarket 'em. Real lucrative for both parties—another reason everybody was willing to let the little matter of WildFyre lie—*both* times she's been stolen."

Away from where grenade launcher tubes were being mated to breeches and locks, a figure loomed far above the workers. Even at this range, Tristan could make out the way the lab coat couldn't help molding itself to a splendiferously rounded ass.

"Say," he said, pointing, "isn't that—"

"Stormy." Jubal nodded proudly. "Someday she'll succeed me as Chief Engineer. A real whiz, she is, though she's still a little too fond of gimmicky innovations. Old ways are the best ways, but she'll learn that in time."

He gave Tristan a shrewd, ancient look. "My little girl Sandy's head of security, by the way. Does a damn fine job; her people tracked you from the instant you rolled your ass off that ferry. See, my little girls are flaky, Lord love 'em. But what they *ain't* is bimbos."

Tristan rubbed his jaw and said nothing.

"Why've you got it in for heroes?" he asked when they were out walking the tunnels again.

"Why? *Why?*" Jubal raised his knobby but powerful hands to the echoing rock walls. "Think about it. Think about your *life*, son. Have you ever known one teeny-tiny moment of peace? Well? Have you?"

Tristan rubbed his long chin and thought about it. Hard. "Well," he said after a spell, "there was when I was living with the Tomlinsons, back when I was in high school."

"Yeah? Well, how'd that end up?"

"I beat the mortal shit out of a dozen or so cops and got given a choice between the army and the mines," Tristan said. He chuckled at the memory. He'd busted both his hands, but every iota of pain had been well worth it.

"See?" Jubal puffed on his cigar. Blue smoke wreathed his face, giving him a demon-imp look. "And how'd things go for your foster parents after they adopted you?"

"Okay. I mean, I was always a handful, even though I did love them and try not to bring them too much grief. I mean, they did put themselves out for me, and they got my skinny adolescent butt out of McGrory, which is definitely an upper story of Hell, and a bro don't bite the hand that feeds him. But the Neighborhood Watch weenies leaned on them pretty hard for taking in scooter trash off the Plains. And . . ." He shook his head sadly. "I reckon things haven't exactly gone well for them since the Purity takeover in Homeland. Those white-jumpsuit butt-stuffers didn't much love me *before* I fired up my one-man war against them."

Jubal was nodding triumphantly. "Uh-huh. Uh-huh. See? You're disaster on the hoof, boy. You're a jinx."

He reached up to pat Tristan's elbow, which was as close as he could get to the tall man's shoulder. "I have a feeling I could get to love you like a son, boy," he said, "but have you caught a clue as to why I don't want you around? The Land Below is a refuge for those people Life dealt to from the bottom of the deck. It's my duty to protect them. Now, come crunch time, I gotta admit, a Hero is a damned helpful thing to have around. But afterward, when the fur stops flying—no way, José."

He shook his head. "You think I'm just pushing wind at you, don't you, boy? Just being a garrulous old fuck who likes to hear himself run on. And you're right. But I know what I'm talking about."

He stuck his hands in the pockets of his slightly scruffy informal robe—purple without the fur trim—and walked and smoked a few moments in silence.

"My son Buddy was a Hero too, see."

"Buddy?"

"My youngest. Born after the girls. Who d'you think swiped WildFyre back from the tailheads in the first place? Dumb son of a bitch."

Tristan's step almost faltered. "Uh, well . . ."

"Worried he's gonna get all hot and bothered 'cause you came to steal her back again? Don't be. Buddy's been gone these three years down. Landslide took him."

"Oh. I'm sorry."

"Don't be," Jubal said. "Buddy was a dickweed. I mean, his given name was Burton. That's not a bad name, nothing wrong with it at all. What kind of self-respecting person would *choose* to be called Buddy?"

He wiped an eye with his sleeve. "Oh, I bawled for three days straight when it happened, of course, tore out mosta what remained of my hair, that kinda thing. I guess I miss him every single day. But the terrible thing is, it's best for the realm that he's gone."

He waved a hand. "See what he's gone and done? He got the

notion he was gonna vindicate the honor of the kobold kind. I mean, I *ask* you—what kind of honor are freaks gonna have? We don't *survive* by being honorable. But honor was a big hairy thing for Buddy. He got a bunch of his pals with more balls than sense, like him, and set off to Osagerie without telling a blessed soul.

"Good thing too; I'da yanked a knot in his tail. Did I mention he had a tail? Didn't take much after the twins. Anyway, the Osage had the sense not to say anything about it. They like to think of themselves as mean-ass Plains warriors, right up there with the Lakota and the Blackfeet. If it got out that us low-down little kobolds had counted coup on them, it'd sure make 'em look like they had miniature tallywhackers, now, wouldn't it?" He grinned and puffed. Obviously, his disapproval of his son's action extended only so far.

He stopped abruptly, angled his head off to one side. His bushy brows furrowed. After a moment he straightened up.

"Uh-oh," he said, "gotta go. Affairs of state and all that. Let's find a way down to the shop floor. I'll leave you in my daughter's hands. You know how capable she is."

Tristan had trouble keeping from choking. *Just how much does this saucy little bastard know?* He had a free-falling sensation that damned little happened in the Mountain King's subterranean realm that he wasn't right on top of.

Jubal spared him further discomfort by setting off down the tunnel at such a brisk pace that Tristan had trouble keeping up, for all his vastly greater length of leg. "So, uh, Your Majesty, I appreciate the tour and all, but I'm dying to know: What's my part in all this?"

"I thought I made that clear. We determine whether you're a Hero or just a chump. If you're the first, we might be able to deal with you. If you're the second . . ." He shrugged. "You get taken out with the trash. You already passed the first test with flying colors. It was the easy one, of course."

"Yeah," Tristan said with a rueful grin. "I thought it was kinda fortuitous you used real gold chains. Gold isn't exactly hard to bust, now, is it?"

Jubal cackled. "You're smart for a Hero, I'll give you that. Course, that only makes you all the more dangerous to those around you, not to mention your own damned self."

He took out his cigar and stabbed it at Tristan, unconsciously menacing him with the ember. "My daughters do have some in-put into how important prisoners are treated," he said. "For in-stance, I *have* had enemies brought before me on poles like dead deer, with their wrists and ankles bolted together. When you're in our position, the judicious use of atrocity is, y'know, an invaluable resource."

Tristan swallowed. He was glad that during his "wet dream" he'd decided to give as good as he got, rather than just lying back and enjoying it.

"That's something there's no point in losing sight of, son," Jubal said more gently, pulling his stogie back out of charring range of Tristan's white linen shirt. "We're not kind and gentle down here. So, I like to kill my enemies clean, and do major cosmetic surgery on 'em to put the wind up their friends and po-tential accomplices after they can't feel pain. I'm not a sadist, but I am cruel. If the surface-dwellers weren't shit-scared of us, and the place we live, they'd pour fifty thousand gallons of gas down these caves and torch it off in a second."

"Okay, Your Majesty, so you're a stone hardass. Now, what about this Ordeal?"

Jubal glared at him. "Still on about that?"

"It does play kind of a significant role in my future plans."

Jubal held the glare a moment longer, then broke into a grin and slapped Tristan's arm. "I like you, boy, crush me if I don't! I'd say you remind me of me, except that's a lie—I was always too damned sneaky to go blurting out whatever came to mind like you do. It's only after I came to power I had the luxury to be long-winded."

"You should've figured what the Ordeal's all about already. You heard all them fairy-stories around the campfire. You read a lot—all the old legends and fantasies and what not. You've come to claim a fabulous treasure."

"Uh—yeah." Tristan still felt a little strange talking so openly about his planned theft with the intended recipient of the ripoff.

"So it's guarded by a dragon, of course. To get WildFyre, you got to get past the dragon."

"Yeah," Tristan said, "Right."

Jubal puffed mightily on his cigar. Blue smoke wreathed his head till it looked as if he were part dragon himself. "You'll see," the Kobold King said, "you'll see."

28

She was standing there when he turned around, all eight pink and blond feet of her. He managed not to jump.

"How do you people keep sneaking up on me like that anyway?" he demanded.

She smiled sweetly. "We teleport."

"All right," he said, "don't tell me if you don't want to. Sit down and take a load off, if you've mind to."

Sandy smiled prettily down at him and plopped instantly into a relaxed jock sprawl in the room's sole chair, apparently at ease despite the wooden angularity that made no compromise with the human form, of whatever size. For all her cheerleader demeanor she moved like a seasoned campaigner, and that included a cat's talent for getting comfortable anywhere and anytime.

That didn't surprise Tristan. By this time nothing surprised him about the kobolds in general, and the King's Power-Lifting Daughters in particular. He had just spent most of the Land Below's "day" shift getting his little legs worn to stumps following Stormy through the various weapons fab, testing, and development chambers.

The chocolate twin displayed an unsettlingly detailed knowledge of his background and career—obviously the kobolds had spies even in Homeland, another crack in the face to Purity's official paranoia and obsession with security. Actually, he doubted they had their own people in there; more likely they had some kind of deal worked out with Osage intelligence. Hell, for all he knew, they were siphoning their skinny from the Indians. They were just that tricky.

Today Stormy was all business. As a former Homeland Defense Force "rag" regular, a Striker, and a biker, Tristan had a unique three-dimensional perspective on real-life weapons use and performance. Stormy seemed as single-mindedly bent on wringing his brain dry of pertinent data as she had been on wringing dry certain other parts of him not so very long ago.

She knew more than just Tristan's not-real-elite grade-point average from high school, or that he'd been reprimanded by a court-martial for scalping a few Catheads he'd downed after they caught his motorized patrol in a fire-sack ambush. She knew her dope, stone cold. Whether it was discussing the optimum balance, cyclic rate, and magazine capacity for a hand-held full-auto 30-mm grenade launcher the kobolds were developing, to the proper detonating height for a new Bouncing Betty "S"-mine—the dreaded Nut Cutter—she was as completely at ease as now Sandy was in the bad chair.

Just on the basis of a SWAG—Scientific Wild-Ass Guess, to use one of Stormy's favorite engineer phrases—he reckoned Sandy would be a mighty tough customer even beyond the fact she could heft him one-handed and chuck him like a javelin.

He kicked off his boots and planted his weary carcass on the bed. He could be a right courtly son of a bitch when occasion demanded—he'd have gotten nowhere fast with Elinor if that weren't the case—but right now he was just too tired. He was still nursing badly cracked ribs, plus the other dings, scratches, and woes attendant on having fallen into a crack between two boulders and lying there in the weather for gods knew how long. The right side of his rib cage was turning all those wonderful drab-rainbow colors of a maturing bruise, yellow and purple and black and green. He had black dots swarming in his eyes. He was a hell of mess yet, no question. Fortunately, the First Family of Kobolddom didn't seem to stand much on formality.

He sighed, settled himself with his hands behind his back, and looked at Sandy. She wore jeans, pointy-toe boots, and a man's pearl-snap Western-style shirt. She looked for all the world like a spoiled Dallasite deb fixing to ride her daddy's back forty to watch the slaves sweat. Brother Wind knew where she got the outfit. He was morally certain no off-the-shelf fe-male clothing had been made in those sizes since Bro Adam came down from the trees. He reckoned you could get all the tailoring your little heart desired when you were a Princess.

"So what . . ." With a horrified start he realized he'd been about to finish *can I do you for*? For all the liberties her not-so-identical twin had taken with him, he wasn't sure how far he could go with the vanilla version before she decided to upend him, wrap those astounding thighs around his skinny neck, and play Pile Driver with his head bone.

"What can I *do for you*, Princess," he said, enunciating *very* clearly.

She smiled. "It's probably a silly question."

"No such thing," he said, quoting old Bayliss the Librarian, a blind old walking-stick of a man who was the wisest soul he'd ever known, and was almost certainly years dead.

Her cheeks colored up nicely. He felt a twinge in his scrotum. "Well, you probably get tired of being asked it anyway," she went on, "but I was wondering if you could tell me about some of your experiences. You know—with the Strikers, out on the Plains. I mean, I've read the files. But they leave out so much. The heart and soul and grit."

Too true. He arched a brow at her. "War stories?"

"If it's not too much to ask."

He laughed hugely, groaned with agony, and laughed again on a more restrained note. "Sister, you're in luck. Swapping lies around the campfire is the second favorite outdoor sport of the High Free Folk, and please don't ask what *numero uno* is. Now, since we still have to breathe in here, let's just imagine that the foot of the bed is a merry old blaze. . . ."

There was no true day or night in the Land Below. But of the three shifts that defined the kobold existence, the one that corre-sponded most to sunlight hours Above was the most active, midnight-to-dawn the least. Asleep in the belly of the graveyard shift, Tristan stirred and murmured something. The shape he was in it was impossible to get comfortable. And of course, he was still trapped between too-close walls deep in the trembling bowels of the Shaking Land.

None of that was the real problem. He was missing his bear. He had never really flaunted it. His squaddies had given him some flak over it in the HDF—but no one more than once, especially after he became a master of the brutal barracks fighting-form called Empty. In the Strikers, carrying a teddy bear had been pretty mild as eccentricities went; Black Jack's hard-core bully boys prided themselves as being as crankily individualistic as any rad-trad Lakota buck on the prod for hair. Among the Stormriders attachment to talismanic objects was the norm, not the exception. Still, he hadn't actually slept with the thing in his arms since before he left the Tomlinsons' house.

But it had been his constant companion for nigh on half his life. It was gone, along with all his possibles. He missed his handy Saskatoon Scout, comrade of many a hunt and fight, and the fine new sword he'd only just purchased and barely baptized in Cathead blood. His Bolo had gone into the crevice with him, and he gathered the kobolds had policed it up along with him, but none of his new friends seemed in much of a hurry to hand it back to him. The cruiser he missed not at all, with its too-long extension and dippy flame-painted tank.

None of that would he weep over; the loss of none got under his skin. In his early years he'd come to travel light, attached to no possessions except his sled. And he didn't even have one of those; he had never really bonded to the durable, handy little Osage scrambler he'd ridden as a Striker, and that had gotten trashed in the Burning Skull fight.

But the little griz was a friend. Its loss left a hole. He hadn't let himself mourn Jeremy yet, which somehow made the lesser loss of the bear all the keener.

He began to slip back under. He was in a black volcanic waste under a dead matte sky. A glow lit the horizon from end to end. It sprang from a burning steer's skull—only instead of being mounted on a pole, it rode the broad shoulders of a tall man cloaked in black.

The figure gazed at him. Then it raised its flame-filled sockets to stare past him, raised a spectral arm, and said, "Haul your ass out of bed if you don't intend to lose it. They're coming over the wire."

He knew it by repute, from bros who'd been downed by City Man's law and lived to tell about it: the Shank Rush. Your enemies bribed the guard to slip the lock on your cell, and they came boiling in in the middle of the night, threw a blanket over your head, and stabbed you till no amount of suturing could

possibly seal up all the holes before your life leaked out of
them.

He was in violent motion while the words still echoed in his
skull, and the *snik* of the door lock registered after the fact on
his conscious mind. He rolled off the bed to his right toward the
near wall, straight out from under the covers, dragging them
with him around his left arm to use as a shield of sorts. In a
badly outnumbered fight—and he already knew this was going
to be one—you grabbed for every tiny little sliver of advantage
you could find.

He heard feet, some bare, some shod, scrabble on the stone
floor and then stop. A beat, and then a voice said, "Hey! Where
the fuck'd he *go*?"

"Right here, asshole." Tristan popped onto his pins, a lopping
overhead hammerfist already on the way. A kobold, short but
damned near as wide as tall, stood hard by the bed clutching an
olive drab City-issue military blanket in cracked black nails.
Tristan's fist bounced right off his sloped forehead. It was a
blow less likely to bust your hand than a straight-on knuckle
punch, and a wagonload more powerful. Tristan's hand didn't
break. The kobold's eyes rolled up, and he went down.

Half a dozen of them were crammed into the little chamber.
Most of them were like the first, not tall but not small either, but
by the dim glow of the night-light that had been stuck in the
room to keep the surface-crawler from going bugfuck in true
absolute dark, Tristan saw a familiar reptile-headed form looming at the rear of the pack.

Somebody shut the door. The lock engaged with a very final
sound. Dull glints danced around knife-blades. Either they
wanted this to be comparatively quiet, or they had enough sense
not to want stray bullets caroming around the stone walls with
all their bodies in the way. Or maybe they just wanted to feel the
steel take him and get his blood on their knuckles. Probably all
of the above.

But they had a little problem: how to get at him with the bed
in between. They dithered in place, deking left, deking right, as
if hoping they'd flush him that way. He laughed in their bat-
ugly faces.

"Rush him, you pissants!" the lizard-man roared. "Push the
bed, damn it. *Pin his fucking legs to the wall!*"

Sometimes there's a guy in a crowd who manages to keep his

head when everybody else is losing theirs. What a pisser that Elvis had to be one.

The two burly boys in the lead put their hairless heads down and charged. As they hit the bed running Tristan threw himself onto it on his side, rolling over. He snapped a front kick into the face of one, dropping him. The bed hit the wall, and the other slammed his midsection full into it, driving the air from his lungs. Before he got himself sorted out Tristan gave him a hooking heel-palm blow and flattened his nose more than it was already. He sat down on his butt, squalling and spurting between warty fingers.

Tristan rolled off the bed and onto his feet. Hands like C-clamps got him by the neck and lifted him right off the floor.

"Pink worm," Elvis gritted through his teeth, "I'm going to enjoy squashing you."

Tristan planted the instep of his right foot at the apex of the mighty scaled legs. He wasn't sure where lizards kept their wedding-tackle, but ol' Elvis was more like a man than an iguana anyway. He released Tristan's throat and doubled over himself with a groan.

Tristan landed on his feet, tossing elbows around as if coming down with a rebound in the old Homeland high school conference. For a half-wild captive nomad kid with a panther's strength, speed, and coordination, City-Boy basketball was a contact sport.

The problem was, there are those who can play through pain, and Elvis happened to be one of those, too. He got some air stuffed back in his lights and straightened to square off with Tristan.

"Is that—the best—you can do?" he asked painfully.

Tristan gave him an A for effort. He also gave him two quick jabs to the snout with his leading right hand as he tried to close. Like a lot of Empty fighters, Tristan fought with his power hand forward, not back, and he knew how to snap his jabs back the millisecond after contact so as not to shatter his knuckles.

Elvis's big bony head rocked back. Tristan's right leg whipped up and around, aiming his shinbone like the blade of an axe at the lizard-man's left knee. Elvis was quick; he leaned his weight forward and took the kick on the meat of the thigh.

"I'm quicker and stronger than you are, worm," he said, "and now you've really got me pissed."

Tristan had guessed that. He fired a front snap-kick at the same knee. Elvis dodged it and charged him with a roar.

Lightning flashed behind Tristan's eyes as Elvis's massive arms closed around his chest. He brought his right elbow down hard on the lizard-man's temple. The deathgrip slacked but did not let go.

Tristan was impressed; that shot could put a man down or kill him outright, as he knew first-hand. He gave Elvis a savage forward elbow to back him up, another.

Elvis's head began to wobble on his thick neck. The lights were on, but the occupant had stepped out for a moment. Tristan grabbed hold of him, jumped up, sledgehammered his right knee into the kobold's short ribs. Something cracked. He came back with a left, then another right, then a left—the Empty death-dance, the leaping knee-kicks he'd used to put the Final Hurt on John Badheart.

And then they swarmed him. Life's a bitch sometimes.

They got the bed out from the wall and held him down on it spread-eagled. Elvis stood over him with a big knife and an even bigger grin. All his teeth were pointy. Tristan didn't know if it was art or nature.

"You know something, little man?" the lizard-man asked. "I have a secret dream I think you can help me with. All my life I've wanted to be a famous surgeon."

He extended the knife slowly until its tip was pressed deep into Tristan's navel. "I think I'll start—right *here*."

Instead he was raised into the air, shaken like a cocktail stirrer, and thrown into the wall so hard it seemed another tremor had let go. Pointy kobold heads turned. Misshapen kobold jaws dropped.

Warty kobold asses were kicked.

It was dark, and Tristan was having some trouble with his head, which felt as if it had recently been used for soccer practice. The details were pretty much lost to him. He just sort of lay there and watched things fly around and around. It looked like the Tasmanian Devil in an ancient cartoon bounced off a satellite from Portage la Prairie had gotten loose among the would-be assassins.

After they had been dragged off under guard—being generally unable to move under their own power—and they were alone again, Tristan's blond avenging angel cradled his head in her lap.

"Poor baby," she cooed, rubbing his cheek with the raw backs of her knuckles.

"Guess I'm not much of a Hero after all, huh?"

"I guess you *are*. There were only six of them to one of you. And you were hurt already, poor thing."

"I, ah, I couldn't help noticing you didn't have much trouble dusting the furniture with them."

"I got 'em from behind. And I do have a few advantages. I'm not one of the King's Power-Lifting Daughters for nothing!"

"Yeah," Tristan said, noticing how satiny and fine her thigh felt on his much-abused cheek. She was wearing nothing but a T-shirt and panties. Her glorious golden hair was piled in a bun on top of her head. "I kinda get the idea. But just how did you manage to catch the fuckards from behind? I didn't hear the door open, and you got loud locks in this joint."

"I told you before," she said, "I teleported."

"I . . . see," he said.

She brushed hair back from his forehead. "Sorry you had to wait so long. But I didn't find out what was going on until the last moment."

He badly wanted to ask how she *did* find out. He decided he probably wouldn't like the answer.

"You cut it pretty close," he admitted. "What'll happen to the boys?"

She straightened up and looked off to the wall. "My father is not a very absolute monarch," she said. "We have a pretty open society here, as you might've noticed. We're not monolithic or anything. Elvis comes from a real important family—he's the Boss Chemist's nephew."

She shook her head. "I reckon, beyond what we did to them, nothing's going to happen at all."

She smiled radiantly. "Of course, between the two of us we *did* manage to give them an ass-kicking they won't soon forget!"

The pain made the world go away for a few moments. When it came back, Tristan said, "Don't make me laugh like that, babe. I think that scaly son of a bitch knocked something loose inside."

She kissed his forehead. "Poor baby. You want me to get a

doctor? I would've already, but I figured, y'know, if you had a broken rib through your lung you'd be coming bloody froth from the nose and everything."

She really did have the damnedest bedroom rap for a debutante. "No, you're right. If he did me any lasting damage I'd know it by now. It's mostly my pride that's hurt." *And I'm a lying sack of shit.*

She kissed his forehead again. Then she looked intently into his eyes.

"You came very close to dying here," she said in a husky voice.

"You got that right."

"You know what I've always heard?" He shook his head. She leaned close. "I've always heard that after a close brush with death, the body needs to reaffirm life. It's, like, a biological response."

"Uh," Tristan said. "Well . . ."

She straightened up and skinned the T-shirt off over her head. Her breasts came tumbling out, all creamy and pink-tipped. They weren't quite as stupendous as her sister's, but he was willing to accord them their place as two of the four wonders of the natural world.

With one hand under the small of his back she lifted him slightly off the bed and skimmed off the undershorts which were all he'd been wearing when his uninvited guests turned up.

"Just think of this as therapy, hon," she said, and leaned on down.

29

"Are you ready to face the dragon?" King Jubal asked in rolling portentous tones. They were so unlike the usual kick-ass Kobold King that Tristan damned near busted out laughing.

"Yeah, right," he said. Jubal glowered at him. "I mean, yes, Your Majesty."

The main reason he was having trouble keeping a straight face, of course, was this whole *dragon* rap. There were some definite off-notes here in kobold land, and no mistake. But among the few things he was confident of in this world was that there were no dragons in it.

The antechamber to the Hall of Ordeals was not much smaller than the Throne Room, and it had a capacity crowd tonight. Stormy and Sandy stood on either side of their father, fresh-scrubbed and cute as cheerleaders, looking as if they ought to be carrying pom-poms and placards that read GO TRISTAN!

Too bad the *rest* of the kobolds looked as if they ought to be carrying placards that said GO DRAGON!

It was damned near all he could do not to give the King an elbow in the ribs—well, okay, so he'd have to stoop pretty far—and ask, *So, Majesty dude, what's the scam here anyway? You got a big-ass old crocodile on a chain? A mechanical toy with hydraulic jaws and a flamethrower snout? C'mon, fun's fun, but we all know the last thing in the world you have on the other side of those humongous bronze doors is a real dragon.*

But Jubal was having his fun and would not let go. He was all got up in his King suit today, with the purple robe with cat-fur trim, and his enormous crown, and his scepter that doubled as a back scratcher. Standing with his back up against the great doors he raised both hands. The room went silent.

"Many years ago," he began, with the air of a man reciting a familiar formula, "we consecrated the space beyond these doors to our own Heroes." Tristan *knew* he was playing ritual now, because he made not one smart-ass dig at Heroes. "In those chambers we trained and tested our craftiest and boldest warriors. In them we stored the trophies of the great victories of the kobold kind. In the heart of them the motorcycle WildFyre, the bikest of the bikes, coveted by all surface-dwellers, was put on display after Prince Buddy returned her to us.

"But lo!" The crowd echoed *lo*! "And woe!" The crowd echoed *woe*! "A terrible Dragon appeared in the Shaking Lands. Many kobolds did it slay, and then on a day dark with portents it found its way into the Land Below, into our Hall of Ordeals, where it remains to this day.

"Should any arise who would challenge this evil, and purge it from the heart of the realm, the joy of the kobold kind would know no bounds, and neither would our gratitude. Comes now a challenger before us. *Let's* get ready to *rumble*: Kobolds of all sexes, shapes, and colors, allow me to present to you—Tristan *Burningskull*!"

The crowd went nuts. Tristan held his arms up over his head and shook his fists in the air like a boxer. He had been ceremonially garbed that morning in a red headband, baggy camouflaged trousers, and Dallas-issue combat boots. The bare-chested *macho* effect was only somewhat spoiled by the bandages still wrapped tightly around his ribs. For armament they had returned his big Bowie. As a final touch giggling kobold maidens with pointy ears had daubed a thumb-wide stripe of lampblack beneath each eye. There was something vaguely familiar about the getup. It made him feel like a ninny.

I still think they'd rather be cheering the dragon. At least they had let him keep the thunderstone. Even though its batting average seemed to be sliding down toward the Mendoza Line of late.

King Jubal turned and extended a hand toward the doors. A

pointy-eared functionary pulled a lever. A locking mechanism disengaged with a metal squeal.

"All right, boy," the Kobold King said. "Go for it."

Sandy and Stormy came up either side of him, and bent down to kiss his cheeks simultaneously. It made him feel as if he were about eight and being sent back home from vacation by a pair of foxy aunts.

Sweating kobolds hauled the two doors open. He strode forward.

Even as he was letting his weight go forward for his first step something was trying to push him back: that *smell*. A stench of decaying meat, combined with a gamy predator odor like that from a panther's cage. *What the fuck, over?* He drove on. The doors swung to behind him with a suitably ominous thud.

On the other side was a brief passageway so low Tristan had to stoop slightly. He stalked forward as boldly as he could, knife in hand. Torches flickered in black iron holders set in either wall. Beyond he could see that the caverns opened out into a big torchlit chamber, broken up by stalagmites and other cave rock formations whose names he didn't know.

He heard motion. A scraping rustle, a squeak and click as of talons on stone. But *big*. He frowned. There was definitely something in here.

Yeah, probably a big amplifier blasting prerecorded special effects, he told himself as he neared the end of the foyer. As if in response a roar of stupefying volume almost blasted him back to the big bronze doors.

Holding onto that thought about amps and F/X, he peered cautiously out around the mouth of the entry tunnel.

Not fifty feet away a dragon stood. You couldn't miss it. A good twenty feet its great head rose from a limestone floor that was smoothed by millennia of trickling water and generations of sweaty kobold feet.

He looked down at his knife. He looked back at the dragon. Yep, there was no question about it: Each of the teeth set in those six-foot jaws was fully the size of the knife in his hand.

The dragon turned to look at him. It seemed to smile. That was probably just an effect of all those big-ass teeth. Probably.

He turned and walked up the short passage and pounded on the doors. A couple of beats, and a panel slid open in the right hand door, right by his hip. Jubal's beady eyes looked through.

"Is there a problem?" the Kobold King asked.

"That's a *Tyrannosaurus rex*," Tristan said.

Smile lines crinkled the corners of the eyes. "*Good* boy. You've done your homework. I knew I could count on you."

"Yes, but it's a real *T. rex*. A *live T. rex*."

"Yes, it is. I told you we had a dragon. How much closer can you get to a real dragon than that? It doesn't breathe fire, of course, but then our science types tell me that's impossible anyway."

"Just where in hell," said Tristan, feeling totally unreal, "did you *get* a Tyrannosaurus?" He successfully fought the urge to scream the question, but it was close.

Jubal held a finger up to the slit and wagged it. "No, no, no. We kobolds have our little secrets. Besides, what does it matter where it came from? It's there. WildFyre's on the other side. *You* work it out."

Rubbing his chin, Tristan glanced back down the short passageway. He jumped. The son of a bitch was bent down, *peering* at him.

"Um, your Majesty," he said sidelong to the King, who had his fingers through the slot now and was waving at the beast, "you couldn't, like, see your way clear to letting me have my Bolo back?"

"Sorry, son. We have very strict rules for Ordeals around here. What kind of an Ordeal would it be if the subject got to use guns?"

"What kind of Ordeals have real Tyrannosaurs?"

"Demanding ones. Very demanding ones. Now run along and play, or I'll haul you out and toss you to your fan club."

"What fan club?"

"The one Lizard Elvis is president of."

Tristan chewed his underlip. "Catch you later, Majesty," he said, and started back down the passageway.

As he turned back to the monster the force of its breath hit him full-on. It staggered him like a punch. *Whoo, does this boy need to floss, or what?*

He glanced down at his knife. He was almost embarrassed by it. It would mainly be useful for slashing his wrists.

If he were a real Hero, or at least a video Hero, he would flip the Bowie in the air, catch it by the blade, and throw it smack into the monster's left eye. At which point the Tyrannosaurus would reel around squalling and knocking over stalagmites with his tail. The difficulty was, the beast had a brain about the size of a walnut. What chance did he have of finding that in a head that massive?

It watched him as he warily approached. It was tipped well forward with its hips for pivots, the keel of its breast and its belly well off the ground, its tail held high for balance. Its eyes were fairly large, and mounted to give binocular vision. They probably didn't get a lot of detail—not much processing power to back them up—but they seemed keen enough.

Okay. I can't hurt the fuckard just yet. But maybe I can back him off. He grabbed a torch, and poked experimentally at the giant snout. The creature pulled its head back slightly. It showed no signs of going away.

All right, he thought. *Now, if I can just* time *this right.* He thrust the torch high, right at those eyes. The monster jerked its head up.

Tristan was racing flat-out forward, beneath the dagger-hung shelf of the lower jaw, ducking below its belly, out between its legs, *gone*—

It had amazing reflexes. It spun around. The tail caught Tristan on the hip and sent him flying.

30

He just managed to get his arms in front of his face and tucked into a ball.

He hit on his shoulder and rolled. It felt as if a seam split in his chest. Then he hit something soft and sprawled right into it.

A new wave of odor assaulted his nostrils. *"Jesus!"* he exclaimed. It was all he could do not to rear up gagging, but he knew if he moved he was meat.

So was what he'd landed in. He opened his eyes to discover he was lying amid a pile of cow parts in assorted stages of decay.

Bastard's a sloppy eater, he thought. Obviously the kobolds, helpful little devils that they were, had been tossing cattle to their resident monster. With those little bitty arms and hands—little by comparison; its biceps were easily as big as Tristan's thigh—it would have trouble hanging onto food, much less scooping up dropped morsels. The monster clearly just ate what it could take in a couple good chomps and forgot about the rest.

In fact, as he watched, the thing visibly forgot *him*. It turned its great head left and right for a few moments, obviously searching for its prey. Then it just sort of wandered away.

Okay, so as long as I don't move, I'm fine. It couldn't see him, and it sure as hell wasn't going to pick up his scent in all this slimy slippery shit. That was great, except a) lying here in a tangle of decomposing cow guts was not getting him WildFyre back; and b) who the hell wanted to lie around in a pile of cow guts any longer than absolutely necessary? Besides, sooner or later the monster was going to wander by and spot a chunk of meat that was big enough to make it worth bending over to scarf it up, and that would be it for Tristan Burningskull, Wanna-Be Hero and Maximum Lord of the Plains.

He took stock of the situation. He had managed to hang onto his knife, which still seemed pretty useless. He had lost the torch. That wasn't a big deal. There were others all around, enough to keep the caverns brightly lit, if well supplied with constantly shifted shadows. In the adventure videos, of course, prehistoric monsters were afraid of fire, and an adventurer armed with a torch could stand them off. This bad boy obviously didn't like the stuff, but seemed unconvinced there was enough of it to do him actual harm. So was Tristan.

So the torches were unlikely to be a big help. But those *shadows* they cast . . .

Tristan was guessing what it mainly saw was *motion*. The torches created plenty of those, darting and shifting constantly among the niches and columns of the Hall of Ordeals cavern complex—if that was really what the kobolds called this place, and they hadn't just made that up to shine him on, as he more than half suspected. The beast ignored the shadows. Obviously its tiny brain had learned to filter that motion out, as it would the motion of wind-stirred giant ferns back in its native Jurassic or Triassic or Coke Classic or whatever you called its time period.

No, he thought, *not native*. He wasn't road-dopey enough to believe this thing had survived 100 million years in some damp cave. He remembered scanning the newspapers from the days just before StarFall, photographically preserved in the Reader units of the Library. There had been a front-page article which he had to read, because he'd always loved dinosaurs, from the campfire nights when Golden Marcia sang of dinosaurs walking the Earth. The piece claimed that scientists had somehow succeeded in reconstituting dinosaur DNA. There was speculation that they might actually try to clone some of the long-extinct beasts.

Obviously, they'd done more than *try*. But that was two hundred years ago. What this one was doing alive—not to mention way the hell down here in a cave somewhere—he hadn't a clue.

He did have a clue as to how he was going to try and handle the monster. He just didn't know if it had a prayer of working.

Ignoring the pain movement sent blazing through his chest, he came up to all fours, propelled himself forward, got his feet beneath him, and ran like a mother at an angle away from the monster, toward the interior of the complex.

He hadn't made six steps before the thing spotted him. It uttered a happy whistling roar that almost burst his eardrums and came for him.

In the days before StarFall when the books Tristan had read on dinosaurs were written, there was dispute about whether the dinosaurs were warm-blooded and fast or cold-blooded and sluggish. Cold & Sluggish had been fighting a rearguard action, and he could now say with complete confidence that it was in fact out to lunch. That puppy whipped around like a cutting horse and came after him like a buzz bomb, firing off those extra-large drumsticks.

In fact it gained on him at a pretty good clip as he sprinted flat-out. He could hear it thundering up on him. *"Fuck, fuck, fuck, fuck, fuck!"* he yelped, and hurled himself into a little grotto with a low-hanging arch of roof.

For all its obvious agility the creature's huge-taloned feet did not give it good traction on the slick stone floor. It backpedaled frantically, and piled into the wall with an awe-inspiring crash.

Tristan was duly awed, and also he was winded and knocked to shit by his landing, but he made himself pop up and dart out again before the horror could recover from being stunned.

He was aiming for another nook about fifty yards in, toward the limit of visibility among the walls and rock curtains and columns of melted-looking stone. He had just gotten halfway when he heard the freight-train rumble on his tail. He dodged between a couple of stalagmites as big around as he was.

He heard them splinter as the monster trucked right on through. He took a running dive into the niche.

Skidding, the monster crashed headfirst into the wall again. *That's the trouble with having a brain the size of a walnut. It takes a while for experience to pound those new lessons home.*

He was winded and hurting but he couldn't rest; the whole plan depended on not giving the monster time to. He dodged past the dazed bulk and raced for another shelter.

And so they progressed deeper into the complex, with the monster banging off the walls and pillars like some bizarre pinball game. Tristan's legs turned to jelly, and he seemed to be breathing torn-away sheets of his own lung tissue. But he managed to keep those horrible dagger teeth out of his hide.

When he was barely able to move, and the fantastic rock shapes of the cave had begun to spin around him, he found himself among a forest of stalagmites joined to stalactites dropping from above, too thick and densely clustered for the monster to bull through. But the monster was on the trail now, and thoroughly pissed off from getting his face pounded in. Tristan was convinced this wasn't a hunter-prey thing anymore. It was *personal*.

The thing was going to get him too. He was too rubber-legged to make any more fast takeoffs. *Once the fuckard picks his way through those columns my ass is an appetizer*, he knew, *unless I can find me another cozy little niche to die in . . .*

And the frozen forest of stalagmites fell away, and the cavern opened up, and there in the middle of the floor stood WildFyre.

Tristan stopped and just stared, despite the inexorable crashing and banging of the monster working its way on his trail. It was the most beautiful sight he had ever seen.

It was *gold*. Instead of silver, the normally chromed surfaces of the machine, the forks with the discreet four-inch extension, the roaster-style bars, the primary cover and oil tanks and pipes, were brilliant metallic gold. The frame was gold-enameled; the gas tank and the cut, flared, and scooped rear fender were red with yellow trim. It was perfection, everything a road machine should be, glowing so bright it hurt the eyes.

In fact it was glowing so bright Tristan got suspicious and glanced up. Sure enough; there were little Fresnel spotlights hung from the ceiling to illuminate the glorious ride.

A furious roar made him wince. The Tyrannosaurus was about to get clear and come for him. Feeling new strength flow through his legs, he ran to the bike.

At close range it was even more breathtaking. Tristan was a piss-poor wrench himself, but he knew enough to appreciate the Art. This was its highest point. He reached a hand and touched it, and it was as if current flowed. He swung aboard.

It was as if the big machine had become a part of his body. As he put his hands on the bars he almost forgot his danger—almost. He was so wrapped up in the bike that it took him a moment to notice what was by his right knee.

It was a kobold-made grenade launcher, 40-mm, hung from the bars in a nylon scabbard.

"Hot *damn*," he said. He pulled the weapon out, broke it open shotgun-style. There was a round chambered. The circles painted on its base around its primer and base plug were red, gold, and yellow. By modern usage that identified it as High Explosive, Dual Purpose. That meant it had a shaped-charge warhead for defeating light armor. It could take down an armored car easy—or an errant thunder lizard.

The monster had almost made it through. Its glittering eyes were fixed on him expectantly.

He raised the weapon to his shoulder, sighted down the fat barrel. There was no need to elevate the rear sight. He could barely miss at this range; his big concern was to fire before the monster got within the ten yards the projectile had to fly before it would arm itself. He held aim right between those folded little two-clawed hands and took up the trigger slack.

Then he lowered the weapon. "Aw, bullshit," he said. "I can't do this."

He'd always loved dinosaurs. He was goddamned if he was going to kill the last one on Earth. Not unless he had no option.

And he had one big option here: He was a Stormrider born and bred, with history greatest ride between his legs. Let the fuckard *try* and catch him now. He slid the launcher back in its holster, not without regret, and kicked the starter.

The behemoth charged.

The big V-Twin engine roared instantly to full-throated life. The monster froze in its tracks.

Letting the engine idle, Tristan stared in surprise at the giant creature. He glanced down at the machine, then back at the monster. It still hadn't moved.

He twitched the throttle. The engine roared. The Tyrannosaurus flinched.

"Oh, yeah?" he said, and smiled beneath the rakish sweep of his mustache. "You're afraid of my little beauty here, aren't you?"

He wound the engine up to full revolutions. The dinosaur turned and fled in terror.

Tristan's triumphant laughter chased it out of sight. Then he rode WildFyre out of the Hall of Ordeals. The bronze doors opened to his approach.

A storm front of applause greeted him. Sandy was jumping up and down and whooping. Stormy grinned and gave him a thumbs-up. Jubal stood there nodding his big bald crown-laden head.

"Good show, kid. We watched it all on the monitors." He jerked a thumb to the big screen TV set in the walls, which had been uncovered since Tristan went into the Hall. "I got just one question to ask you."

Tristan swayed in his saddle. Everything was starting to catch up to him again. "Ask away."

"Why didn't you go ahead and kill the ugly son of a bitch? You had him right in your sights."

Tristan blew out a long breath between pursed lips. "I couldn't do it."

"Why not? That's a monster in there. An abomination."

"Actually, I think it's kind of cool, now that it's not on my case any longer. Once I had my bike it was no threat to me, so I, uh, well . . ."

A smile had begun to play around the corners of Jubal's ugly mug. A bomb went off behind Tristan's eyes.

"You little motherfucker," he snarled. He snatched the launcher out of its scabbard, aimed it up one-handed toward the ceiling, and started to take the slack back in on the trigger. The crowd gasped and shrank away.

"If I pull the trigger a whole bunch of us are gonna be toast, right?"

Sandy giggled and bounced up and down, clapping her hands. "See, Daddy? I told you he'd figure it out."

"He took his own sweet time about it." Tristan lowered the weapon. The King deftly plucked it from his fingers.

"You guessed right, Junior," Jubal said, cracking the launcher open and pulling out the round. "The ten-yard free-flight safety has been disabled, and—as you can see—the barrel's blocked. If you'd tried to pop our little pet, you'd be resting in pieces now."

If Sandy and Stormy hadn't suddenly been holding him up on either side like well-upholstered bookends, he would have fallen. "Why?"

"Because we've decided the Catheads, and more particularly the Fusion, constitute a major threat to our safety. We're going to lend your bike-trash buddies a *hand*, son. That little fact added to your possession of WildFyre would make you a big bastard indeed on the Plains.

"If your gut reflex was going to be to to go ahead and waste something because it was different and ugly . . ." He shrugged. "We figured you'd be better off dead. No hard feelings?"

"My *ass*," Tristan said. He started to climb off the bike in order to punch the Kobold King in the nose.

He fainted instead.

He was awakened by a weight coming onto the right side of his bed. He started to roll away, going for his Bolo, which he'd tucked under the mattress after they returned it.

A hand caught his arm and rolled him back over. He found himself staring up between Sandy's imposing bare breasts at her smiling face.

"There, now, baby," she said. "Don't worry. It's only me."

He grinned up at her in the dark. "I feel better already."

He was reaching for her when there was a soft *pop*. Stormy was standing on the far side of the bed. She was buck naked too.

"Uh, hi, Stormy," Tristan said, thinking, *Great. I survive confrontations with Tyrannosaurs and rigged grenade launchers, only to be crushed to death in the world's biggest cat fight.* "I, uh . . . you can see, I'm a little busy . . ."

For a handful of heartbeats the twins' eyes held each other in silent communication. Then Stormy grinned.

"Don't worry, hon," she said. "My sister and I are *used* to sharing."

31

"Your Majesty," panted the black-clad biker with the bloody bandage knotted around his head, covering one eye. "We're taking heavy casualties. But their fire's slackin' up big time. We're fixin' to take 'em down."

King Billy nodded his crowned head. He was piled atop his gleaming black Carondelet with his staff clustered thickly around him—the High Free Folk snipers were persistent and too damned accurate for comfort. The five-hundred-rider Cat-head reserve winged out in battle array to either side. The growl of their idling engines sounded in his ears like continuous thunder. Over it you could still hear the savage crackle of a firefight, like hail on a tin roof.

"Good," he said, rubbing his thickly bearded jowls. "I'm ready to get this over with."

A thousand yards away through the drizzle lay the low ridge behind which the defeated army of the High Free Folk had finally been brought to bay. It was a good defensive position. John Hammerhand had been a far more formidable foe in abject defeat than he had when he was riding off to war, confident in his own success and contemptuous of niceties like *tactics*.

King Billy, that scowling mountain of a man, had waited long enough for the final triumph he was about to claim. The first victory west of Plattesburg had been convincing, sure, but it had left Hammerhand with much of his force intact. Worse, it had inflicted heavier casualties on the Nation than Billy had ever thought possible.

They would suck casualties this day too, may the Demons of Dissonance and Discord tear out Hammerhand's liver. But counting the yellowrobe Fusion troopies from east of the Missus Hip—and King Billy would no longer discount them with a motor nomad's reflex contempt, not after seeing them in action—he had upwards of two thousand fighters, well armed and supplied. Against him Hammerhand could muster maybe seven hundred, exhausted, depressed, low on ammo, and lower on options.

So let the casualties fall where they may. The Fusion missionaries said they would all fly away to join that great and cosmic One which was the goal of all life anyway. For hundreds of miles Billy had been striving to pin down Hammerhand's still-highly mobile and elusive force, throwing sweeps first around his left flank and then the right. His continuous one-two punches had never connected solidly—until now. Now the nomads had been pinned with their backs to a loop of the South Platte, gorged white and wild with runoff from the Rockies rising blue to the west. However well they fought now, when the sun, unseen above clotted yellow clouds, finally set, they would be destroyed. King Billy would at last be undisputed Lord of the Plains.

He smiled.

"Remember not to become too entangled in the ropes of your self, fellow soul," the Most Effaced said at his elbow.

King Billy grunted. The shriveled little bastard—that is, his most exalted and beloved spiritual teacher—had an uncomfortable knack for reading his thoughts. Which should not surprise the King, since the Most Effaced claimed to be able to do just that.

King Billy glanced away. The Fusion missionary's Acolyte forked her own sled nearby with the ease of a nomad babe. She inclined her totally bald head, which the King always found provocative, ever so slightly, narrowed those almond-sapphire eyes, and smiled.

King Billy felt a twinge at the base of the royal nut-sac. *Damn good job the Most Effaced can't read* all *my thoughts*. He sometimes, deep down in his majestic belly, wondered what he had won himself and his clan by accepting Fusion. The spiritual peace they offered he only got in snatches, and in truth even a hard, brutal bastard like King Billy felt a certain queasiness over some of the deeper Mysteries to which he had been initiated. The power of the Fusion was undeniable, of course. It had been King Billy's conviction that their Medicine was too great to withstand, not any spiritual yearning, that led him to join.

But looking at the way the damp saffron robes molded themselves to the Acolyte's long, wiry-muscled form . . . he replayed in his mind the line about getting spiritual peace in snatches. Yes, indeed, there were fringe benefits to his Oneness with Fusion . . .

The Most Effaced laid gentle brown fingertips on his black-clad arm. "Fellow soul, there is one matter that concerns me."

King Billy inclined his head on its dais of chins. "Yes, Soul?"

The missionary pointed back to the east. The clouds back there were a muddy yellow, drawn down toward the Earth in points. "Wolf's Teats," the nomads called them. They meant one thing and one thing only.

"Tornadoes," the Most Effaced said. As he spoke, tapering blackness stretched down from the clouds like fingers, to brush tentatively at the ground and then withdraw. "They are a manifestation of Nature, herself one of the purest manifestations of that Oneness we adore. Yet they are very powerful, and very random. Should they not concern us?"

King Billy had to choke down a laugh. The Most Effaced was wise and powerful, but he was still an Easterner, with an Easterner's ignorance of the Plains.

"They always head east, soul," he said. "They're behind us. They'll only go away from us." *Which will put the hard damned arm on all this defeatist talk I've been hearing today, how there's a relief column out of Osagerie bearing down on us from behind. As if the Osage had any interest in pulling scooter-trash nuts out of the fire, or would dare try if they did, what with Dallas giving the hungry eye to the Red Earth oil fields.*

Besides, even if the tailheads did try to intervene, they'd never make it this far. The Plains themselves would destroy them. The floods and ashfalls and quakes and, of course, the Stalking Wind. And the Catheads would've heard their radio traffic by now, even with atmospherics bad as they were; your City soldiers loved to hear themselves talk. It was all total bushwa. Still, the bros had a way of talking things up bigger than they were. King Billy had been compelled to bust a few heads.

"If you're sure, fellow soul," the Most Effaced said. He clearly wasn't.

The King smiled. Though the Cathead King had given himself and his people over to the Fusion after its missionaries had shown him secret and unmistakable proofs of its Power, part of him still enjoyed seeing their serenity fucked with. They were just too cool sometimes.

He laid both big hands upon his bars and gunned his engine. "The moment has come," he said. "Let's finish this."

A whistling noise rose in his ears. He cocked his mighty head to one side. There was something awfully familiar about that—

A bright flash off to the right. A handful of bikes fell over and began to burn, alcohol and gas fumes pale in the misting rain.

"What the—" the whistle again, much louder this time "—fucking *fuck*?"

Explosions raked the Cathead reserve, tossing parts of men and machines in all directions.

"What is going on, fellow soul?" the Most Effaced asked calmly.

"We're being mortared, you skinny little quack!"

Through the ringing the blasts had laid on his ears he heard another, even more ominous sound: the slow, heavy stop-and-go drumming of .50-caliber machine-gun fire. Cathead riders started to fall like wheat to the scythe.

King Billy had time to see even bigger flashes go off way ahead, among the ranks of his attacking army. Then he turned.

The yellowrobe foot soldiers were racing for their vehicles. A canvasback truck exploded as he watched. Fusion initiates came tumbling out flapping and reeling like drunk crows, their yellow robes aflame.

Over a swell to the east came a line of light combat cars, with machine guns winking from their roll bars. *Osage! What the fuck!*

But it wasn't just the tailheads. In the center of that onrushing line, leading the entire pack, came a lonely figure mounted on an outlaw sled that seemed to glow with a golden light of its own.

• • •

"*Yee*-haa!" Tristan yelled, though nobody could hear him but him. He was in the wind again for true.

It had been a desperate wild journey across the storm- and quake- and Caner-racked Plains. He had re-enacted his ancestor's famous Hard Ride, but this time there was help. On the other hand, the Cats weren't the sag-nuts little band of child-molesters and chicken-stealers they'd been in Anse the One-Eyed's time.

A quarter of the men and machines his force had left Osagerie with two days before lay strung out behind them. Some could be repaired and recovered, some could not. They'd taken more losses during the last two hours, when Tristan had led his reluctant joint command on a real, live Stormride through the tornado zone. The Osage were not crazy with joy at the prospect of Dancin' with Mr. D—much less the kobolds, most of whom had never seen weather before. But they weren't about to let some scooter-trash nomad on a shiny bike show them up. Even if he was a Hero.

They came through the Stalking Winds with maybe four hundred troops. Less than half the numbers of the joint Fusion/Cathead reserve they were tackling now. But they had surprise, they had awesome firepower, and they had WildFyre.

The shave-headed Fusion groundpounders hadn't bothered to dig in. Why should they? They were truck soldiers, and if there was any fighting to do that day they were going to be mounting up and riding to it, not the other way around.

They were well armed and had good discipline, plus they had the fanatic True Believer's certainty of Ultimate Victory. But there's nothing to make a soldier's heart go bad like getting hit good and hard in the rear.

By the time Tristan led his cage cavalry in among the yellowrobes' transport they had come apart as a fighting force under savage physical and moral shock attack. Tristan laughed and slew them. If they stood he ran them down. If they ran he shot them in the back with his Bolo.

He wove WildFyre in and out among burning trucks ignited by mortars or the Osage heavy machine guns mounted on their precious few surviving armored cars, which were hanging back to give fire support. A few last mortar bombs cracked off and the barrage lifted. It had done its work.

Tristan snarled past the flat snout of a Quad Cities transport

into the midst of a bunch of Fusion troopies, who immediately
scattered like quail. All but one, standing thirty yards away,
calm as if he were on the rifle range, lining a Water Horse storm
carbine for a shot at Tristan. Tristan pointed the Bolo at him and
pulled the trigger.

Nothing happened. He had made the sag-nuts Civic soldier's
worst mistake: fired his piece dry without knowing it. Cursing
himself he prepared to lay WildFyre down, hoping it would take
him out of the imminent bullet-stream—

The yellowrobe exploded like a bag of tomatoes dropped
from a height. An open-topped Bison armored carrier had come
bucketing out on the far side of him from Tristan. Standing up
in it, firing over the side, was none other than Sandy, the Kobold
King's blond Power-Lifting Daughter.

While her sister was back directing the main kobold contingent, which was pouring all that lovely tube and rocket artillery
fire into the Cats, Sandy was riding to battle, leading a picked
platoon of her security goons.

Sandy was armed with a custom storm carbine. Of course, a
"storm carbine" to an eight-foot kobold Valkyrie babe was an
automatic rifle in full-power .50 caliber, which she whipped
around as lightly as a Homeland rag ever did his M52. It put a
man in a world of hurt when it connected.

He gave her a thumbs-up and skidded WildFyre to a broadside halt. They had gone all the way through the Fusion contingent, scattering them beyond hope of a rally. Now they faced
the Cathead reserve line.

Kobold mortars and Osage river guns had torn great gaping
fiery holes in the Cat line. But the Cats weren't like City soldiers, or even their Fusion allies. They were better organized
than their hostile Plains cousins, but at base they were similar:
an army of warriors, each fighting, ultimately, as an individual.
They were more likely to melt away under the hammering of a
face-up firefight than rags—regulars—but when something
really unexpectedly horrible happened, like an assault from behind, they were less likely to shatter. They could, if their hearts
were right, display a resiliency City commanders could only
dream of.

Today was one of those days. King Billy himself was head of
this body, and he had not won kingship of the Cathead Nation in
a raffle. The Cats believed in their giant monarch with all their

black and mingy hearts. For all the bad things you could say about him—he was a torturer, a rapist, a murderer, a treacherous bastard who'd embrace a man like a brother and leave his dirk in his back—he had never let them down.

Tristan made a hacking motion of his arm. The Bison stopped and began to disgorge kobolds in coal-scuttle helmets. The combat cars began to peel away to positions where they could fire from the cover of wrecked or abandoned trucks. The Osage troops carriers, following closely behind the assault line, halted. The rifle squads dismounted and went to ground, quickly and efficiently.

Tristan circled WildFyre back among the dead transport, dismounted, and laid her down. No point in hanging his dick in the breeze for every Cathead in the line to make a target of. He was not exactly inconspicuous on WildFyre.

He reloaded his Bolo and put it away. He drew the Water Horse M52 from its scabbard, and checked to make sure the ancient cavalry saber Randy Firecloud had given him as a good-luck parting gift was loose in its sheath. He didn't like either as well as what he'd lost to Pud and his low-down Chosen Few backshot buddies, but they'd do the job.

The Cathead charge was doomed from the outset. Even without their beefy armored cars, already rolling up to join them, the Osage had a real shitstorm of firepower at hand. But the sole alternative was to beat cheeks left and right and fight again some other day.

That would doom the greater Cathead force engaged with the trapped nomad army a thousand yards ahead. It was enormously larger than the relief column, sure enough. But if the column hit it from behind—and Stormy's big rocket tubes were already pasting it—it would be shattered against the anvil of Hammerhand's dug-in desperados and desperadettes.

King Billy still wanted his victory. Bastard though he was, he was a Stormrider too. At the crunch he was willing to put his faith in raw guts and hard riding. Hammerhand had not been *completely* wrong: Sometimes ballsy works.

The Cats came on. The Osage automatic weapons and kobold grenade launchers just reaped them. It tore steaming chunks from Tristan's heart to see nomad saddles relentlessly emptied by disciplined City-soldier fire—but he was lying in a regulation prone position, cracking single aimed shots at the enemy, and most times when he pulled one off he drained a saddle too. This was no time for sentiment.

The relievers' fire was awesome and well-directed. But it wasn't enough to halt the Cathead charge.

Screaming like wounded catamounts, the black-clad riders rolled over the rifle line.

32

Tristan hauled WildFyre upright, swung abroad her, kicked her alive. A Cathead rode at him swinging a chain. He slashed his face open with the saber.

He rode among the wrecked Fusion trucks, dodging Cats when he encountered them, only laying about with his sword to get clear. He had no time to lose.

What with the dead and fled, the relievers now outnumbered the Cats by a space. But what was happening here was what King Billy had been hoping for, what City commanders most feared: The nomads had got to grips with the regulars, where the fighting was bad-breath to bad-breath and the stunning City firepower wasn't worth a pinch of dried owl shit.

He came around a burning truck and saw what he was looking for. Catheads had caught an Osage armored car parked and were swarming over it like ants. Astride his bike nearby, a spiked ball-head mace with a three-foot handle in his hand, stood King Billy his bad self.

"Billy!" Tristan roared. "Your fat ass is *mine*!" He charged.

The king turned to face this new onslaught. His vast ugly face split in a grin. "Oneness bless you, boy! You've gone and brought me WildFyre! I love you so much I think I'll fuck you before I finish you off."

"Fuck *this*." Tristan aimed an overhead slash at the Cathead king. With surprising agility King Billy leaned back out of the way. The whistling blow cut only air.

Tristan ducked a return swipe that would have ripped his head off his shoulders, went past, and wheeled his bike around. And then they were going round and round like dogs, engines snarling, steel clanging off steel, speed against strength.

Tristan quickly found he could nick his opponent, but King Billy wasn't slow, and never gave him a clearing for a solid cut or thrust. And King Billy was damned near as strong as the King's Power-Lifting Daughters. Tristan could not block his blows directly, only try to deflect them enough so he could bend out of the way.

"See, boy?" King Billy puffed, grinning hugely. "You ain't strong enough for me. Give it up, boy. Accept the One. Cease to exist."

Tristan hawked and spat. The glob caught King Billy full on his black-bearded cheek.

"You butthole surfer!" King Billy exclaimed. He fired a whistling blow full overhand. Tristan threw himself back almost out of the saddle momentarily letting go of the bars.

The spiked mace-head glanced off WildFyre's gas tank. It didn't even scratch the finish.

King Billy goggled. While he was coping with that Tristan leaned forward and stabbed him in the belly.

King Billy bellowed. Tristan barely yanked his saber back in time to avoid having it knocked spinning from his hand. The problem was, nailing King Billy in the gut wasn't the same as getting him in the *guts*. All that flab was backed with hard muscle and an extremely tough abdominal wall. It was good armor in its own right.

But if Tristan hadn't done him lasting hurt, Tristan had still hurt him. He could see the bigger man's eyes narrow with pain every time he swung.

"Give it up, fatso. It's over. Your Fusion friends ain't shit. You sold your soul and the Cathead Nation for chump change."

The Cathead's eyes went red. He threw his mace high over his head for a blow that would hammer Tristan into the planet, WildFyre and all. Tristan watched it, timed it. When King Billy dropped it with a steam-whistle scream he yanked the bars way over and spun out of the way.

With a backhand cut he chopped King Billy's overextended mace hand clean off.

King Billy bellowed in agony. He turned the black Carondelet to flee. He had no hand to work the throttle now. Tristan raised his saber to follow.

He froze.

It was the strangest feeling he'd ever known. He was still awake, still full of adrenaline strength and fury that the constant throbbing in his chest only served to hone. But he could not control his body.

As if of its own accord, his head turned. A little brown guy with an enormous head stood fifty feet away, all dressed in yellow robes. He smiled at Tristan.

"You doubted the power of the Fusion, young Burningskull," the man said. "Now you see it cannot be resisted. The time has come to return to that Oneness you thought, in your folly, to flee and fight against."

King Billy's bodyguard was circling round him, grinning like wolves. He struggled to win command of his limbs, but it did no good. He couldn't find anything to fight *against*.

Someone stood behind the little man. Like him she wore yellow. She was taller. Her eyes were slanted, and so blue they pierced Tristan's head like jacketed bullets when they met his.

She smiled. "You perceive correctly. We have met before." She laughed. "A pity we will not meet again, this side of One."

"Daughter," the yellowrobe said without turning, "beware the traps of ego."

The fine bald head hung. "Forgive me, Most Effaced. Permit me to atone by sending him to One."

The little man shook his head. It had yellow and white lines painted on it. "No, daughter, I fear that's still your Self talking." He nodded. "Let *them* take care of him. It will help them work out their karma."

They were King Billy's bully boys, who had him surrounded now. "Get ready to do some serious screaming," a blond-bearded one said. He plucked the saber from Tristan's helpless fingers.

The yellow-robed man's head exploded.

Instantly Tristan was back in control. He grabbed a fistful of yellow hair, and dragged the startled Cathead's face forward into a head butt. Then he let himself go slack and slide from WildFyre's saddle.

The sled went over the other way, toppling a rider. Tristan's sudden dead weight dragged the stunned Cathead out of his own saddle on top of him. Fortunately his bike didn't follow.

With the blond Cat a stinking weight on top of him, Tristan grabbed the man's Leech & Rigdon .44 Magnum revolver from its cross-draw holster. Pinning the man to him with his left arm he reached around his bulk with the piece, put the muzzle practically against a Cathead's leather-clad knee, and blew the leg off.

He cranked off four more shots, dropping two more Catheads and sending a third away bleeding. The man whose gun he'd borrowed got both fists on the ground and broke Tristan's grip, rearing up with a roar of triumph.

"Really fucking stupid," was Tristan's comment. He put the man's own pistol to the bridge of his nose and blew away the top of his head.

He threw the flopping, splashing corpse off him and rolled to his feet, dropping the empty revolver and drawing his Bolo. The remaining Catheads were in full flight, bearing their injured King with them. Sandy was there, giant storm carbine in her hand, her warty little bastards with her.

She caught him as he swayed and almost collapsed. "That's two I owe you," he said. "You might have made it three if Blondie had been a little quicker on the uptake."

She frowned. "What are you talking about? I shot that one guy who was holding down on you by the truck."

"You didn't pop old Baldy's head for him?"

She shook her head. "When we got here you were lying in the middle of like a bunch of Catheads blowing parts off them. The only bald person I saw was that little girl, and she was riding off as fast as her motorbike would carry her."

"Little girl?" It took a moment to register that she was talking about the Acolyte—who stood six feet tall if she stood an inch. Being eight feet tall gives you a different perspective.

He patted her arm that was holding him up. "I'm okay, now. Let's wrap this thing up."

She grinned.

King Billy was right to launch his final frantic charge, though it cost him his hand and most of his surviving men.

The Osage motorized infantry closed to within four hundred yards of the Cathead main force in their trucks, dismounted, and deployed into a firing line again. Then they massacred the Cats and Fusion soldiers with their support weapons, their machine guns, mortars, and grenade launchers.

The trapped Catheads mounted three countercharges of their own. None got close. They had too much ground to cover, and the Osage riflemen chimed in once they got within three hundred yards. Not one black rider made it closer than a hundred.

When it was done, over a thousand Catheads and allies lay dead between the two fires. At least three hundred more of the reserve had fallen. The proud Nation was demolished.

The record for the worst military disaster in nomad history had stood for sixteen days.

EPILOGUE

With Tristan riding WildFyre in front of the line, there was no chance of a combat-shocked Stormrider mistaking the relief force for enemies and opening fire. No one seeing that splendid bike rolling forward, radiant gold in the light of the sun that had broken through the clouds, could doubt what had just happened.

The last of the Hardriders had ridden WildFyre to the rescue of his embattled friends, just as the first one had.

From the rifle pits and trenches they had scooped out of the merciless earth rose the survivors of the High Free Folk. They were too drained by all they had been through to do much more than stare.

Except for a group way off to the left, with a heap of Cathead slain before them. They were standing up, whooping and hollering and waving their shirts. Tristan turned his front wheel that way and lined WildFyre out full-bore.

It was the Jokers and Outlaws. There was Jovanne, and Pony, and Tooth, and the others. A pitiful remnant, though they seemed not to have lost many since he had taken leave of them. He rode WildFyre right into the middle of them. They swarmed him in a laughing, crying, back-slapping mob.

He swung off. Jovanne was standing right beside him. "Do you always have to be such a showboat?" she asked. What started off coolly snide ended in a tearful rush, and strong arms wrapped around his neck.

"Oh, Tristan," she said, "I never thought I'd see you again."

"I never thought you'd see me again either," he said.

He noticed Little Teal standing with the butt of her 7-mm Magnum—almost as tall as she was—grounded and her arms wrapped lovingly about it. She was smiling. He hadn't seen her do that since the Burning Skull fight, when her man Big Jupe fell.

"You like my shot?" she asked.

"Which shot."

"The one that busted that Fusion fuckard's bald head at a good thousand yards," she said with enormous satisfaction. "I've been waiting for a decent shot at one of the Cat bosses since this whole fandango began. That was the first one they let me have."

"Glad to be of service," Tristan said. "You saved my ass."

The clans had gathered around WildFyre to make appropriate oohing and ahhing sounds. "A hell of a ride," Jovanne murmured in his ear.

"In more ways than one."

"I didn't think you could pull it off."

"That makes two of us. Say, could you not hug me so tight, babe? I got a few busted ribs over on that side."

"What happened?"

"Some sumbitch blasted me with a Shocker at about five feet."

She took a step back and looked at him critically. "I let you out of my sight for a few days and look what happens," she said.

"That isn't half of it."

"By the way," she said, patting him on the uninjured side of his chest, "there's somebody else waiting to say hi."

His eyes followed her nod, and there to one side stood—

"Jeremy? *Ferret?*"

When the little man finally pried himself free of the rib-crushing embrace, Tristan said, "How the hell did you survive that mace-shot to the head? You must have a thicker skull than I thought."

"I don't, but you must. You think the Black Avenger went around with all that metal in front of his face without having a helmet under the hood? Get real. The fuckard put me down, but not to stay."

Tristan saw Vengeance lying on its side behind a bush thirty yards away. "So the Avenger's come out from behind the mask?"

Jeremy shrugged. "The gag ran long enough. It was getting to be kind of a pain, going around in that mask. Say . . ." He brushed his grimy cheek with a thumb, a gesture Tristan remembered well from Dorm C days. "Just how was it you were able to ride up those bastards' tailpipes without their hearing your traffic? No way you kept a force that size together without plenty of chatter on the airwaves."

The answer was *kobold telepathy.* Only a tiny minority had it, and most of them were relatives at one remove or another of the royal line. A few of them scattered among the force had been enough to keep decent command and control.

Tristan put his hand on his friend's shoulder. "I'll tell you later." He wasn't sure how his ultra-rational friend was going to take this. Gods knew *he'd* had trouble with it.

The shadows fell across them. *Big* shadows.

Jeremy turned around and stared up at the King's Power-Lifting Daughters. "Jumping Jesus on roller skates," he said.

"Tristan," Sandy said, "we met the *nicest* man. He says he's a friend of yours."

And yes, standing between them like a *nouvelle cuisine* slice of meat between a sesame-seed bun and a pumpernickel, his arm around either giant's waist, stood Jammer his own black self, grinning wider beneath his wraparound mirror shades than Tristan had ever seen him grin before.

"Well, Tristan, you've gone and done it. One-upped old Anse big time. And these two delightful little girls have been telling me you used WildFyre to defeat an honest-to-good *Tyrannosaurus.*"

He shook his head. "I tell you, son, you Hardriders are the best thing going for us Bards. I'll be cranking out songs about this for *years.*"

A step behind him, Tristan sensed a familiar presence. Stormy seemed a little out of it—she had been throwing her guts up the last time Tristan saw her. She had never before seen first-hand the effects of the destructive hardware she lavished such love and genius on.

Sandy, though, had seen the elephant back in the Shaking Lands. She was as alert as ever. Her blue eyes narrowed.

"Who's this?" she asked. "Your little girlfriend?"

An arm slipped around Tristan's waist. He smiled feebly. "Uh, this is Jovanne. President of the Jokers MC. Uh, Jovanne, you've heard of the Kobold King's Power-Lifting Daughters? This is them. Stormy and Sandy."

Jovanne looked up at them like a border collie eying a pair of Great Danes. "Tristan," she said, "don't tell me you're boffing *both* of them?"

If the Earth is planning on opening beneath my feet and swallowing me at any point in my life, Tristan thought, *now's as good a time as any to do it*.

"Yo! Tristan! Tristan Burningskull!"

Never in my whole did I expect to be glad to hear that voice, he thought. He turned out of from Jovanne's possessive grasp to face the speaker.

"Hammerhand," he said. "So you're still alive."

John Hammerhand smiled. "I'm way too mean for the likes of King Billy to kill."

Tristan felt anger boil up inside him. *About a thousand of the brothers and sisters who trusted you enough to follow you into battle sure as hell weren't*, he thought.

Hammerhand laid a hand on his shoulder, said, "Excuse me, ladies," and guided Tristan away from the standoff. He still had a cloud of ManLodge Death Commandos drifting along after him, Tristan saw. A lot of the starch and swagger had gone out of them, though, and in their eyes Tristan saw the thousand-yard unfocused stare of men who seen too much for one lifetime.

Yeah. All your goddamn chest-puffing and drum-beating. How much do all those stack up to when you've got Hell staring you in the eye? Maybe it was after-battle reaction setting in, but he was seething with a desire to tee off on Hammerhand, so great he was practically jumping out of his skin. *This isn't the* time, he told himself.

Hammerhand was talking in that deep rich voice of his. ". . . done a real service for the High Free Folk. But tell me one thing, son. Are those *kobolds* I see with you?"

"Yes."

He shook his blond head admiringly. "How did you manage to get them to come out of their caves and lend us a hand in our hour of need?"

• • •

The truth was, wily old King Jubal had intended to do it all along. The Fusion missionaries who had visited the Land Below had made a big impression on him, and it wasn't favorable.

"They're powerful sorcerers," His Majesty had said, when Tristan's cuts and scrapes from his personal Ordeal had been seen to, and they were sitting alone in the King's chambers knocking back a few. The word for those chambers was *opulent*. Jubal was a creature who liked his comforts.

"Almost as powerful as we are. Take 'em all together, you got trouble. I've been looking to take a hand for months, but I didn't see a way until you turned up."

"So it was all a setup?" Somehow the urge to punch the king out had evaporated. Which was just as well, since a calm, reflective Tristan wasn't sure he could.

Jubal beamed. "Of course. More brandy?"

"Sure." Tristan held out his goblet. As the King poured, he said, "So you staged it all—my being dragged to you in chains, the hostility of the crowd—"

"Hold your horses, there, boy. *That* part wasn't staged. The hostility was real enough; it's why we had to stage the rest."

He paused to take a swig of brandy and a hit from his cigar. "*Ahh.* See, I did have to test you, to make damned sure I wouldn't be setting up an even greater menace to my people than the Fusion if I helped you out. That was part of the reason for the test. But the big reason was to get the people onto your side. That's why it's a damned good thing you passed the test *exactly as you did*. Otherwise you'd be topside with the ravens pecking out your eyeballs right this moment, even if Rex and the rigged launcher hadn't nailed you.

"You okay, son? You're looking mite peaked there. Here, take another shot of this. It's good for what ails you."

"It's a long story," Tristan said. It wasn't one he felt like sharing with Hammerhand right this moment. He couldn't help but admire the way Hammerhand had handled his people after their disastrous defeat, but that didn't wipe out his stupidity in leading them into it in the first place. Right now, all Tristan wanted was to get away from him.

"You've earned yourself a major part in building up our new Nation of the Plains," John Hammerhand said. "A big part."

Tristan stared at him. *The fool thinks he's still sitting on top of the hill! He thinks I've saved his political ass as well as his physical one.*

"Yes," Hammerhand was saying, his voice booming and expansive, "we're going to see some changes made. Some changes for the better. For one thing, we're going to instill a little more respect for order among the clans. This anarchic lifestyle of ours almost got us killed off. It's time to see which way the wind is blowing and blow with it.

"Another thing, son—and I hope you've had time to see your way clear on this one—another thing is, we're going to get women off bikes and the battle line and back home raising babies. That's what our Mother Earth intended, that they be nurturers like her. Leave the fighting to us men—women just have no grit for it—"

He broke off then, because he realized he was hemmed in by a pair of what seemed like ambulatory mountains, one light, one dark.

"What was that you said—" Sandy began.

"About women?" Stormy finished.

"Why, I'm sure you young ladies would agree with me, if you examined your souls—"

"Are you saying we can't fight?" Sandy demanded. She grabbed one arm. Her sister took the other. Together they hoisted John Hammerhand into the air as if he were a doll.

"You and us are going to have a little *talk*, Mister," Sandy said. "And if we don't like your answers—"

"—we're gonna make a wish."

A touch on Tristan's shoulder brought him around. "What now?"

It was Jammer. "That Hammerhand," he said, shaking his head in mock admiration. "He do have a way with the ladies, don't he?"

The Electric Skald took Tristan by the arm. Jovanne came up and slid her arm around Tristan's waist again.

"C'mon, son," Jammer said. "It's time you took your place as Maximum Lord of the Plains. Bro Wind knows you've earned it."

And with his friends around him Tristan walked among the Children of the Plains, to receive their love and acclamation.